The Dragon's Eye, Reign of Shadow, Book Two

Copyright © 2024 by Rayna L. Stiner

Printed in the United States of America

ISBN-13: 978-0-9967959-7-5

Visit raynalstiner.com to learn more about the
author and her other works.

Join the conversation on facebook.com/raynalstiner
or Instagram @rlstiner.

*This is a work of fiction. Names, characters, places,
and incidents are the products of the author's
imagination or are used fictitiously. Any resemblance
to actual events, locales, or persons, living or dead, is
entirely coincidental.*

Content warning: domestic violence.

The Dragon's Eye

Reign of Shadow, Book Two
By Rayna L. Stiner

TAGORBI PUBLISHING, LLC

ACKNOWLEDGMENTS

Jessica, my best friend and beta reader, thank you for everything. You continue to inspire me to tell the best story available, both in writing and in my perspective on the world and its inhabitants. Thank you for your constant compassion, and support on so many levels.

James, my love, we've been doing this partner thing now for over two decades and I am consistently in awe and gratitude that you are in my life. Thank you for being the amazing human you are!

Thank you to all my friends and family who support me regularly and consistently. Many of you have watched Tyrinth grow from a tiny spark of an idea to random writings, short stories, and then novels in a variety of versions. You've been brave supporters of a growing artist, alpha readers, beta readers, champions, financial supporters, and cheerleaders. I'm stunned at your generosity, and I am forever in your debt.

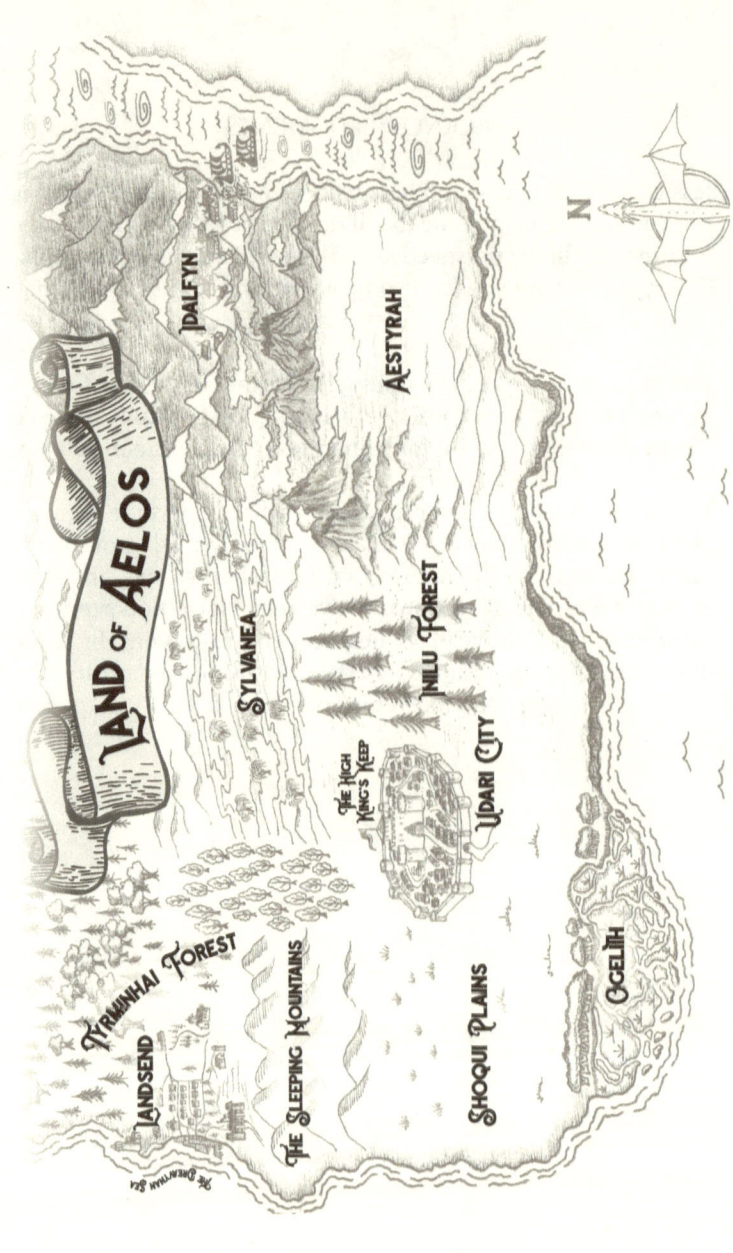

CHAPTER ONE

Riana - Age Eight

Riana pelted through the field under a canopy of blossoming stars. Under one arm, she clutched a glass jar, its burden on her small frame tilting her steps through the tall grasses. The looming tree line of the TyrMinHai forest rose over her left shoulder, silent and steeped in evening's shadow.

Her breath hitched and a pain stabbed her side, but she ran anyway. Every step rattled through her eight-year-old body and sparked hope. Her leg muscles ached from the circuit she'd been running since sunset, desperate to capture the prize that would make her mother well. Sweat pasted her silver hair to her forehead, ears, and the back of her neck. They were close. It was as if they raced and then stopped to watch her catch up. She gave an exasperated grunt and willed her scrawny legs into a sprint.

"Wait!" she called. She stretched her hand out and caught air. Ahead of her, the fire nymphs darted away. Their blue skin shone coolly against the darker shadow of evening and their opalescent wings bore them away on a whir of color and light. The small cloud of nymphs, seemingly tired of their sport, fled into the forest.

Riana pulled up under the safety of awakening stars, sweating, and heaving. She collapsed onto the ground, her play skirts soaking in the dew. Clunking the jar down beside her, she wrapped her arms around her legs, frustration blooming where hope withered. She pounded her knee with a tiny fist and growled into the air. What she wouldn't do to have a fire nymph's blessing on her mother, to make the sickness go away. She breathed in deeply and exhaled in a spluttering whoosh.

Once her heart and breathing calmed, she stood, dusting herself off and frowning at the forest. If she were braver, she would go in after them. Grandmother would skin her alive if she caught her out under the trees this late in the evening. That was a scarier prospect than anything she might encounter among the trees. She sighed and began her journey back to the house, expertly catching firebugs in her big, glass jar. When a dozen or more of them darted and blinked, blue-green inside the glass, Riana heard her grandmother's voice ring out, "Riana! Come in!"

She looked at the firebugs. "You'll have to do." She shook the jar and felt the clanking of the bugs against the glass. Wrapping both arms around the jar, she tromped to the entrance of the house and General Store, leaving the night to its own devices.

Behind her, from the safety of the TyrMinHai, the fire nymphs chatted in a melody amongst each other as they watched the strange girl with silver hair disappear from their view.

***

Mother had been sleeping, so with a prayer to keep the bugs alive overnight, she had gone to bed with her present blinking in the corner of her room. In the morning, Riana dressed quickly and made her way down the short hall from her room to the living area. Yellow firelight danced on the floral rug and cast its partner, shadow onto the outstretched form of her mother.

Riana approached her dozing mother with the jar clutched to her chest. Her mother's pale eyelids twitched under pinched, golden eyebrows. Her head rocked against a teal couch pillow and a golden, curled lock of hair fell onto her sunken cheek. Riana tiptoed to her side and brushed the hair behind her mother's ear as she lowered herself beside her.

Riana reached next to her and pushed the blue oil lamp over to make way on the oak side table for her mother's gift. The glass jar scraped against the oak tabletop and cast the blue-green light of the firebugs against the yellow glow of the wick's flame.

Riana watched the bugs dart and blink then turned to her mother. Blue irises surrounded by reddened whites looked up at her.

"Such a beautiful girl you are," her mother said through cracked lips. Her breath smelled of medicines and the mint leaves she used to cover the taste. Riana reached for the pitcher and water glass, but her mother's skeletal hand stopped her.

"Mother, you need to drink something," Riana urged.

"No," she replied. "Not thirsty." Her hand slipped from Riana's small arm. Her eyes slid down.

"Mother, I got you a present," Riana said, hoping to wake her mother before she drowsed again. Riana looked around to make sure her father wasn't near. "I made you a lamp. The fire nymphs were too fast for me." She frowned down at her empty hands, remembering their flight.

Her mother's eyes went wide. "You saw...?"

Riana frowned. "I tried to catch one for you, but they got away." Riana picked up the big jar of firebugs, smaller than fire nymphs and greener, lacking the opalescent wings that shimmered like rainbows in the dark. "But maybe you can pretend that these are fire nymphs and maybe they'll help you feel better."

Her mother's face split into a wide smile that showed her teeth and made her look beautiful despite her weariness. Riana's heart twisted around love and fear.

The smile on her mother's face faltered. A vice-like grip encircled Riana's upper arm. Her body yanked from its perch. This loosened Riana's grip on the firebug lantern. The jar crashed to the floor. Her father's face whipped into sight as the firebugs floated past her. Hideous in the red glow of the firelight, his watery blue eyes burned under nettled eyebrows.

CHAPTER TWO

Riana - One Month From Her Sixteenth Birthday

Riana closed her eyes to the memory. Roy Fraely had been her father, once upon a time. But that had all changed when Grandmother, Sela Starliss, had discovered the bruises and welts. Everything had changed at once. Her grandmother had discovered Roy Fraely's abuse, her mother had died, Sela Starliss had changed Riana's adoption to herself instead of Sela's daughter and son-in-law, and Riana had moved in with Sela.

Riana scuffed a boot over the dust-laden floor. Storm-smeared daylight spilled through a small window. The oil lamp on a nearby side table hissed and flickered, its light casting a glow onto a meager bed. Being back in this room, raw with emotion from her grandmother's death, brought an onslaught of unpleasant memories.

She picked up the urn on the bedside. It was engraved, "Sela Starliss. Born under the Waning Crescent of Rylitre (third month in the third season), 449 P.D. Died under the Full of Meritre (third month of the first season), 512 P.D."

It had been two weeks since her grandmother's death. She clutched at her chest.

It had been two weeks since Riana had murdered Luther, Captain of the High King's Tyrmini Guard, and murderer of Riana's grandmother, Sela Starliss. Her clutching hand turned to a fist.

It was one moon until her sixteenth birthday, which would fall under the first full moon in Tijilou, the first month in the second season, just when the weather would begin to heat and the days would last longer. Her hand fell to her side.

Which meant Riana could not claim the inheritance of her grandmother's estate, including the home she'd grown up in, until then. And that meant Riana now stood in a tiny room with piles of her belongings surrounding her, listening to the chime of the doorbell at the General Store.

Roy Fraely – owner of Landsend's General Store, widower to Sela Starliss's deceased daughter, only living semblance of a relative to the Starliss family through marriage, and now Riana's legal guardian – spoke to the customer who'd entered. The walls were thin enough Riana could hear his voice, but thick enough she couldn't distinguish his words.

Riana let the voices drop into the background of her awareness. She picked up a box, stacked atop another box and placed it on the bed. A cloud of dust puffed up from the blanket. Riana coughed, covering her nose and mouth with the back of her hand. She moved to the window and opened it to fresh, rain-washed air. From here she could see the northern stretch of the TyrMinHai. She folded her arms and placed them on the windowsill, resting her chin on her hands.

Out there in the expanse of giant evergreens, the wild elementals roamed free. Protected by the townsfolk's fear, and her grandmother's expansive land ownership, fire nymphs flitted, antoli hunted, a young and orphaned amatsu swam the forest's slough, and a relocated berubula slurped up crabs near his muddy home.

No one besides herself, her best friend Elynda, and her newly found friend and past bully, Donny Derringer, had seen evidence of these creatures' existence. Riana meant to keep it that way. The last travelers who'd discovered them were now dead.

Riana ran a hand over the red slashes on her arms. The wounds had healed, but the scars were still fresh and new. Treyor's handy work had nearly killed her. If it had not been for the elementals everyone else hated and feared, Riana would have been dead. Instead, she had survived. The fire nymphs survived the fiery death of their mother tree with the replacement of a new tree.

THE DRAGON'S EYE

The bond between Riana and the elementals had grown. Riana had once felt torn between two worlds. Now, she found it harder and harder to marry herself to people who murdered and slaughtered not only innocent creatures but their own kind if they were different and possessed power.

Riana turned away from the window and forced herself to open a box. Bright, cheerful, delicate handkerchiefs spilled out. Her grandmother's. She froze, a punch of pain in her gut. She sobbed as she closed the box, tears spilling freely. She replaced the box to its previous place.

In her mind's eye she saw Captain Luther's dagger drag through her grandmother's fragile skin, blood escaping like a long-kept prisoner. In reaction to seeing her grandmother's death, Riana's explosion of anger, shock and grief had transformed itself into physical substance. Spears of light had burst from her hands with a gesture. Captain Luther had had no time to react. He was skewered through, left to die, and be consumed in the fire he'd set on the nymphs' mother tree.

Riana had killed him.

She felt two ways about this. She was smugly proud to have avenged her grandmother. And ashamed of her own ferocity. Afraid of how cold and calculating she'd felt as she'd set her intention on killing him.

Who could do such a thing? Riana had always maintained a person capable of murder had to have evil in them. Was she evil? She didn't feel evil. Except, maybe in her revelry of Captain Luther's death. Yet even that emotion sparked shame. It was as if there were two sides to her: one that would risk all to save someone; and one that would murder to appease her anger and mourning.

Riana opened the box once more and pulled out a beautiful blue handkerchief. In one corner an expert SS was embroidered. Riana clutched the cloth to her chest and let the tears spill freely.

Pounding at the door startled her from dark thoughts. She gasped, swiped at her face and turned to answer the door. She pulled the door wide to Mr. Fraely's sneer. "It's been two weeks. Time to stop crying and start working," he said.

Riana cocked her head to the side. "Working? You mean at the winery?"

"No," he shouted, making Riana jump. "Ungrateful. You live here for the next month, you work."

Riana pulled herself straighter. "I wouldn't want to put you out. Perhaps I should ask the Heilbees if their home may be open to me for the next month?"

"I insist you stay here," he ground out.

"Why?" she asked flatly. "It's not as if you want me here. We both know that. At least at the Heilbees, I'd be treated kindly."

"How dare you," he whispered.

Riana crossed her arms and cocked an eyebrow, meeting his watery blue eyes with her multicolored ones. The silence between them stretched. Even the air seemed to be holding its breath. A caustic anger bubbled in her. Why hadn't they just allowed her to stay in her home? She ground her jaw. She opened her mouth and inhaled to speak. She wanted to point out as her legal guardian all he needed to do was say she could stay with them, and it would be fine. There was no need for either of them to suffer this way.

The words never made it to her mouth. Sharp pain splintered her vision, shot through the bridge of her nose, and permeated her head. Her head snapped to one side. Stunned, she looked at her guardian.

He'd hit her.

Nasty memories of days gone by flashed in her mind. A knot formed in her gut as she grasped her face.

"I am your guardian," he said. "I will say where you live. And you will live here until you are sixteen summers. That is that."

He turned, grasped the doorknob, and pulled it shut.

Riana stared at the door, mouth still hanging open. Shock stole her emotions, her pain, for long minutes as she worked out the reality of her situation.

CHAPTER THREE

"Where is Apprentice Elynda?" an elder healer called. "I need her."

Elynda heard the call and scurried from behind the desk where she'd been reviewing inventory of the healing tinctures to ensure they were well stocked.

"Yes, Elder," she answered, "I'm coming." She turned to hurry out of the healers' station, paused, turned around and grabbed several tinctures from the shelf on a whim. She hurried to the Elder Healer.

The woman wore a minimalist blue dress, as was customary for her rank. Over her soft blue dress was a white apron, same as Riana's. The healer's hair was pulled back and tucked under a decorative cap. It was the only piece of attire they were allowed to wear that expressed their personality. Elder Healer Santh's cap was an iridescent blue green that reminded Elynda of amatsu fur.

Elder Healer Santh waved impatiently at Elynda. "There's not much time left," she said. She stood in front of a patient room and glanced into the swath of sunshine spilling out into the hallway. When Elynda drew close, the woman hurried into the room, clearly wanting Elynda to follow.

As soon as Elynda stepped over the threshold her hands ignited in tingling warmth. Energy flowed into her from the crown of her head and set her insides singing with purpose. Whoever was in this room was very, very sick. She didn't know how she knew, except the energy flowing through her seemed to be telling her so.

Elder Santh motioned Elynda to the patient's bed. "This is Lieutenant Will of the Baron's Guard."

Her description was unnecessary because Will was still dressed in his navy and silver coat, although his hat had been laid on the bedside table.

Elynda smelled rotting flesh. Infection pulsed through this officer. "He has blood poisoning from a wound," she said and pointed to the guard's left leg.

Healer Santh blinked furiously. "Did someone speak to you of this patient?"

"Just a hunch," Elynda said, looking at the healer through the curve of her dark eyelashes. She turned quickly to the patient and pulled away the covers. "Can you help me remove his boot?"

Healer Santh paused, opened her mouth as if to speak, then seemed to think better of it and followed Elynda to the man's boot.

The man wheezed, unconscious and struggling to breathe.

Elynda and Healer Santh pulled the boot off. The smell of advanced infection rolled over them. Elynda fought back a wave of nausea, gagged silently, and prayed her elder did not notice. When she looked at her teacher and mentor, Healer Santh was looking at the wound with pursed lips and a furrowed brow.

Elynda pulled scissors from one of the many apron pockets and ripped through the fabric of the man's pants, which were wet and sticky. Green pus and pink blood oozed down the sides of his bloated leg, soaking into the pristine white sheets. The wound gaped open, a raw cavern of red flesh with a heart of yellow and green fluid.

The leg surrounding the wound was a deep red. Heat radiated from the leg. She shook her head. "Why'd he wait so long to get help?" Elynda asked no one in particular. It looked as though he'd had the wound for weeks. A simple clean and stitch could have prevented the catastrophe now laying in the bed in front of them.

Elder Santh shook her head. "Sometimes men have funny notions of what strength is. What are you inclined to do about this patient, Apprentice?"

Elynda gripped her hands at her sides, surveying the wound as she pulled up the mental list of actions she would take if this were her patient. Movement caught in her peripheral vision. She turned quickly and barked at a passing healer. "We need hot water and towels in here immediately."

"We also need antiseptic -,"

"I've got it here, Healer," Elynda interrupted her. While she waited for the hot water and towels to arrive, Elynda moved to the man's head. He was burning with fever. She pulled a tincture from her apron pocket and turned to the Elder Healer. "Shall I administer fever reducing tincture now, Healer?"

Healer Santh nodded but made no move to help.

Elynda unscrewed the stopper. "I shall give him a full dropper since his temperature is so high. He is an average weight and height. In thirty minutes, I recommend another dose. Does that seem appropriate, Healer?" She was nervous. She did not want to hurt anyone with a wrong dosage. Many healers had made that mistake, sometimes with fatal outcomes.

"That is precisely what I would prescribe," Healer Santh stated. She held her hand in front of her apron and regarded Elynda with quiet apathy.

Elynda nodded, set the tincture on the bedside table, opened the man's mouth and carefully squeezed the medicine into his cheek. She rubbed at his throat which triggered his swallow reflex. The man was red with fever, but otherwise handsome through the scruff of several days of hair growth. His reddish-brown hair was close-cropped and clean. His dark eyebrows framed closed eyes lined with thick, curling eyelashes that would make a woman jealous.

"Mr. Will, I promise we'll make sure you're patched up and ready for service in no time. Next time, you'll do us the favor of seeing us immediately when you're wounded. Understand?" The man did not respond, of course, but Elynda was happy to make her point clear.

She nodded at him. "Yes, that's what I thought," she said. The water and towels arrived, and she set to work on cleaning the wound. It was foul work and tedious, but she was patient with her ministrations, allowing her hands to transmit that strange warm energy she felt coursing through her. Determination stole through her several times. He would live, though the odds were in Death's favor.

She treated the man with several tinctures. One for blood poisoning, another an antibiotic, another for pain and yet another for the fever. She reviewed each one carefully with the Elder Healer, ensuring her dosing and the interactions between the medicines would not cause an adverse reaction.

When at last the wound had been treated and bandaged, Elynda washed up thoroughly and turned to the man. Elynda's hands tingled. The sensation had appeared several times before. Her body throbbed with excess excitement, eagerness, and compassion. The heady emotions blurred the outlines of her vision. An overwhelming need stole over her. She must put her hands on the wounded guard. The odd compulsion was accompanied with a knowing that this man would heal.

She approached slowly, her body trembling. Her hands were magnets to the patient. She laid a hand on his shoulder and head, a gesture the head healer would take for testing his temperature. Within her, a door kicked open and flooding out of it was pure love. It navigated its way up from her core, through her arms, into her hands where it found its target. Elynda watched in amazement as his color shifted and his fever dropped. She stayed this way for several moments. It was difficult to school her features to deny the inner workings of what Elynda had come to understand as bliss and love. Luckily, her back was turned toward the head healer. The feeling of power climaxed as the flood of energy spilled from her to the patient. When the energy slowed, Elynda moved her hands away.

The man's eyes fluttered open. He exhaled and his eyebrows pinched together.

"How are you feeling?" Elynda asked.

"Awful, but better."

Elynda covered her mouth and laughed quietly.

"You sir," began the Elder Healer, "were on Death's doorstep. I asked this young apprentice in to help me send you on your way. She had other ideas. You owe your life to her."

Elynda stared at the Elder Healer in stunned silence. The woman's intention had been to teach her about a patient dying. Instead, Elynda had healed him.

The woman was old with paper-thin skin and sagging eyes, but those eyes were sharp and sincere when she turned to Elynda and pronounced, "Well done, Healer."

It was the first time she'd been called that. She'd been called Apprentice for the duration of the months since she'd started at Healer's Hall. Her nerves sang in exultation. An Elder Healer had called her a Healer. Elynda bowed her head in humility. "Thank you, Elder," she said.

CHAPTER FOUR

Elynda scurried down the stairs, humming as she went. She hit the floor of the den at a steady clip and stomped over the carpet. The fire cast a happy glow over the armchair and bookshelves while gray sunlight made an ambivalent appearance through a nearby window. Elynda glanced out the window, frowning at the dreary weather, before pulling her thicker cloak from the coat rack.

"Hold on, honey," her mother said.

Elynda threw her book bag over her shoulder and headed back to her mother.

Mrs. Heilbee was a mature and beautiful woman, with raven dark hair Elynda had inherited and two different colored eyes. She smiled at Elynda and handed her a bowl, covered in a blue checkered cloth. "Riana's probably starving. Take these to share with her."

"Is it cinni rolls?" Elynda asked excitedly.

Mrs. Heilbee nodded, handed the bowl over, then pinched her daughter's cheeks. "You make sure you give that girl a hug."

"I will, mama. See you this afternoon at the hall," Elynda said. She turned to go.

"Wait," Mrs. Heilbee said. "I almost forgot." She stalked out of the room, into the kitchen and back again. "This is for your pack." She pulled the flap up on Elynda's book bag and pushed a small container inside.

"What is it?" Elynda asked.

"A compound jelly I make myself and use at the hall."

Elynda jigged. "Oh, goody!" She was just starting to build her own medicine bag.

"I just made a fresh batch. Keep it on you in case someone has minor injuries, or sore muscles. It's not for cuts, though. You want to be sure the skin is closed before you apply."

"And how should I apply it?" Elynda asked.

"Gently and sparingly," Mrs. Heilbee said, pointing a finger at her daughter for emphasis.

"Got it," Elynda said and smiled. She hoped she'd get to use it soon, maybe this evening at her apprenticeship shift at Healer's Hall. She didn't know how the other kids felt, but she couldn't be happier with her apprenticeship assignment. She was thrilled to work alongside her mother and Healer Bastian.

"Now, off you go and I'll see you this afternoon," Mrs. Heilbee said.

Elynda bowed her head to her mother, who grabbed her face, turned it up and kissed her on the forehead.

"Mom," she complained, but secretly, she didn't mind.

"Oh, alright, off you go." Mrs. Heilbee turned her around by the shoulders and gave her a playful push toward the door.

Outside, Elynda made her way out into the cool morning mist with the ocean waves crashing against the cliffside of Landsend. Over her left shoulder, on the highest point of Landsend, the lighthouse shone like a distant candle in the gloom.

Elynda couldn't wait for Spring to fully make an appearance.

"At least it's not raining, though," she consoled herself.

The North Road was mostly quiet. At the Snow residence, Ribbit came out to greet her. "Hullo, Elynda!" he said.

Elynda smiled and nodded. They'd walked together to school for as long as they'd been going to school.

"What's that?" he pointed at the blue checkered towel.

"Oh, cinni rolls. They're for Riana," Elynda told him.

"Oh," Ribbit's shoulders slumped and his face turned to gaze at the ground. "I see."

"But you can have one," Elynda said. She didn't want to give up her pastry, but she would for Ribbit. She pulled the cloth away and the aroma of vanilla, cinnamon, butter and yeast filled her nostrils. She salivated and was relieved to see there were three pastries. How did her mom always know?

"Yes!" Ribbit pumped his fist in the air and jumped in exultation. Smiling broadly to reveal slightly crooked teeth, he snagged a roll.

Elynda watched him devour it in three bites. "Hungry?" she asked.

Ribbit licked his fingers of gooey frosting before replying. "Always," he said. "How's Healer's Hall?"

"Amazing," she said. "I think I might have a real talent at this healing thing."

"Oh yeah?" Ribbit tucked his thumbs into his overalls. "You really like it, huh?"

"Yeah," she confirmed. "What about you? How's everything going with the horses?"

"Fine," he said and shrugged. "Not much different than what it used to be." He kicked a stray white rock. It skipped down the road. The gray clouds overhead broke momentarily and Ribbit was cast in a pillar of golden light. "I guess he's giving me more responsibility."

"Don't you like working with horses?" Elynda asked. Ribbit had always seemed really happy with his family's occupation. Maybe she'd missed something.

"Well, yes, that's the part I like. It's all the other stuff I don't like. Give me a horse to deal with and I'm just fine. People, on the other hand..." Ribbit rubbed the back of his neck and gave her a crooked smile out of the side of his face.

"You and I do fine," she teased and shouldered him.

"Anybody'd do fine with you," Ribbit said. "You're Elynda. Kindest, caringest, sweetest -,"

Elynda shoved him, laughing heartily. "Stop that, Ribbit Snow! You flatter me too much."

Ribbit recovered, brushing himself free of imaginary dirt. "Now, there is no need for violence." He wagged an admonishing finger at her.

Elynda laughed, grabbed Ribbit and squeezed him. "Fine! I shall hug you instead."

Ribbit wheezed. "You'll break me!"

"It'll be worth it," Elynda said. She squeezed him once more before releasing him.

Ribbit rubbed his ribs. "I think you broke them."

"Then I shall take you to Healer's Hall and patch you up until your health is fully restored. So have I vowed as a Healer of Healer's Hall," she intoned playfully, bowing to Ribbit with a hand over her heart.

"Oh, don't I know it. Hopefully, your healing is more gentle than your embraces. I feel for the man you marry."

Elynda waved off the comment, not sure she'd ever feel deeply enough for a man to take him home and to her bed.

"You picking Riana up?" he asked, gesturing to the General Store ahead.

"Mhm," she said.

They covered the last few feet to the store. "I'll see you two at school," Ribbit said. He tipped his hat and headed off down the road.

Elynda turned to the store front. The General Store was gray with age, moss sprouting from the roof tiles, windows grimy with dirt and sea salt from the ocean air. The sign announcing one was at the General Store had once been white, but now it was faded and chipping, so the font was ragged and worn.

Elynda recoiled from the store. If her best friend were not in there, she wouldn't step foot into Mr. Fraely's business. Old crook. Old, unsavory crook. She harbored no compassion toward him and if the man ended up in Healer's Hall, well, she'd heal him, but only out of duty and commitment to her oath.

She inhaled deeply, steeling herself before she walked into the store.

CHAPTER FIVE

Sunlight speared Riana's closed eyes, and she knew the light wouldn't give up until it woke her.

She squeezed her eyelids tighter but stopped when pain pinched her brow bone and nose. As the pain in her eye eased, horror gripped her. The prior night's ordeal washed through her memory, coating her insides in fear and shame. She rolled to her side and pulled the covers over her head, wishing the sunshine would respect her mood and go away.

The shadow that enveloped her relaxed the pit in her stomach. She had just enough time to doze off when her door burst open with a rasp and clang. Riana didn't bother to move but groaned as weight sank the edge of her bed.

"I've got a surprise for you," said the familiar voice of her best friend.

"Ijustwannasleep," Riana mumbled. "Goway." She lay there, waiting for the argument, but none came. Instead, the bed shifted, and warmth pressed into her back. She could smell Elynda's lavender scented dress and that other something that was just Elynda. Another body part, Riana assumed it was Elynda's arm wrapped over Riana's shoulder. Through the thin blanket she could see a shadow disrupting the muted glow of the morning sun. Riana was just about to protest Elynda's weight on her when she caught a whiff of sweet, spicy warmth.

Riana wiggled, working to free herself of Elynda and the cover. "Is that cinni rolls?" Riana asked as she shoved the covers aside. She looked at Elynda, blinking away the sting of sunshine. Something was wrong with her view. She could only see a slit of the world with her left eye.

Elynda's green eyes went wide. The hand holding the bowl of pastries trembled.

Riana rolled off the side of the bed and tripped the short distance to the closet door. Every step caused an angry throb in her face. Her head was splitting; a fact she had missed until she'd stood up. Thoughts chased themselves in her mind. She relived the night before, calling up the moment he'd blacked her eye.

Over what? Why had he been so adamant about her staying? And then to hit her seemed obvious he didn't want her there. Why argue?

"What happened?" Elynda asked.

"He hit me," Riana said, her throat clenching around a sudden lump. Grandmother had rescued her when she discovered he was abusive. But Grandmother was gone. The weight of her aloneness sunk to the pit of her stomach. "He struck me with the back of his hand when I suggested I move out."

Elynda gasped and put her hand to her mouth. "Mr. Fraely? Hit you?"

Riana nodded; certain speaking would be impossible.

Elynda was silent for so long that Riana turned to look at her, afraid she'd see Elynda looking disgusted at her. Afraid Elynda would leave her too so she didn't have to be around the ugliness of Riana's current living arrangements.

Elynda looked like her hair might catch fire. She shook, her green eyes blazing, arms rigid at her sides and ending in white-knuckled fists. Her lips were pulled back and her teeth bared. Her sweet and loving friend had transformed into a snarling beast.

"I will murder him," she said, and turned to leave, as if she meant to do it right that moment.

Riana reached out in time to wrap a hand around Elynda's arm, just above the elbow and pulled her away from the door. "Don't," Riana said. "It won't do any good. He's my guardian and he won't let me leave."

"Why? So what if he says you can't. Just come live with me. I'm sure mom and dad won't mind," Elynda said, her face softening as she implored Riana.

Riana paused and thought. Perhaps it didn't matter what he said. Perhaps she could just leave. "Maybe? But what if he somehow uses my leaving to grab at my inheritance? I can't let that happen."

The look of ferocity eased on Elynda's face. She cocked her head. "Is that a possibility?" Elynda asked.

"I'm not sure," Riana stated. She let Elynda's arm go and slumped to the bed. She grabbed the blanket off the bed and wrapped it around her. "I know I can't claim my inheritance until I'm sixteen. Until then, as my guardian, he's the executor of my estate. He is next in line if something happens to me. But I don't know how much freedom I have to do as I wish without risking losing everything," Riana said.

Elynda's face melted to surrender, her shoulders drooping and chin falling to her chest. She huffed. "Alright. I won't murder him yet. Let's just see if we can find out what can be done. I'll ask mom and dad if they can help."

"Thank you," Riana said. "It seems Grandmother didn't think I'd be underage when I inherited the vineyard." She paused as the all-too-familiar ache of her grandmother's absence threatened to consume her, starting with her gut and then working its way to her heart and finally to her throat. She swallowed back bile and squeaked out, "She didn't count on being murdered."

Elynda set the cinni rolls onto the bedside table, next to the oil lamp and settled down next to Riana. She took Riana's hands into hers. Elynda looked at her, searching her face, for what, Riana didn't know. "Until we figure this out, we'll do our best to keep you away as much as possible. I'll be here for you."

Riana nodded, very carefully, so as not to set her throbbing eye into a panicked drumbeat of pain. "Thank you. I knew I could count on you."

"Okay, mom just gave me some salve that will help. You eat this while I get it out." Elynda handed Riana a cinni roll before turning to her book bag.

Riana held the roll in a trembling hand but didn't take a bite.

Elynda unscrewed a small jar of green jelly. The bedroom immediately filled with herbaceous odors of rosemary, thyme and arnica. Elynda turned to Riana with a glob of the jelly on her fingers.

"Here, let me see," she instructed.

Riana turned her body toward Elynda and allowed her gentle ministrations to begin. Her eyesight throbbed, and as she looked through the slit of her black eye, green and gold light shimmered around Elynda. She didn't know black eyes did that.

"It's smelly," Riana noted.

"True," Elynda said, "but, the odor fades pretty quickly, and the effects last all day. You'll have to reapply this evening, so I'll leave the jar with you."

The jelly was cool on Riana's skin, but there was a tingle of electric warmth to Elynda's touch. "Your touch is amazing, Elynda."

"That's funny you say that. I've been getting told that a lot lately."

"Mm," Riana answered, and let Elynda help heal her wounds.

CHAPTER SIX

Elynda's salve pulled at Riana's eye. It was enough she noticed the sensation, but more noticeable to everyone else was the blooming bruise on her face. She wanted to hide out in her room, but she knew she'd then have Mr. Fraely to deal with.

She sat in the back corner of the classroom, pulling her hair down over her face, but Donny saw it anyway.

He stomped over to her desk, stooped low and pulled the hair from her face, examining her abused eye with shock. "What happened to you?" he asked, loud enough a couple of youngsters turned their direction.

Riana pulled away from him, casting a nervous glance around the room. "Would you shut your mouth?" she hissed. "I don't want the world in my business."

Donny straightened, more shock making his mouth go slack. "It used to be I was the one who did this sort of thing to you."

"Well, it seems title of Abuser has been passed to another. You jealous?"

The words were out before she even thought about them. His face softened as he took a step back, like she'd pushed him. Which he didn't deserve. After all, he'd helped her with the rescue of several elementals. And if they'd been caught anywhere near elementals, they all would have been imprisoned. Who was she to judge him so harshly after the danger she'd put everyone in?

She let a long, slow exhale. "That was uncalled for. I'm sorry. I guess my nerves are on edge."

"It's okay," he said. "I probably deserve it."

The bell rang outside. Kids filing in from the cool morning brought the scent of the ocean mist and budding grass and trees.

"How about we talk after school? It's been a wretched two weeks."

She held Donny's gaze. Light filtered in from the window to her left and cast Donny in a warm glow; a glow she was careful to avoid.

Donny's shock and hurt seemed to melt a little. He nodded and turned slowly away, his shoulders slumped, his pace slow as he made his way to a desk and folded his considerable height into the chair.

Riana leaned forward and put a hand over the left side of her face, hoping it appeared as though she were simply lost in thought, instead of hiding the damage Mr. Fraely had done.

"Alright, class? Good morning," Mrs. Tomly greeted. She rang the little bell on her desk to call the class to attention. They settled in, but there was a general restlessness to the group that could only be associated with the oncoming spring.

"First order of business," Mrs. Tomly said. "Riana, you're to head to the vineyard at lunch for your apprenticeship." She smiled softly at her, but the gesture didn't make it to her eyes; those held only sorrow.

Riana nodded shortly, careful to not disturb the hair concealing the bruise.

After the morning's lesson flew by, Riana welcomed the escape of the schoolhouse. Lunchtime was the mark for the last years to make their way to their apprenticeships. Elynda rushed off for Healer's Hall. Riana headed for the winery, butterflies jigging in her belly. She hadn't been to Starliss Vineyard since her grandmother had been killed. Since Riana had murdered that bastard, Captain Luther, right-hand man to the High King. He'd been in Landsend sniffing out the golden elixir for the High King whom Riana had surmised was ill.

The golden elixir was fashioned from the unique fruit Sela's childhood friend and Tyrmini, Kaely had created to sustain the fire nymphs that lived deep in the forest. The fruit held healing properties. Riana had learned her grandmother's father, the late Baron of

Tarbyrwin, had been saved at a young age by the fruit. Unfortunately, they learned with the Baron that the fruit was addictive to humans. Sela Starliss had been forced to come up with a way to provide the fruit in a smaller dose regularly to the Baron to sustain his habit.

And so, the elixir had been born, and somehow, rumors had spread of its existence – from Landsend all the way to the heart of Aelos, to the High King's ears. Kaely's tree had been dying when Captain Luther had come to Landsend on his master's command. That hadn't stopped him from sacrificing Sela to grasp at the last remaining fruits. The elixir was gone now. The Baron of Landsend had consumed all that was left. The last anyone knew except for Riana was that the fire nymph tree had burned to ashes. No more fruit, and no more Sela Starliss meant no more elixir, and no more of the High King hunting it down.

She hoped.

There were so many secrets buried in the cellars, the vineyard, the wine, the forest. The shadows of the whole ordeal gained more substance the closer Riana got to the vineyard.

If that weren't enough, she faced the knowledge that none of the workers at the vineyard and winery liked her. It was strictly because of her grandmother that they had ever even allowed Riana into the establishment. Riana didn't know which worker at the vineyard would apprentice her since her grandmother was gone. Or if maybe they were forced to apprentice her because of her grandmother's will.

That would make a miserable apprenticeship, to add to a miserable living situation.

Riana wrapped her arms around her stomach and kept walking. She didn't know what she'd do, except not let her grandmother's sacrifice go to waste.

She was only a few yards past the school when Donny's voice rang out. She looked over her shoulder. Donny ran toward her and she couldn't help but notice he looked different. She regarded him as he ran. He moved naturally, pumping his arms and legs, his head up and looking at her. He'd gotten his hair cut, so his bangs weren't in his eyes and his eyes caught her up and refused to let her go. It was more than his hair that had changed too. He was thinner, she realized. And the muscles of his shoulders, chest and neck could be seen under the loose tunic he wore. Loose because of the weight loss, she guessed.

He was still formidable, but in a way that struck Riana as... she grappled to find the word that matched this teen she'd disliked her whole life... hunky. Yes, he was handsome. Strong. When had that happened? Just a few months before he'd been more chubby than muscle-bound. She supposed that was just as he'd begun his apprenticeship at the Baron's Guard. And before they'd become friends. Riana was struck by the idea. They were friends now, weren't they? They'd been through a lot together, rescuing creatures, hiding from the authorities, witnessing a power being born from within Riana. He'd even helped rescue Riana when Treyor had sliced her up. She'd nearly died from her wounds. Donny had held her in his arms all the way to Healer's Hall, cradling her close to him until he deposited her into the care of the healers.

Of course, Riana had heard this second-hand from Elynda since Riana had been unconscious. It was as if from that moment on, Donny had secretly vowed to make up for the years of bullying he'd put her through.

"So, will you tell me now what's going on?" Donny asked as he closed the gap.

The sunshine was bright in a clear blue sky. A tiny breeze picked through Donny's hair, ruffling the dark strands. Riana realized without all that hair on his forehead, his eyes were very pretty. Even though they were smallish, they were hazel, with tints of green and brown and gray.

"What -?" she asked, too deep in thought and observation to think properly. What was she feeling? There was a warmth that had started in her chest upon seeing Donny. And it felt a little squirmy in her stomach.

"What do you mean, 'What'? What happened to your face, Riana?" Donny gently cupped her chin and tilted her face up toward him.

Riana's hair fell away from her injured eye. Donny studied her. Riana froze and melted all at once. His hands were warm against her skin.

"I-," she started.

"He did this to you, didn't he?" Donny scowled and the fullness of his lips disappeared.

Riana hesitated. Then a thought occurred to her. "He did," she began, "and I'd like to leave and stay at the Heilbees until my sixteenth birthday."

"Sounds like a solid plan to me," he said, but let the statement trail, seeming to know she had more to say. He crossed his arms. Riana watched his muscles bunch, impressed all over again.

"I'm not sure the law allows it," Riana said. "He is my legal guardian. Do you know anyone who can tell me if leaving will mess up my inheritance?"

He rubbed his square jaw. "Let me ask around. See if there's something we can do that will keep your inheritance intact. And your face."

The spell of his new physique evaporated. She tried to look disapproving, but it hurt so she gave up. "Funny," she said.

"No," Donny said, and shook his head. "No, it's not funny. I'd like to demolish that –,"

"Now, now," Riana interrupted what she assumed would be foul words describing Mr. Fraely accurately. She drew close to him and surprising herself, put both her palms against his chest. He looked down at her hands, eyes wide. Riana felt his heartbeat beneath her palms, under the layer of muscle. She dropped her hands as though they'd burned. "I just appreciate any direction you can give."

Riana wrapped her hands together and backed away to prevent any further sudden impulses.

"Okay. Yeah. Definitely," he said, and his voice cracked. He cleared his throat. "I'll find you when I figure something out."

"Thank you, Donny," she said sincerely.

CHAPTER SEVEN

Riana's day couldn't get any worse. She'd started the morning off with the shocking reality she was living in an abusive home. Her old bully now wanted to protect her. A bully she was pretty sure she was at least physically attracted to. Her emotions spun wildly.

The accompanying emptiness she felt since her grandmother's passing drummed in the background to the other acute and new feelings. The all-consuming loneliness was edged in horror of the deep secret that she had murdered Captain Luther. She was tainted by the reality she held some powerful magic that could kill simply by having compelling motivation.

Riana had seen a side of herself she didn't know how to reconcile. Her grandmother had been murdered and so Riana had exacted swift punishment to the tune of revenge. How did a person overcome such a realization? Riana tasted the word 'murderer' in her mind and wanted to hurl it out. But the word stayed, branded on her soul.

Riana was a murderer.

Riana was also Sela Starliss's beneficiary. The fact didn't ease her loss. In fact, it made it worse. As she shuffled down the long drive that led to Starliss Vineyard & Winery, she knew her grandmother would still be alive if it hadn't been for her. She uttered her silent, ceaseless apology once again to her grandmother. Her shoulders drooped as she closed the space and entered the winery, unprepared for what may lie ahead.

It was Ms. Hightower who met her. She was sitting at her grandmother's desk; a fact that set Riana's nerves blazing with anger and loss. Words and emotion mixed in her gut and rose through her aching heart and then stuck resolutely in her throat. She swallowed at the lump of unsaid sentiments, took a deep breath and addressed the cellar manager.

"Ms. Hightower," Riana started.

"Ah, Riana," Ms. Hightower said. Riana couldn't help but notice the lack of anger and disgust. In fact, Riana thought she saw a welcome sense of relief on the cellar manager's face. "I'm glad to see you were able to return to your internship."

"You are?" Riana asked, unable to keep her stunned question from escaping her.

Ms. Hightower nodded slowly. "I am. I know that comes as a shock for you since I minced no words previously about my perspective on your ability to take over and take care of your grandmother's legacy," she said.

Riana stood silently and waited for the woman to explain herself. She did not speak or nod or even blink. She was even reluctant to breathe.

Eventually, Ms. Hightower continued. "Losing your grandmother hit us hard here. Not only were we at a loss with how to move forward without her leadership, but we were also lost without her presence. She was more like family to us." The hard, hard woman Riana had grown up knowing for scowls and sharp remarks suddenly dipped her head as a sob wretched from her mouth – a sound that Riana could hear came up from her stomach, from her toes, from the depth of her as a person.

Riana's tears seemed to think Ms. Hightower's tears needed company, and poured from her eyes, despite Riana's bidding them to stay put.

Ms. Hightower lifted her head suddenly, catching Riana's multi-colored gaze and immediately softened with a look of chagrin. "Oh, I'm so sorry, dear. I didn't mean to upset you. This was all just so unexpected. She was in the best of health. She was a pillar of the community. She was my boss, but she was also my friend. To think someone could murder her..." she broke into a fresh wave of sobs.

Riana watched as the cellar manager pulled a handkerchief from her sleeve, wiped her face, blew her nose loudly and then regarded Riana with red eyes. Riana took her own handkerchief – one of the many her grandmother had given to her – and wiped at her face. Her eye now throbbed with refreshed pain. Crying and black eyes didn't mix, it seemed. As if her thinking of it called attention to it, Ms. Hightower's face turned stunned.

"What happened to you?"

Riana breathed in deeply and let it out long and slow. She was tired of discussing it, she decided, and wanted to immerse herself in work. "Oh, I just slipped and fell when I was moving things into my new living quarters at the General Store. Right into a doorknob. Silly." She waved away Ms. Hightower's concern, inside loathing Mr. Fraely.

Ms. Hightower cocked a dark eyebrow over an equally dark eye. Her gaze bore into Riana and Riana felt color creep into her cheeks. "Fell, is it? Into a doorknob?"

"It was very clumsy of me," Riana confirmed.

Ms. Hightower hmphed and slowly shifted her gaze to a corner in the small office. "So, now I know what he's up to," she whispered.

"Excuse me?" Riana asked.

She nodded, coming back to the present, and looked at Riana. "Your father – "

"Guardian," Riana interrupted.

"What do you mean?"

"I mean, he's no father of mine," Riana said.

"Ah. I understand. Very well. Mr. Fraely would like nothing more than to gobble up Starliss Vineyard. He was by here last week and proposed we halt your apprenticeship. He also offered his 'help' to run the business. Your fa-, excuse me, Mr. Fraely has a well-known reputation in Landsend. And it isn't good."

"I see," Riana said.

"So, I politely declined his help and asked him to relay to you that we would be looking forward to seeing you this week, upon your return to school."

"He didn't tell me," Riana said.

"No, I figured he would not. That is why I left the message with your teacher."

"Thank you. I wasn't sure what would happen now that she's gone."

"I will tell you, Riana. I didn't much care for you, but I cared deeply for your grandmother. And she wanted you to have Starliss Vineyard. Believed in your capability implicitly," she said. She pointed a finger at Riana, her expression growing steely, back to the face Riana was so accustomed to seeing. "And I'll tell you something else. I'll be dead before I let Sela Starliss's son-in-law take over this vineyard."

Riana couldn't help the smile creeping up one corner of her mouth.

"So, we've got work to do to get you ready for your sixteenth birthday. Let's get to it."

Riana extended her hand as Ms. Hightower rose from the chair. At first the cellar manager regarded it as if it were a snake about to strike. She grabbed the hand and shook it firmly, nodding her satisfaction with stern approval.

"The first thing we must do is prepare for the Spring Ball, welcoming in our new Baron with wine galore. Your grandmother was much better at this aspect than I am. I'll expect you picked up a trick or two from studying her." Ms. Hightower turned to the desk upon which lay a large book. Riana recognized it as the ledger; a book her grandmother had trained her to read when she was tending her internship.

"So, today we'll be reviewing the many types of wines we have in the cellars and I'll be showing you which the baron has ordered most frequently, and which are even better than those. While we're doing that, we'll go over all the stock so you can comfortably speak about our wine to the denizens of the ball to promote Starliss Vineyard most accurately."

Now, there was something Riana could do.

The rest of the day was spent perusing the cavernous cellars, Ms. Hightower stopping at various racks of wines to quiz Riana on them. Riana grew up in these cellars; Grandmother Sela had been educating her on the making of wine since she'd adopted her at the age of eight. Her apprenticeship had been going on much longer than the months leading up to her grandmother's murder.

Ms. Hightower had been pleased with Riana's knowledge and praised her in short, emotionless responses. Nevertheless, Riana knew a compliment when she heard it. The cellar manager was so impressed with her work, she had released Riana early, with daylight still to burn.

"I think I'll just walk through the cellars for a bit longer before I leave," Riana told Ms. Hightower.

Ms. Hightower was sitting again at Sela's desk. Her features softened. She didn't speak but nodded and gave an understanding smile.

Riana walked down the sloping ramp from the production room into the cellar. She passed through the rows of aging liquid until she reached the open area with the chandelier, a wine barrel propped under it as a table on which to uncork and taste the various vintages. She passed this and headed for the ancient vintage room. Before she pushed the door open, she twisted the knob of her oil lamp, extending the wick higher to cast more light into the utter darkness.

She closed the door behind her and moved swiftly through the aged racks and bottles collecting dust, taking a left at the last row and stooping to the hidden door. It was the first time she'd been back since her grandmother had died.

She put her hands over the place a door should be but was not apparently there. She pushed, the wall rattled, slid, and revealed an opening. She set her lamp on the dirt floor and crawled through the opening. She retrieved the lamp and closed the door. It gave a click, satisfying Riana that it was firmly shut. She turned as if she were about to see her grandmother there. The room was empty.

Well, it was empty of people. But it was full, too. Full of dried plants, fire nymph wings, antoli fangs, talismans, charms, instruments and most importantly, books. Riana couldn't help the welling of tears. Soon, this place would be hers. If she could just make it through the next few weeks, she would leave Mr. Fraely's, take up residence at her grandmother's home, and work here in the winery. She would escape whenever she wanted into this room where she could find not just solitude and comfort, but information.

Riana looked around at the familiar shelves, tasting the thrill at seeing spines boasting ornamental titles: The Secret Study of Etyr; Why the Magys is Extinct; The Five Dragons; An History of the Inilu; Creatures of the Shoqui Plains; Elementals of Aelos: A Catalogue. The smell was even comforting. Dust and paper, wood and dried herbs hanging here and there.

Riana went to one of the shelves adorned in various items. There was a stray fire nymph wing, a lonely necklace and a glass case containing what looked like a twig. Riana picked it up and turned it over. There was an inscription. Lock Pick, by Kaely.

The chair she'd read in was still flanked by a sturdy and ancient side table. Unfamiliar, though, was what lay on the table. Riana shuffled toward it.

"Another book," she mumbled. She picked it up and turned it to its cover, curious which forbidden knowledge this book outlined. The binding was a rich, soft chocolate leather, so supple Riana immediately set the lamp in the place of the book she held and stroked the outer casing.

The front had neither pictures nor words to illustrate its contents. Riana turned it to its spine, but there was nothing there either. Her arms tingled as she held the book and then was followed by a shiver down her spine. She held the book to her thumping heart, tilting her eyes heavenward, toward a sky she couldn't see. Could it be?

Finally, she stilled her shaking hands enough to crack open the book. She hurried over to the seat, feeling herself sway. The words on the page blurred and cleared, blurred, and cleared as the tears ran.

THE DRAGON'S EYE

Journal

Of

Sela Starliss

The word 'journal' was embossed in gold. Riana ran a finger over the fine work of it. She'd never seen such beautiful printing before and with golden ink. Under the word 'of' a line opened the possibility of the book's ownership. Her grandmother's name was written in perfect handwriting, which Riana recognized immediately as Sela's. Riana gripped her chest at the ache there. How many times had she been down into this little dungeon cavern of secrets, yet she had never seen this journal. Riana wondered if her grandmother had left it here for her to find.

She was careful to hold the book away from her enough that her tears fell onto her leathers rather than this new keepsake she'd discovered. She continued her hand's exploration of the page, running fingers over the indentation made by the quill where the paper had soaked in the ink. This handwriting was so familiar, Riana had to wonder how old it could really be. It seemed intact, new even.

She turned the page and found her answer at the top, right corner of the page. Sela Starliss had started writing this journal in 512 P.A. (the time frame after the genocide on Tyrmini and revolution of High King Achyla), the year she'd been born.

Dear Riana,

I am keeping this journal in the hopes one day you will find it useful. You will likely have many questions about your origin, your power and your heritage, even your very existence. This is not a pretty tale. I caution you to read these writings knowing your view on your current reality may shift entirely.

Everything you've known about our history on Aelos,
the nature of Tyrmini and elementals has been a lie. I
have kept so much from you to keep you safe from harm,
because even knowing the truths hidden in this journal
may paint a target on your back. So, my child, proceed
through these pages carefully.

It was a cool spring day in Landsend. I had taken to the
north road to stretch my legs and hike to the Lighthouse.
When I arrived, I was stunned to discover two women
in the field. One of the women was clearly from the
Aestyrah Desert and the other was laboring in childbirth.

The Aestyran named herself Mylah, a powerful fire and
Tyrinth Tyrmini. They could not travel to Healer's Hall for
fear Mylah would be discovered and more importantly
her laboring companion. I helped to birth you, but your
mother did not survive.

As to who your mother was...

Riana snapped the book shut. Her heart pounded in her chest and in the still of the room, it thundered in her ears. After all the years she'd asked about her mother, all the years of wondering and imagining, she now didn't want to know. She was afraid of knowing. She puzzled over the fear. Why didn't she want to know? This new aversion of curiosity, of knowledge about herself and her heritage stunned her. And then she realized. She didn't want to know because she had already claimed Sela Starliss as her grandmother. Any other knowledge would contradict that. She wasn't ready for it.

As she held the journal in her hands, savoring the warmth of the leather binding, she noticed an ear mark on a page at the end of the book. Riana opened the book once again.

A drawing stretched across the page. In the upper corner the familiar shape of the lighthouse was sketched in ink. Underneath it, her grandmother's writing labeled a small hillock at the east side of the lighthouse, the side behind the Dreavynan.

> I'm not certain, but it seems to me you may be able to open this entrance. I have tried and failed. It must take a Tyrmini, or you, a Magys, if my theories are accurate, to open it. I don't know how, but if you've awakened your power, there is a way you can ask it to show you the way. It is imperative you search out and learn how to open this portal immediately after you've discovered this journal.

> If you've found the journal, I'm dead. If I'm dead, you're most likely being hunted by the High King. The Dragon's Eye may not work on you, but he has other ways. You may need to transport yourself quickly across Aelos. Mylah has assured me the High King cannot use these portals.

Riana's head spun. What did she mean The Dragon's Eye may not work on her? And, portals? She might not be curious enough to read the passages of her life's beginning, but she was certainly curious about a portal. She checked her pendant watch. There wasn't enough time now, and as she considered, she wanted to have Elynda with her for the discovery. She read back over the passage to secure the information in her mind. Once she closed the book, she held it to her heart.

"Thank you, Grandmother," Riana said. "You're still looking out for me, even after you're gone."

She set the book back in its place on the side table next to the chair, sending a mental promise she would return tomorrow and read further.

For now, she had to return to the General Store. Mr. Fraely wanted her home before sunset. She crawled back through the hidden door, carefully peering around to ensure no one else had come here, then hauled her lamp and herself out into the must and gloom of the forgotten cellar room. After she replaced the door, she made her way past the ancient vintages and carefully pushed open the door that led to the great expanse of the wine cellar. No one was around, but as soon as she had closed the door and walked past the tasting barrel perched under the candelabra, she spied workers down several aisles, stowing, shifting, boxing, and turning the wines.

Soon they would be her responsibility. She would need to lead them as Sela Starliss had. Her stomach flopped at the notion. She didn't know if she could handle that much responsibility.

Outside the winery, a breeze met her face. She inhaled deeply, loosening the dusty clutch of the cellar from her nose. Riana relished the walk back to the General Store without relishing the thought of arriving. The sky was a peaceful teal fading into navy blue. In the fields on opposite sides of the road, frogs tuned up for their nightly performance. Crickets picked out a tune. The rush and hush of the ocean kept rhythm. This was a night of springtime joy.

Riana hoped the evening would have the same effect on Mr. Fraely as it had on her. The leaden ball in the pit of her stomach told her otherwise.

The twilight swallowed the horizon in light blues, save one small smudge of yellow that illuminated a window of the General Store. She cast a worried gaze to the sky.

"If there's truly a Mother and Father up there watching out for us, I could use your help right now." Her boots scuffed in the dirt. She felt as if someone were pulling her away from the old wooden building. The sign boasted loudly: "Landsend's Prized General Store". But in the near darkness, their painted letters looked dingy and foreboding. As if they warned her away instead of welcoming her in.

She took several long, slow breaths to calm her suddenly racing heart. Her instincts goaded her to escape.

She stepped up the three short stairs, crossed the porch and pulled the screen door open.

The first thing she saw was his watery-blue stare glaring at her from behind the counter.

CHAPTER EIGHT

The second thing she saw was Ms. Hightower, who stood across the counter from Mr. Fraely. Her thin lips pulled away from teeth yellowed by the repeated sampling of wine. Her dark eyes tried capturing Mr. Fraely's, but his were locked on Riana.

Riana's gaze darted between the two angry adults, waiting for the eruption.

At last, Ms. Hightower broke her lock on Mr. Fraely's face enough to dart a glance toward what had distracted him from her. When she saw Riana, her face softened.

"Ah, Riana," she started.

"Ms. Hightower?" Riana asked and couldn't help the nerves shaking her voice. She wondered if the repeat of last night would take place after she left. She was sure she'd said something to Mr. Fraely, even if Riana had claimed the doorknob had blackened her eye and not Mr. Fraely.

Ms. Hightower turned toward Riana, set her legs in a wide stance, and folded her hands together in front of her. "Yes, your – Mr. Fraely – and I were just having a discussion about your apprenticeship in regard to his responsibility as your guardian," she said.

Riana looked between the two of them, waiting for one to continue. Mr. Fraely's spectacles slipped down his shiny nose. He nudged them up with a thick knuckle, then peered at Riana through the square glass.

"There's nothing to discuss," Mr. Fraely said. "Your grandmother saw to it to saddle me with an orphan."

Riana's stomach squeezed in on itself at the mention of her grandmother, the slander at her station as an orphan, and the hatred with which he spoke of her.

"If you think I won't use you to do some work, though, I'll be swallowed by the Throne!" He shouted and Riana flinched away.

"I think you've asserted your power enough for a day or two, Mr. Fraely. Have you no decency? Hitting a young girl."

"I just took a spill, Ms. Hightower," Riana lied. She had not been fooling Ms. Hightower, it seemed.

"What are you talking about?" Mr. Fraely said. "The girl is clumsy."

Footsteps sounded off and then Ms. Hightower's hand gripped Riana's chin and hoisted it up to the light of the lanterns illuminating the stock-stuffed room.

"This," Ms. Hightower said.

"I don't see a thing," he said, and crossed his arms in defiance.

Ms. Hightower looked at Riana and her eyes widened in shock.

"What?" Riana asked. She didn't think it had been hurting as bad, but maybe the bruising had gone a really nasty shade of purple in the last several hours.

"It's gone," Ms. Hightower whispered.

"Gone?" Riana asked.

"A little bruise from being a klutz that's already healed," Mr. Fraely said. Riana couldn't decide if he looked disturbed, relieved, smug, or worried. Maybe he felt them all.

Ms. Hightower's hand slipped from her face.

Riana was dying to run to her room and look at herself in the mirror. But her mind was also hyper focused on the fate of her future at her grandmother's winery. "What of my apprenticeship?" she asked.

"You're my apprentice," Ms. Hightower said.

Riana's nerves eased at this announcement, right up until her guardian's voice barked out his own assertation.

"But you'll be doing chores when you're not at the vineyard," Mr. Fraely said.

Great. Two apprenticeships, Riana thought.

CHAPTER NINE

He slipped and swirled down dark tunnels. Distantly he heard screams of terror, shouts of agony and wails of despair. Reddish, ruddy light illuminated his path by the meagerest means and set his nerves throbbing with the sense of danger. Danger. It was always dangerous to traverse these tunnels.

While he was sucked through the neverwhere, he lost his sense of self. As if the place pulled at the unique pieces that made him who he was. It pulled at his memories, his purpose, his personality and abilities, and connections to others. He could not recall why he was in this place or what had led up to his venturing into this shadow realm. At last when he was hollow, the place began to fill him with new emotion: first with regret, then with agony and finally with sheer panic. The most maddening part of it was the lack of logic as to why he felt the way he felt.

Luther plunged through the aching, red darkness, his teeth gritted against an urgent scream for help to be saved from the unholy landscape of the damned. Perhaps this was the time Luther's master would leave him here. Perhaps the High King would at last be rid of the Captain of the Tyrmini Guard and find another.

At that thought he recalled one thing that made his life unique. His daughter. His daughter needed him.

He held on to the thought like a lifeline and let the pull of his master haul him through the wilderness of eternity.

Luther fell through a clinging barrier that rent open with the weight of his body, like skin being torn to birth him. He landed hard against a stone floor and felt his shoulder pop at the impact. He lay there, eyes pressed tightly closed, heaving in a great lungful of air that burned. His body shivered, his teeth clattering together. There was an unpleasant throb behind his eyes and his stomach lurched. His abdominals squeezed and he vomited as the vertigo that set his head spinning became too much.

"Are your wounds healed?" the High King asked. His voice was paper thin. He must have aged further since Luther had seen him just a few short months ago.

When his head stopped spinning and his body calmed from the uncontrollable quaking, he took stock of himself; primarily his midsection which the girl had skewered with – what had it been? – light spears, was the only way he could think to describe it.

He tentatively looked down at his body. His clothes were torn and blood-stained and smoke rose from him. He touched the exposed skin of his stomach. The wounds were still there, but they were no longer life-threatening. He supposed he should be grateful the journey through the neverwhere had the pleasant side effect of healing his wounds. The peace of death had been postponed twice now. He was consumed by a soul exhaustion that eclipsed his gratitude for living.

He tried speaking to confirm he would live, but he only managed a squeak. He swallowed to wet the dry tissue in his throat and mouth. He pushed himself to a kneeling position.

"Yes, High King," he managed, his voice like sandpaper, both in the sound of it and the feel of it. "I will live." There was regret in his voice, but also relief. He could only assume his daughter would be slaughtered as soon as he died.

"To be healed. If only..." the King dissolved into racking coughs.

Luther scrambled to his feet, fighting the wave of dizziness. He stumbled into the table set in the middle of the room, dragging remnants of herbs and salt from the circle that had been created to bring him back. He rubbed at the tattoo over his heart. It always burned after it had been used to pull him through.

Luther tipped a pitcher of water into a waiting goblet and staggered to the High King's chaise chair. It was his comfortable place when he was working his own brand of elemental magic. He was in his sleeping gown and rich, red velvet robe which set off his blonde hair and pale complexion. He was skinny and sickly – not the strapping man he'd known when the High King had first appointed him to his post. The king was too young to be so sick and weak.

The High King took the cup and drained it noisily. Then he sat back into the cushions and heaved as he tried to recover.

"Be grateful for your health," the King said. "Being without it makes everything so much more difficult."

"Yes, my King, I am grateful," Luther said, ducking his head and backing away from the ruler of Aelos. "Please forgive me if I sounded ungrateful."

The High King waved away his comment. "Enough," he said. "Tell me about the girl."

"She is powerful," Luther confirmed. "But, something entirely different. Entirely un-elemental. I've never seen such a power before," he said.

"Go on," the King demanded.

"It is as though her intention is sculpted from light or energy. It's not Tyrinth, Water, Air or Fire or any combination of those things. She is altogether new. Altogether unique. And altogether dangerous. I sense she could cause real trouble." A fact he counted on to carry out his plan.

"Light, you say? Light," the High King asked this as if he wanted to believe it weren't the case. As if he wanted to believe the Captain had conjured from imagination some new power source aside from the elements, rather than being skewered by it.

"I have not witnessed any power its equal," Luther said and for that he caught the full and overbearing gaze of the High King. His eyes were a prominent watery blue with red rims of fatigue and illness. He wondered how much time he had left; if there was really time to produce an heir.

The High King narrowed his gaze. The room grew fiercely quiet. Shadow roiled and spread from the corners of the room. Luther's body grew heavy and chilled as tentacles of darkness reached toward him. He mastered his fear only because he'd practiced so often.

Luther had faced dangerous Tyrmini, their raw power explosive, even murderous, and none of those elemental powers disturbed him quite the way his king wielded this dark magic.

Few knew Achylla's little secret: that he possessed magic. It would do no good for a man who insisted on the slaughter of magical people to have magic himself.

The High King's handsome, but sickly face seemed bent on Luther's destruction. His frame quivered slightly. As suddenly as his temper flared, it washed away. He blinked and exhaled. The tension in the room deflated. The shadow abated, dark tentacles slithering back into the corners, like dogs tugged away on their leashes. Luther let go of the breath he was holding.

"You have failed me once again. If there were any other choice of guard, you would be ashes." The High King's words whipped out at Luther, one lash after the next. "Do I need to remind you who's being kept in a cell, in my dungeon, at my mercy?"

"No, your majesty," Luther croaked, his throat dry.

"Do I need to tell you what fate your daughter would be granted should you fail me again?"

"No, Majesty," Luther said.

Silence stretched between them as the High King surveyed Luther, his gaze uncomfortably stripping him down to the soul, laying bare his vulnerabilities and weaknesses and failures. When he seemed satisfied, he looked away, back into the flames.

"Bring me the eye and let us look in on our new and strange friend," he said.

Luther wobbled toward the hidden altar. His bootheels first scraped the castle's original stone floor, then softened as he crossed the intricately woven crimson and gold rug. The fire hissed and crackled

like a faithful pet, casting warm, orange light onto the ornate furniture.
Oil lamps installed in sconces on the walls, cast yellow light in globular
pools into the room. A trip through the neverwhere always made his
bones feel like jelly, but then facing the High King of Aelos liquified
them, rendering him weak as a kitten.

Luther approached the cabinet. Its lustrous wood shone with fresh
polish and the mounted golden decorations, fashioned in the shapes of
dragons, sparkled with a high shine. Luther stood in front of the cabinet
for a moment, stilling his raging nerves, hoping his hands weren't
shaking too badly. Finally, he pressed the tiny panel on the upper-right
corner of the cabinet's top. It sprung out into a handle. Luther pushed
the handle to the left. From there, he pulled at another section of wood
which sprang free. He then pulled at a larger panel that resulted in
the right dragon ornament shifting clockwise thirty-five degrees and
revealing yet another false panel. He continued with the puzzle, pulling,
pushing, twisting and turning various pieces of the furniture hidden to
the inexperienced eye, until at last the doors clicked open. He swung
the cabinet door wide cringing as he always did at what lie inside.

Magloryn's eye was a rainbow of colors. Encased in thick glass,
suspended in fluid, the disembodied eyeball of the dragon shifted up
to stare at Luther, the pupil narrowing, as if accusing him. And oh, did
his sins call to him when he looked in this eye. The shame of his deeds
dropped into his belly and burned.

He lifted the eye from the cushion while it bored into his soul. His
hands vibrated with energy. The irises shifted, the many colors bleeding
away from the black pupil to form a solid silver, the fibers reflecting
like strands of diamond. As he turned away from the cabinet, the color
trembled and burst into a vibrant, sunset orange. When he aimed the
eye at the High King, making his way over the carpets, past furniture,
the eye shifted again to a brilliant violet, then blue, then green and
finally it settled to a purest black.

He nearly dropped the eye. He had never seen it shift to black
before. He glanced at the High King, who, sick or not, straightened in

the chaise, his mouth opening like a fish out of water. Luther's spine prickled in warning. But, in the warning was something so much bigger. Something so profound, Luther could not help a surge of excitement. As if change were inevitable. Be damned. I'll see a new reality, so I will, I swear, he thought as he walked slowly toward the High King and gazed at the blackness of the Dragon's Eye.

He could only surmise his excitement could be aimed toward one ending: safety for his daughter. He stowed the thoughts and emotions and placed the eye into the waiting hands of the High King.

Luther backed away. Holding a disembodied eye of a deity dragon was one thing; watching the High King perform the ritual spell to see through it evoked a dread in him he could never explain to another living soul. It was horrific.

Flames danced in the fireplace. The High King gazed into the eye. Luther had done dreadful, awful things in the name of saving his daughter. What the High King did through him and his other Tyrmini guards was damning. Yet, the High King looked into the eye of Magloryn with no hint of remorse or guilt. That was the thing that bothered Luther most about his position and the duties he carried out. If true genocide was the only way to keep the vast majority of Aelos safe from certain destruction, wouldn't the weight of those other lives he was supposedly saving mean he had a heart? Luther knew better. The High King was threatened by others having power. There could never be a Tyrmini left alive whom he couldn't control. Their collective power could overthrow him. Even Mylah on her own was a threat to the High King. Which is why he had not seen her in so long.

Deep, guttural words jerked out of the High King. There was an ancient rhythm to them that tainted the room in shadow, thrusting the here and now away and replacing it with an old reality. It was as if the room disappeared and Luther and the High King were in a cave with nothing but a glowing fire between them. Luther folded himself to the ground, swearing it felt of jagged stone instead of rich carpet.

Shadows slid into view, gliding across the wall and then away. The High King continued his chant, the eye gripped in his bony hands as he rocked forward and back. The shadow gathered like a cloud over the High King. His chants stopped. His head lolled forward. The black cloud hanging over him descended, concentrating until it seemed substantial. The cloud formed a crown and then locked onto the head of the High King. The High King inhaled violently, his body ratcheted back, greasy hair flinging off his face. There between his eyebrows burned the man's third eye, a deep indigo spot that reflected the flames of the fire. A tendril of shadow snaked out of the third eye, twisting and seeking as if hungry. At last it found Magloryn's eye and darted forward, viciously attacking the eye, penetrating the glass and fluid. It sank into the vertical pupil. The eye shivered as if struggling against the shadow then stilled.

The High King kept his two eyes closed while the third indigo eye remained open. He beckoned Luther over with the wave of a hand. Luther crawled across the floor and looked at the surface of glass encasing the eye. He watched as the image cleared, eventually becoming so vibrant it blocked the visibility of Magloryn's eye.

Images of Riana walking along the North Road in Landsend danced across the surface. She was talking, but there was no sound. One could only see with the eye, not hear.

"This is the girl," the High King said, although maybe he'd meant it as a question.

"Yes, Majesty," Luther confirmed.

"I see nothing about this girl that makes her unique," snarled the High King. "How is it she bested you?"

"My King, truly, I do not know. The girl possesses a power –,"

"Wait," the High King said, although his voice was layered and dripping with deep, unfamiliar notes. "Watch."

Luther obeyed. He was a wise enough man to know the shadow that inhabited his master's body was not one to be trifled with.

"We sense something," the High King and the Shadow breathed.

The view in the Dragon's Eye zoomed out, revealing more of what surrounded Riana. Behind Riana, a vibrant aura pulsated in hues of green, orange, yellow, blue and red. The High King shifted, breath catching. Their view was over Riana's shoulder and the aura of elemental power grew. Luther could sense the desperate hope rolling off the High King. He could almost smell his eagerness, a sweaty aroma with sharp and tangy bitterness. He recoiled from the sensation, pulling away enough so he was not overwhelmed by the need he felt from the High King.

The concentration of the multicolored aura grew so bright it nearly washed out all other details of the scene playing out before them. The High King shook with excitement, his mouth stretched in a maniacal smile that showed all his teeth and pulled his purple lips to near nothingness.

He slumped forward, uttering several guttural words which were more the sound of shadow than the voice of the High King. The shadow retreated, drawing out of the dragon's eye, out of the High King and finally out of the room.

When the High King sat up, he was shaking and sweaty. Luther's heart dropped into his stomach. He knew what this vision meant, and he hated what would come next. Luther hung his head as he scooped up the eye and carried it back to the cabinet. Movement across the eye captured his attention. The vision zoomed out and overlooked the whole of Landsend. Pricking the vision like pillars of lights were columns of elemental auras. Many of them. And all concentrated around one strange girl.

CHAPTER TEN

Elynda had been dismissed for the evening from her apprenticeship and Riana had begged the night off from Ms. Hightower, due to the ensuing chores assigned by Mr. Fraely. It had only been a week since she'd restarted her apprenticeship at the winery again, and Ms. Hightower had been hesitant to allow her the time away. Yet, there was something warm in her eyes when Riana had asked for the time to spend with Elynda. In the end, she'd crumpled under Riana's insistent pleading and let her go.

Riana didn't dare ask the same of Mr. Fraely, but as it turned out, he'd dismissed Riana on account of training his new apprentice.

Riana and Elynda had the full evening to themselves, a weekend unencumbered by responsibility in which they would spend at Elynda's home. Riana was ecstatic to escape the drills of Ms. Hightower, the abuse of Mr. Fraely, and the confined space of her small and bare bedroom behind the General Store.

She'd also spirited out her grandmother's journal with full intentions of visiting the mound behind the lighthouse. They walked together along North Road, Riana buzzing with excitement and Elynda firing questions off about Sela Starliss's journal.

"What else does she say, Riana? What else have you read aside from this page talking about a transport stone?" Elynda asked.

"Not much, really. Grandmother basically gave me homework. She alluded to other books in the secret room I should read to understand some history we aren't normally taught."

"Like what? Tell me! Don't hold out." Elynda whined at her best friend.

Riana snagged her hand in her own, pulling her close. There was no one else on the road, but she couldn't bear to speak loudly of information she was sure was forbidden by the law.

"Did you know that the High King is himself possesses some form of magic?" Riana started, her mind whirling with the information she gulped down in spare moments between her apprenticeship and the chores doled out by her adopted father.

"No," Elynda said. "But why does he assassinate Tyrmini, then?"

"I don't know," Riana said, her face downcast. "Well, I mean he doesn't assassinate them all, does he? He saves the powerful ones to be his soldiers. The ones who go and kill the others."

"The Tyrmini Guard," Elynda said, hanging her head and looking at the rock road. "Serve or die."

"Yes, exactly," Riana confirmed. "Grandmother suspected I was Tyrmini, but she says I'm different."

"Did she explain what that difference is?" Elynda asked, her round eyes suddenly fixated on Riana. A light wind buffeted them and Elynda's curls of dark hair swirled around her heart-shaped face.

"She called me a 'Magys', but so far, I haven't read what the difference is between Tyrmini and Magys," Riana said, thinking of the beginning she'd chosen not to read. Perhaps that explanation was laid out cleanly for her on pages she wasn't ready to read.

"Oh," Elynda said. "I see."

"I haven't read it all yet. So, I'm not sure. Maybe she tells me what I am. Maybe she knew."

"Maybe she didn't but she has enough information she's given you a place to start the research?" Elynda asked.

"It could be," Riana said. "I brought the journal, in case I wanted to read more this weekend." Riana said this and suddenly wished she hadn't. She didn't know if she was prepared for the truth hidden in the pages she'd chosen to skip. Maybe she wasn't. And could she explain that to Elynda? Could she tell her best friend she couldn't bare the truth of her own existence? Riana felt weak and pathetic. Her grandmother had gone through extreme efforts to ensure Riana had all the information she needed to survive, and yet Riana couldn't handle it. She couldn't handle reading it. Because she couldn't stomach the fact she was truly without living blood ties. Riana was sure Elynda's next words would be to push her to read more of the journal.

"That's got to be really difficult and emotional to read. You should take your time getting through it," Elynda said.

Riana's eyes welled with tears. She swiped them away before Elynda could see. "Yeah, I'll take it easy," Riana said.

They made it to the lighthouse by midafternoon. Riana shouldn't have been surprised by their progress since she'd kept a quick pace, her curiosity pushing her. She'd waited almost a full week to see the place. Now that she was able to look at it, it didn't seem real.

The crash of the Dreavynan against the ancient black cliffs of Landsend warned them from the cliffside. No light burned in the white tower, but a friendly old man's face could be seen through the glass between the passing circles of his rag on the windows. A stump of a pipe was bitten between his teeth and his white hair was partially concealed by the dark cap of a sea captain.

Riana ducked past his potential gaze, heading for the land side of the lighthouse. To its east, they would find the hillock her grandmother mentioned. And find it, they did. The trouble was, it seemed to be nothing more than a sturdy mound of dirt and long grasses and lavender, fragrant and covered in bees. Riana and Elynda circled the mound, looking for some indication of an entrance.

Elynda stopped and stared into the dirt and grass. "Look here," she said.

"It's grass," Riana said, disappointment filling her and wondering about Elynda's judgment. She looked at her friend. Elynda radiated energy. Riana thought she saw a nimbus of blue and green around her, but as quickly as it came it was gone again. Riana shook her head to dispel the odd vision.

"No, look closer," Elynda said, sounding cross.

Riana looked in the direction Elynda pointed and after a long stretch of silence, gave up. "I don't see any-," she started. Yet, as soon as she began to claim a lack of anything out of the ordinary, something extraordinary began to happen.

"What is that?" Riana whispered.

The soil beneath the grass shimmered in a subtle opalescent. Riana dropped to a sitting position and pulled her grandmother's journal from her rucksack. She opened the book up to the dog-eared page.

Her grandmother had said she was a Magys and as one, she could call upon her power to know what she needed to do to open the secret entrance. Riana thought about this and knew what she had to do.

"So, how do you open it?" Elynda asked.

"You know when we were rescuing the berubula?"

"Yes?"

"Well, when it attacked me, the light energy inside me? It automatically protected me. But, when I was trying to protect myself from Luther, I tried to call on it. At first, I failed, but later when I needed to protect grandmother, it came out no problem."

"How so?" Elynda asked.

"I called on the dragon of light, Magloryn," Riana said.

"Dragon of light?" Elynda asked. "I didn't know one existed."

"Neither did I, but when all of this started happening, I began having dreams about a beautiful white dragon with one eye. Then, when the power stopped the berubula from eating me-" she paused to shudder – "her name kept repeating in my mind. As if she were speaking to me."

Elynda shifted, inching closer to Riana. "So, what if you do that now? Call her name in your mind?"

"Yes," Riana said, "I think that could work."

"What can I do to help?"

Riana thought about it. "Um, I don't know. Maybe..." She held out her hand to Elynda, somehow wanting the comfort and reassurance her friend's touch could lend her.

Elynda placed her hand in Riana's and they both turned their gaze to the mound before them.

Riana drew up the memory of the power that had manifested during the berubula incident. The white dragon who called itself Magloryn had felt like a companion spirit to her own. A part of her, yet somewhat separate.

Riana called the name in her mind. She felt a glimmer of light spark within her. She repeated the name again, calling on the memory of the energy that had captured and protected her. The light flickered into a warm flame. She focused on it, continuing the chant, as if stoking the fire with her intention.

The light within her pushed through a last barrier inside her soul and burst through the physical plane. It filled her blood, bone, and muscles with a surging buoyancy. She looked down and found her body was outlined in white-blue light. She squeezed Elynda's hand before releasing it. She stretched forward toward the shimmering spot in the grass, reaching for an invisible handle. When her hand closed around it, her heart jangled at the very real sensation. She twisted the knob and pushed the door open.

Beside her, Elynda gasped. Riana crawled through the opening. As her feet touched the floor, carvings in the stone beneath her grew luminescent. Light spread out from where she stood as if soaking in the energy cloaking her. The carvings lit the room with slow spreading succession, first the floor, then the walls until the energy touched sconces and invisible wicks flared to life.

The room was circular and much larger than Riana could have imagined. The pattern of carvings depicted a maze that led to the center where a gem-studded golden disc glittered in the energy light.

Elynda crawled through the opening, stepping down with care. "Wow," she said. She absently dusted at her dress as her wide eyes canvassed the room with what Riana thought was growing wonder. "This has been here all our lives and we never knew?"

"Grandmother says it was hidden when the High King began the Tyrmini genocide. They were afraid he would destroy them, so they hid them away."

"And what does it do again?" asked Elynda. She took several steps toward the center of the room.

"It's a transport," Riana replied. "Grandmother wanted me to know about it in case anyone else showed up and tried to kill me."

"How did your grandmother know about this?" Elynda looked at her, green eyes searching Riana's face for answers.

Riana swallowed. "I guess this is where my mother gave birth to me. And then died." Her voice quavered.

"How was your grandmother here for that?" Elynda's green eyes narrowed.

"She was walking along North Road to the Lighthouse when she saw a woman in the field. The woman asked for help and she followed her in here." Riana gestured around her, taking in the wide, open circular room. The lights on the wall flickered in their ethereal blue flame.

"So, your grandmother has known all this time about your mother?"

"Yes," Riana said. Her stomach knotted at the next question she knew would come.

"And why didn't she tell you?"

Riana didn't want to be mad at her grandmother, but she had been asking the same question many times since reading the beginning entry in the journal her grandmother had written for her. "She says in the journal she was keeping the truth from me in order to keep me safe. That knowing may have put me at risk."

"How?" Elynda asked. She had turned to Riana and now crossed her arms over her stomach.

Riana's nerves grew jagged. "I don't know, Elynda. I didn't keep reading to find out. That's my fault, not Sela's." Riana stopped. She had just referred to her grandmother by her name rather than the title she had for her. It hit her hard. She had no claim to her grandmother. Sela Starliss had no claim to her. She was an orphan, but more than that, she was on the brink of adulthood and she was acting like a scared child.

Elynda's mouth dropped open. The significance of Riana calling her grandmother by name had not been lost on her it seemed.

"I'm sorry," Riana said. Her fear and confusion, loss and hurt bubbled to the surface and before she could stop herself, tears poured from her eyes as gut-wrenching sobs burst from her belly and out her mouth. She fell to the floor, fingers sliding over the strange lit grooves of the carved stone.

Elynda scurried over, kneeling beside Riana, and wrapping a warm arm around her shoulders. "You don't need to be sorry. I'm sorry I pushed you. I just think there's a lot to know and a lot you seem to be ignoring. What if Sela was right? What if you are in danger? What if her telling you before you finding this journal could have prevented everything you went through before her death? Maybe you could have been more prepared when Treyor attacked you. And then Captain Luther."

Riana sobbed in response. She had had such thoughts and had stuffed them quietly down, thinking no one else in the world would consider these things, and wanting nothing to tarnish the memory of the only woman she had called family.

"I know your grandmother loved you deeply and I know she was doing what she thought was right and that's commendable. It doesn't, however, mean it was right."

"She couldn't know. She couldn't know what I'd go through."

"Is that really true? It seems like she may have known. Otherwise, why would she have kept this meticulous journal entailing all the information you need? You know Riana, maybe she just wanted to pretend you weren't who you really are. She'd lost her daughter. Her husband died ages ago. Maybe she needed you just as much as you needed her."

Riana's heart throbbed, and the energy of her love expanded through her chest. "So, you're saying Grandmother may have made a mistake by not preparing me for the inevitable, but she did it because she loved me so much?"

"That's exactly what I'm saying," Elynda said. "You've got to own that she may have made a mistake. You may have some similar situations come up in the future, and you have the opportunity to apply the wisdom then that you're gaining now, as long as you can embrace it."

Riana looked up at Elynda's determined and loving gaze. "When did you get so wise?"

Elynda chuckled. "It's nothing special, Riana. I'm on the outside looking in. A fresh pair of eyes. It's tough to see things clearly when you're in the middle of it."

"I need to read this journal. All of it. Even the parts I don't want to hear," Riana determined.

"Yes. Captain Luther may be dead, but the High King has a whole retinue of Tyrmini Guards. He could appoint anyone of them to come after you. What your grandmother has given you in the journal may be the key to keeping you alive. And by all the dragons of all the elements, I'll be damned if I stand by and watch you stumble into danger through ignorance because you're turning a blind eye."

Riana could barely hold the steely gaze of her best friend. Framed in dark, distinguished eyebrows and peachy soft skin, the emerald of her eyes flashed in warning: dare not deny this truth. "I won't. Not anymore. You're right."

Elynda's eyes softened and a small smile lightened her features. She pushed herself to standing and extended a hand to her friend. "Good. Now, what did you learn about this portal?"

Riana took Elynda's hand and pulled herself off the floor. It was time to stand, she decided. No more lying around waiting for things to be sprung on her. She had what she needed to equip herself for what may come. Including information at her fingertips, both in the journal and in the hidden library at Starliss Winery.

Riana strode toward the center of the maze-like pattern on the stone floor. As she stepped, the light in the grooves pulsed in shifting colors. Curious, Riana looked back as Elynda followed her. As Elynda stepped over the grooves, the colors pulsed green, blue and red.

Elynda watched the shifting colors as she stepped over the grooves, seemingly fascinated.

At the center of the maze, a large golden tile was square shaped, surrounded by a silver circle, and studded with four gems. Each gem, positioned in the corners of the square, was a different color. The center of the square descended in a funnel. Suspended above the center of the tile was a clear stone that glittered in the white-blue light.

"How is it doing that?" Elynda asked.

The stone suspended in the middle was held by nothing. Elynda and Riana stared at the stone. It was the size of Riana's fist and perfectly spherical. In its depths the crystal sparkled in rainbows of color.

Riana circled the golden tile, deciding its base was at the point with a vibrant green gem with veins of brown. To her left was a blue gem with waves of aqua; to her right a red gem with swirls of yellow and orange, and in the top corner a light-yellow with streaks of pink. Riana peered down into the center which descended past the plane of the stone floor. Its depths twinkled but without color. Riana got down on her knees to look closer.

"It's black," she told Elynda.

Riana pulled her grandmother's journal out and flipped to the page on the portal. On one side of the page her grandmother had sketched the hillock. On the other side, she'd sketched the tile. She set the book on the edge of the tile and beckoned Elynda to sit beside her.

"Look, Grandmother has some notes on how the tile works," Riana said, pointing to the sketch which had the tile diagrammed. Without looking up from the book, Riana pointed to the green and brown stone.

"Tyrinth," Elynda and Riana said together.

An arrow drawn on the page pointed to the stone to their right, which was also notated in parentheses as "(west)".

"Fire," they noted. Another arrow pointed to the topmost gem, or north.

"Air." The last one on the perimeter was...

"Water." It was in the east. There were two more stones indicated on the illustration.

"Creation."

"Love."

Riana's hair stood on end. Elynda rubbed at her forearms. The clear stone hovering in the space above the tile sparkled, casting far-reaching rainbows that danced across the stone walls. Each of the gems grew luminescent and colorful. Riana shielded her eyes from the growing light. The floor beneath them vibrated. They pushed themselves off the floor and tripped back from the tile. A deep rhythm started to pulse through the air and wind sprang up around them. Fog rolled around them as sparks of fire flashed in the convalescence.

"What's happening?" Elynda shouted.

Riana shook her head, unable to speak. On one hand, she was scared to death; on the other, she thrilled with excitement.

The storm in the center of the room grew, pushing Riana and Elynda back inch by inch until they were at the room's edge. The air was scented with grass and Riana wondered if the hillock would cave in on top of them and this new wonder. Tendrils of fog and flame snaked out of the encroaching storm. Elynda screamed.

The storm stopped. Frozen in place, the fog, fire and wind all stilled without being extinguished, as if time itself had paused. Riana and Elynda clung to each other. On the far side of the room, Riana could make out sunlight, as if someone had just opened a door on the opposite wall. Just as suddenly as the door had opened it crashed closed, the storm dissipated into shrinking mist and the room cleared again. The stones slowly extinguished and Elynda and Riana were steeped in darkness, alone with their wonder and surprise.

Or, at least, that's what Riana thought.

CHAPTER ELEVEN

A low mewling echoed through the cavern. Riana blinked away the blind spots from staring into the disappearing door of light. Elynda clutched at her arm, giving her a sense of location in the semi-darkness as her eyesight adjusted.

"What is that?" Elynda hissed near Riana's ear. Elynda stared straight ahead toward the golden tile studded with what Riana assumed were elemental gems.

Riana's vision cleared. Crouched on the southern corner of the square a small, golden creature with a sapphire gaze cast a worried look around the room. Its pointed black ears laid against its head while three, long tails swept over the stone floor in agitation.

Riana inched toward it, holding out a hand. She was somehow drawn to the creature in a way she had not been with others. She felt an inexorable need to be near it. As if it had been a part of her life before and she'd just forgotten. Its blue eyes caught hers and held them intently in its stare. What Riana had thought was a thick tuft of fur on its head rose, displaying black sections of spike-like scales that shimmered with undertones of blue, aqua, violet and pink. The creature's large white nose wrinkled as it opened its mouth to reveal large canines. It hissed at Riana.

Riana thought that was weird, given how she felt drawn to the creature. "It's okay now, little one," she told the creature.

Its large paws were spread wide to either side of its body. Strips of curving lines that shimmered in the blue light created a subtle shifting mirage of opalescent black. Around its neck a collar of white fur looked soft as down. The contrasting textures of black scales to soft fur gave Riana pause. What sort of creature was this?

"Where did it come from, Elynda?" Riana asked.

"I think it came through the portal," Elynda answered.

"How?"

"We turned it on," Elynda said.

Riana shot her a glance that said, no way.

"Well, I don't know; what other explanation is there?"

"Okay," Riana said, thinking. "We did this. Where did it come though from?"

"Perhaps the book says where the portal connects?"

Riana looked around for the book. "Where is it?"

"You left it over by the..." Elynda pointed in the direction of the creature, who hissed at her gesture. The book was gone.

"No," Riana said. She rushed toward the tile. The gold and black creature darted away. There was no book. It had vanished.

"No, no, no," Riana said, her stomach turning to steel. "We did not just send my grandmother's journal through the portal."

"I think that's exactly what we did." Elynda cradled her head with both hands and rubbed at her temples. The creature sniffed toward Elynda and took a tentative step forward, nose outstretched, eyes searching. Elynda was oblivious to this; she had her eyes squeezed shut while she massaged her head. She dropped her hands in her lap and sighed. The creature skittered away, looking between Elynda and Riana.

Riana fought tears building in her eyes. She'd finally decided to read the journal only to mistakenly send the journal through a mystical portal to an unknown location. She slumped to the floor as the emotions crashed over her. She'd gone from tentative about the knowledge her grandmother had meant her to gain, to accepting it, to tossing it away. It was too much. She covered her face with her hands as the tears ran.

She felt Elynda's soothing touch on her back as she consoled her.

"It just doesn't seem like I'm ever going to get this right," Riana said through sobs.

"It's okay, we'll figure out how to get it back. The spell was simple enough. We'll just try –," Elynda started.

Something warm and soft brushed against Riana's hands. Riana uncovered her eyes and found herself staring into the sapphire eyes of the creature they'd pulled through the portal. Its ears were straight up, rather than laid back against its head. Its white nose sniffed in her direction. Riana froze in place, her hands held out in front of her in the cupped position she'd used to cover her face.

The creature chirped, a breathy sound that somewhat resembled birdsong. The creature bumped its head against Riana's hands. Riana reached toward its head. The creature purred, a low grumbly noise. Riana wasn't sure if it was a warning growl or a sign of acceptance. She paused her hand's forward movement. The creature's tails lay still against the floor. When Riana didn't move, the creature tilted its head toward her hand, sniffed and then licked it, continuing its grumbling purr.

Riana figured that was a good sign and tentatively touched the animal's head, tracing a line around its ear. The creature's purr deepened as it stretched its body forward, stepping over Riana's legs to curl its head into her lap. Riana continued petting the creature as it purred contentedly. She looked at Elynda with wide eyes.

"I'm certain any other person wouldn't get this sort of reaction. Something about your power makes them content. As if you're a member of their pack," Elynda said.

"Wish I knew more about my power," Riana said.

"We'll figure it out. There has to be more information on it in the winery library. It would be easier with the journal, but since we don't have it, we'll just have to find it the old-fashioned way," Elynda said.

Riana stroked the creature's head. "But, what do we do with him?"

Elynda blinked. "Uh – how do you know it's a 'him'?"

Riana shrugged. "I don't know. It just seems like a boy."

"Do you know what kind of creature it is?"

Riana mentally perused the catalogue of books she'd read on elemental creatures. She looked down at the elemental in her lap, trying to match the living thing in front of her to the sometimes-crude sketches and descriptions in the books. "It's cat-like. And these scales are unique," Riana said as she ran a finger over the collection of solid plates forming a mohawk on its head.

Riana looked at the rest of the creature. It had three long, slender tails fur-covered, banded in the same black scale-like material and barbed at their ends with more scales. They looked sharp, as if the creature could use them as a defense against attackers. Riana rubbed the bridge of its nose as she thought. "What are you?" she asked it.

The creature's eyes fluttered open, looking drowsily at Riana. It chirruped. Riana was bowled over by a wash of mental images. Breath caught in her throat as her body went rigid with an overwhelming deluge of information pouring into her.

Riana first saw deep darkness, an absolute lack of light. A single pinprick of starlight expanded into a glowing sun. In its expanding brightness Riana could see a familiar outline of Magloryn. She was struck with the sensation of warmth and thrilling excitement, a fullness and joy for life. The image then shifted as the light faded. This new creature, Riana also knew. This was the elemental dragon of Tyrinth, the Tagorbi. It was joined by another dragon and while Riana was less familiar with it consciously, the knowing came easily: this was the dragon of air, Aerylia. After Aerylia, Uelymer, the dragon of water soon joined. And finally, the dragon of fire, the Tijhi, joined the throng.

Each dragon in turn blew into the face of the creature. Soft chirps emitted from Riana's perspective, giving her the odd sensation that she was the creature. She looked into faces of the elemental dragons. Love surged through her. She chirped again as the five dragons retreated and was replaced with a vista of blue skies and open fields. In the distance she could see collections of trees, lonely islands in a sea of grass.

A breeze sprang up and hushed through the tall vegetation, lulling the creature to sleep.

Riana mentally pulled free from the images and inhaled a long, desperate breath.

"Riana! Are you okay? What just happened? You were turning blue!"

Riana took a moment to breathe before answering. "This is one very unique creature," she said.

"How so?" asked Elynda.

"The fire nymphs are fire elementals. The antoli is air and Tyrinth. Haisyl, the amatsu we rescued, is water. The berubula is water and Tyrinth."

"So, one or two elements?" Elynda asked.

"Yes. And this creature is all of them," Riana said. She stroked the creature's head. It continued to look into her eyes and purr. "And I keep feeling like we're connected. Like this is a long-lost companion who I have a deep, but forgotten relationship with," Riana tried to put words to the sense of familiarity she felt toward the creature.

"I've got shivers," Elynda said. She shook her shoulders, as if the shivers had taken over her body for a moment.

Riana looked from the creature to Elynda. "I don't think it has a name. I don't think it's ever existed before. I think it is a whole new creation of the elemental dragons." As Riana spoke, drawing conclusions from the visions transferred to her, she knew what she said was true.

Give it a name.

The disembodied voice in her head she'd come to know as Magloryn echoed through her.

"We're meant to name it," Riana said.

"So, the elemental dragons created this creature using all of their resources," Elynda said.

Shadow, Light, Tyrinth, Air, Water and Fire, Magloryn confirmed.

"And not just the normal four," Riana voiced to Elynda. "The creature is also constructed of Light and Shadow."

As are all living things.

Riana nodded. Of course. All things living were born to live and to die.

Yes, but that is not the entire nature of Light and Shadow. Do not worry, you will learn in time.

Riana puzzled over the voice's direction and sudden appearance after months of quiet. Why now?

Look around you. You are in a place of magic. Your companion is magic. It is much easier to speak to you when you are so rooted and surrounded in power, when you have exercised power, as you did to open the portal. That is why we have sent this new creature. Your companion will help you hone and harness your power.

So, Riana thought back to Magloryn, I'll be able to speak with you whenever I want now?

No, Magloryn said and her voice sounded sad. My energy is very, very low so I'm not able to speak with you often. But I will try. Your companion helps. Visiting places of great power also helps. Surrounding yourself with other Magyses helps. Using elemental tools helps. You'll find many aids in your journey. For now, I must fade and rest.

Why are you so tired? Riana asked.

I exerted a lot of energy to assist in the creation of this companion. Stay strong, Riana. The answers are not so far away.

And then she was gone. Riana clung to Magloryn's presence with desperate mental fingers. Wait! She called out, but she was gone.

Sorrow spread through Riana as a sense of loss bloomed. The creature in front of her purred, pawing at Riana with gentle pads, as if to get her attention.

It worked. She scratched the creature's cheek, just behind its overly long black whiskers. He leaned into the affection, closing his eyes and purring loudly.

"Let's give you a name," Riana said. She wracked her brain. The creature was all elements. Each dragon had helped to bring it to life. Tagorbi and Tijhi, Oelymer, Magloryn, Aerylia and the power of

Shadow. Riana switched the letters around back and forth and then her eyes lit up. "Tomas."

"Tomas?" Elynda asked. "As in our classmate? The baker's son who was executed?"

Riana nodded slowly. "I hadn't thought of that connection, but it couldn't be more perfect. An homage to our innocent classmate." Riana stroked the creature's fur. "I was also thinking T for Tagorbi and Tijhi. O for Oelymer. M for Magloryn. A for Aerylia. S for Shadow. I don't know if there's a shadow dragon. If there is, I don't know its name. So... what do you think?"

"Tom," Elynda said. "Okay, I can handle that. Tom, it is."

"Tomas," Riana corrected.

Elynda turned to Tomas. "Hey, Tom. What do you think? Do you like your name, Tom?"

Tomas turned in her direction, smiled a toothy grin with eyes closed and chirped its consent.

"Tomas," Riana muttered, but knew it was a losing battle. "What are we going to do with him? We can't let him be seen."

Elynda regarded Tom, deep in thought. "No, definitely not."

Tom plopped on his haunches and exchanged glances between Riana and Elynda.

"Maybe he has an idea," Elynda said.

Riana cocked an eyebrow. "Yeah?" she asked.

"Tom, what are we going to do with you?" she asked.

Tom chirped at her in response.

Riana shrugged. "What's that -," but something had started to happen before she could get the rest of her question out. Tom had hunched low to the ground, rubbed his chin back and forth on the stone before rolling to his back. He wiggled back and forth, his tails thrumming against the ground. Occasionally, he chirped or purred. He rolled back to his paws, shook himself thoroughly, stretched, yawned and stalked in front of Riana and Elynda, appearing as nothing more than a run-of-the-mill ginger cat.

"He's a little on the big side, but I suppose that will work," Elynda said.

Riana felt her eyes burning and realized she hadn't blinked while she'd watched the creature transform itself – no, she corrected herself – disguise itself as a cat. "Wow," was all she could muster in her shock.

They exited the portal and made their way to the North Road, continuing to Elynda's house, with this Tom at their side. Riana looked around her, fighting the nagging sensation the group of them were being watched. She saw no one, and decided the paranoia stemmed from the presence of their new companion – even if he was disguised as a cat.

Riana cast a look about her, watching Tomas walk alongside Elynda, his nose high in the air as he sniffed his new surroundings. They both seemed to be at ease.

Riana continued walking and glancing around. You just couldn't be too careful.

CHAPTER TWELVE

Riana didn't want to return to the General Store after the long weekend with Elynda and Tom – whom Mrs. Heilbee was extremely tolerant of and even affectionate toward. Riana wondered if part of Tom's magic was that everyone he met fell in love with him. She looked down at him as he trotted by her side. Just a normal ginger cat, no scales, only one tail. She figured her theory wouldn't be a good one to test on Mr. Fraely, though.

Before she reached the porch of the General Store, she took a detour. She walked alongside the building until she reached her bedroom window. It was still open. Tom sat in the scruffy grass and looked at Riana.

"You go through the window and I'll meet you inside, okay?"

Tom chirped but didn't move.

"Do you want me to pick you up and put you inside? Can't you jump?" she asked, feeling slightly disappointed. A magical companion disguised as a cat couldn't jump five feet into a window?

Tom looked at the window, at Riana, then out into the field behind the house and store.

"Oh," Riana said. "Alright, then. Go on. I'll leave the window open for you when you're ready to come in."

Tom nodded. At least that's what Riana thought she saw, then chided herself for thinking such a thing. He turned for the field and bounded away. As he leapt into the concealing length of grass, she thought she saw the swish of three tails, instead of just one.

Out in the darkening forest, Riana knew there were fire nymphs flying, an antoli roaming, a happy berubula eating, and maybe somewhere in the slough an amatsu playing. She watched the sunset, catching glimpses of Tom's scales glinting in the fading light through the grass, and almost followed him in.

She resisted, turned toward the front of the building, and re-entered her temporary prison.

The store was as it always was. Oil lamps perched around the shopping area hissed and cast yellow light over Mr. Fraely's inventory. Her adopted father was behind the long counter, looking over a large book of records. Riana did a double-take. She recognized that particular book of records.

"Is that the Starliss Winery records?" Riana asked. Ice snaked down her back and left gooseflesh in its wake. Riana stepped toward the glass counter, anger rising from her guts. "What do you think you're doing with those?"

Mr. Fraely didn't lift his eyes from the rows of numbers. "I never realized how profitable your grandmother's business was," he said. His lip curled on one side, he reached a finger to his tongue, licked, pressed the wet fingertip to the parchment, and turned the page. Above the hiss of the oil lamps, and Riana's rising heartbeat, the sound of paper scraping over paper ripped through Riana's composure. She grabbed at the book.

Mr. Fraely gripped the book and yanked it toward him. "What's the matter, Riana? Does it bother you so much for me to see the insides of the business you're meant to inherit? Are you afraid I'll use what I find in here to some personal means?"

"Not only do I not trust you with those numbers, I know you have no right to that business information."

"See that's where you're wrong," he said, now smiling in a wicked way. He closed the book with a thump.

Riana balled her fists by her side and gritted her teeth.

"As a matter of fact, as your guardian, I am the executor of the Starliss estate until you come of age. When is your birthday again? Three more weeks is it? Hm... I wonder how much gold I can siphon from your inheritance in that time."

"You wouldn't dare," she said, but she thought he would.

He barked out a laugh. "You don't know me well, darling. And if I were to run your little vineyard and winery into the ground, what would you do then? I bet you'd be pretty angry." He leaned over the counter, offering his chin, as if goading her to punch him.

She thought about doing it. Then stopped herself.

"Wait," she said, sobering. "Why are you trying to anger me?"

"Oh, I don't know," said Roy Fraely. He inspected his fingernails through his spectacles. "Perhaps, I'm simply testing a theory."

"A theory about what?" Riana asked, confused.

"I hear Tyrmini powers are activated with heightened emotions," he said. He captured her eyes with a watery blue gaze.

Riana stepped away from him, stunned. She let his words sink in. He was trying to expose her – whether for legitimately being Tyrmini, or for doing anything he could call elemental magic, Riana didn't think he cared.

"Are you feeling emotional?" he whispered, cocking his mouth into a vicious grin.

Riana backed away, shaking with anger and fear, turned without a word, and escaped to her bedroom.

CHAPTER THIRTEEN

Elynda walked along the North Road in the morning mist. The smell of the Dreavynan filled her nose and its crashing tide filled her ears. The day started out cool, but Elynda thought the day would shape up to be warm and sunny by lunchtime. She relished the idea of walking to Healer's Hall in the nice afternoon air before she was hard at work tending the sick. Her feet found their way to the Snow estate of their own accord while Elynda reviewed her list of patients in her head.

When she reached the gate at which Ribbit met her, she found him not present. She headed down the drive to the Snow residence. The home was modest; the barns were exquisite. In the pasture beyond the outbuildings, horses of all sizes and colors roamed, cropping at dewy grass, and swishing away the mist with busy tails. Elynda spotted Ribbit's white-blonde cap of hair peeking out from behind a horse's leg, inspecting a raised hoof. A Baron's Guard stood nearby.

The guard appeared to say something to Ribbit, because Elynda saw Ribbit look up at the man. Elynda trotted closer to hear the conversation, curious about the horse's ailment. Just as she entered earshot, she heard Ribbit's reply.

"Sir, I assure you I am working as quickly as I can. If the horse had been brought to me immediately, this wouldn't be so much of an inconvenience for you," he said, fire in his blue eyes, nostrils flared.

Elynda had never seen Ribbit angry, but his flushed face and clipped tone made it obvious. As she came near enough to see the horse's hoof, she understood his anger. Her nose identified the problem before her eyes did.

She pointed. "That hoof is infected," she pronounced.

"Very infected," agreed Ribbit. "How long has the horse been limping?"

"Dunno," said the guard, his voice deep and gravelly. He was average in height, a little on the plump side, somewhat disheveled and needed a bath.

Ribbit's red face went redder. "You 'dunno'?" Ribbit asked. "Is this your horse? The horse you ride in service each day?"

"Yeah," the guard said and rubbed his dirty nose with his dirty hand. "You gonna fix 'er or you gonna lecture me? I've got a job to do, you know."

"This horse came from these stables and you may well have sentenced her to death. She's been in service for less than a year and you bring her back in this state? I want to speak to the Baron's Guards' stable master, and I want to speak with that person today. The horse hasn't been bathed, treated, brushed, and what is she being fed? She's all skin and bones!"

Elynda agreed the horse was anorectic.

"This horse is your partner," Ribbit went on. "Not a slave, not a servant, a partner. And partners deserve better."

"You better watch your mouth, Stable Boy. I am the Baron's Guard. You will respect me," said the guard.

Ribbit carefully let go of the horse's hoof and stood upright, which was unimpressive since he was so tiny. Elynda wanted to throw herself between Ribbit and the guard but stood frozen.

Ribbit walked toward the guard until he was toe-to-toe with him. Elynda's mouth hung open.

"The Snow family has served the Baron for seven generations, sir. Do not speak to me like a lackey," he said. His voice trembled, which might have made him look weak, but the energy rolling off him was mightier than anything Elynda had ever seen.

The guard, however, was unthreatened. He chortled, took one shuffle back, pulled back one meaty hand over his opposite shoulder, and let it fly. Ribbit was knocked to the ground. Elynda ran to him. He crawled to his knees and hands and spat blood.

"Ribbit! Are you okay?" Elynda asked.

"I think he knew I was bluffing," Ribbit groaned.

She helped Ribbit to his feet.

"What's that?" the guard said.

Ribbit and Elynda looked in the direction of his open-mouthed gaze.

Streaking across the field was a stream of golden light. Within the light was the vague shape of a horse. Yet as it drew near in the passage of seconds, Elynda was certain it was a horse, but unlike any she'd ever laid eyes on.

"Does that horse have wings?" Elynda asked.

"Goldy, no!" Ribbit shouted.

Thunder reverberated through the ground. The horse was wrapped in a golden nimbus and flew toward them, hooves meeting Tyrinth but each stride achieving massive lengths. Even as Elynda thought of it, she could see the hazy outline of giant wings on the animal. Her mind caught up to her observation in time to correct her identification to not a mundane animal but an elemental.

Goldy, as Ribbit had called it, charged toward the guard, stopping inches in front of him, reared on hind legs, wings stretched wide. The guard's eyes went wide in fear, his hands just beginning to lift to protect himself when the front hooves of the creature smashed down. Goldy hit the guard square in the chest knocking him down and back.

"What have you done?" Ribbit said to the elemental. Goldy shook her head and pranced, seeming to be proud of her actions. "You'll get yourself killed. Get out of here before he comes to."

Elynda went to the guard and checked his pulse. A kick like that could very well kill a person on its own and who knew what the kick from an elemental would do. The man groaned, his eyelids slotted showing just the whites. Elynda backed away from him. The guard rolled his body to one side.

"He's getting up!" Elynda reported.

"Go, Goldy!" Ribbit shouted at her.

The golden horse stamped, then lowered her head.

"Go with you?" Ribbit asked. And his moment of hesitation sealed his fate.

"The guard!" Elynda shouted.

The guard, having risen and shambled toward Ribbit, wrapped Elynda's small friend into a grip which protected his body. "You're under arrest," he growled.

"Goldy, go. Just go."

Tears slipped from Elynda's eyes as she backed away from the scene. The golden horse bowed to Ribbit, turned and in a streak of golden light was gone.

"Now," said the guard. "You get us a new horse to ride. I've visited your place and I think it's time you visit mine."

Ribbit looked at Elynda, eyes wide.

"No, you can't," Elynda said.

"Elynda, no!" Ribbit said. "Just go. I'll be fine."

The guard pushed Ribbit toward the main barn and spared not a glance toward Elynda.

Tears streaming, Elynda ran from the Snow residence, toward Riana. Riana would know what to do.

CHAPTER FOURTEEN

Riana left the General Store early, slipping out the side entrance without stopping to speak to Mr. Fraely. She felt bad for not waiting for Elynda, but she knew when Elynda got to the General Store and Mr. Fraely told her Riana had gone, she'd simply follow her here. She would explain when she saw Elynda.

Her walk to the schoolhouse had been stiff. She'd barely noticed her surroundings as her mind whirred on Mr. Fraely's expressed intention. She'd hardly slept last night; her anger kept a steady roar through the night hours. Tom had accompanied her in silence, having returned to his guise as a normal ginger cat.

She'd arrived at school before any other student and perched herself at its front steps. Tom sat next to her on the wide front porch. Occasionally, he butted his head against her elbow, and she indulged him with comforting strokes. She watched the trickle of students walking toward the building, hoping to find the face in the crowd she searched for.

At last when Donny Derringer came into view through the morning mist, she pushed herself up and jogged toward him. He was talking before she could even ask her first question.

"I found out some things," he said, and stopped in the schoolyard near the giant oak.

She looked up at him, eager to hear what he'd learned about what she could do about her situation in Fraely's General Store.

"Captain Steph knows a lot about this, especially your particular case," he said.

Riana nodded, unable to help the worry knotted in her stomach.

"I'm so sorry, Riana. It's not good news."

Riana hung her head, tears stinging her eyes. It was so unfair. As if it were easy being an orphan, then to have her adopted mother die, and then her adopted grandmother die. Then her adopted father was trying to steal her inheritance by way of inciting a Tyrmini outburst . Riana inhaled deeply through her nose and let it out of her mouth in a giant whoosh. "Tell it to me, anyway," she said.

"Mr. Fraely is your legal guardian and is the sole person who can say where you live," he said.

Riana nodded, the worst confirmed.

"But he can't obstruct your internship since that was in play before Ms. Starliss... died," he said the last word quietly, as if to soften the blow to Riana's mourning.

"What about his power over the estate? Last night he said he was the executor and could utilize the winery's profits as he wished. Is that true?" Riana asked.

Donny crossed his arms, widening his stance and cocked a head to one side. "Unfortunately, that is also true, according to Captain Steph. But there are rules to what he can do and what he can't do. Steph and Sela were close. You can talk to him anytime."

Riana knew this. Steph and her grandmother had conspired to provide the Baron with the golden elixir he was so addicted to. She remembered his frequent visits to the winery, which toward the end had become tense, leaving Sela flustered.

Riana nodded. "Okay, where can I find him?"

"He said to be sure and speak with him at the Baron's Ball."

"But that's another six days away," Riana protested.

"It's this weekend, isn't it?" Donny said, a sudden look of panic written on his face.

"Yes," confirmed Riana. It was a big day for the winery; she and Ms. Hightower had been working feverishly on calculating the wine needed for the event based on invitations sent. Riana had received her own invitation at the winery.

Riana looked past Donny into the morning mist. A familiar image emerged. Elynda ran toward them. Riana's hair prickled. Elynda didn't run for the joy of running.

Donny rubbed the back of his neck. "I've been meaning to ask you, Riana - ," he started, but Riana cut him off.

"Elynda?" she said and jogged toward her friend.

Elynda held her side and panted once she'd reached Riana.

"What's wrong?" Riana asked, her worry intensifying.

"It's Ribbit," she said. "He had an elemental, Riana."

"Robert Snow, Jr.?" asked Donny incredulously.

Elynda nodded, moving from one foot to the other and still working to slow her breathing.

"Did anyone see the elemental?" Riana asked.

Elynda sobbed. "Yes," she said, and relayed the story to them.

"They have Ribbit?" Riana couldn't help the questions tumbling out of her mouth. Her imagination was painting horrific visions of Ribbit's execution. Had they already done it? Was her friend dead?

"They're holding him at the Baron's Keep. They say he's to stay there until the High King sends a retinue. They say he's potentially dangerous."

"You're kidding," Riana whispered, sounding stunned, but all she felt was the knot of worry release at knowing Ribbit was still alive. Maybe there was still a chance he could be saved. Maybe they would test him and discover he was safe. She knew better though. Tomas, the boy for which she'd named her new ginger, blue-eyed companion had been seen with fire nymphs and they had been executed for being in company with each other. Riana reached out and stroked Tom's fur, grateful he was camouflaged, worried nonetheless of his possible discovery.

"What happened to the horse elemental, Elynda?" Riana asked.

"It ran. Took off when Ribbit refused to go with her," Elynda said. She plopped onto the porch next to Tom and stroked his back furiously. Tom patiently endured, though his tail smacked the porch in a staccato rhythm.

Riana thought of the bubbling light that was Ribbit being kept in a cell in the Baron's dungeon and wanted to throw up. It was unfair in the extreme. Ribbit was anything but dangerous.

"What are we going to do, Riana?" Elynda asked her, suddenly grabbing at her friend's hands, holding them painfully tight. "How are we going to keep him safe?"

"It's going to be okay. We'll find a way," Riana promised, but she didn't know if she could.

Donny looked fierce, arms crossed, eyebrows nettled over hazel eyes. Elynda and Riana looked up at him. His gaze caught them staring. He looked between them. "What?" he asked, sounding on guard, and lost all at once.

"Well," Riana started. "The thing is..."

"You are a Baron's Guard," Elynda said.

"And you might be able to help us?" asked Riana.

He didn't speak for a moment, his gaze shifting back up and out into the sky.

Riana shook her head. What was she thinking? She couldn't ask Donny to get involved. He'd already risked too much helping her rescue elementals. What did she expect of him? To break Ribbit out of jail?

She opened her mouth to tell Donny he needed to stay out of it. That it was too much to risk. She was sure that's what he was contemplating. Donny's voice cut into her thought process.

"Don't worry," he said. "I'm way ahead of you, girls."

CHAPTER FIFTEEN

Riana had finished her morning at school, gone directly to the winery for her apprenticeship solving a crisis in the vineyard where the viticulturist had discovered the presence of downy mildew on the mulgoveign fruit. They'd spent the entire afternoon thoroughly checking through the rest of the vineyard for further signs of the fungus, and luckily had found none.

She arrived to the General Store tired, mentally drained, emotionally exhausted after hearing about Ribbit, and hungry. She was swaying as she crossed the threshold to the chime of the doorbell.

Mr. Fraely took one look at her and grinned. It wasn't a cheerful grin. "Tired?" he asked.

Riana straightened. "No. As a matter of fact, I'm energized by the day's activities."

Mr. Fraely nodded. "Well, then you won't mind lending me a hand."

"Of course not," Riana said, determined to play the game to win. She smiled as if she really meant it.

"There's a shipment of sugar coming in tonight." He cleared his throat and nudged his spectacles up his nose. "The boat is the Jade Lady and her captain is Svelt Rustofo."

She fought her fatigue to soak in the instructions. Her stomach growled loudly. Mr. Fraely scowled, as if she'd purposefully done it to interrupt him.

He twitched the side of his apron, stretched his neck, and continued. "Take the mule and cart to the dock and bring back the sugar. You'll need to unload it to the back storeroom."

Riana barely suppressed a groan. Her feet throbbed already from the day of walking the property, and now she had to load and unload pounds and pounds of sugar. She inhaled, steadying herself. Mr. Fraely looked at her, eyebrows raised in a question. She smiled in response.

"Not too strained from your apprenticeship, are you? Not feeling... pressured?" he asked.

She cocked one eyebrow. The fire in her belly burned, despite her exhaustion. "I can do this all day," she said.

One corner of his lip pulled toward his nose, making his face ugly. He looked away from her and reached into one of the various hidden drawers behind the counter. He pulled out a small stack of silver pieces and a leather pouch. He lined them up on the counter and counted, watery blue eyes peering over the rim of his glasses and pointing with stubby fingers while he muttered the numbers indiscernibly. Satisfied, he straightened and scooped them into the open leather pouch. "This is enough coin to purchase one hundred pounds of sugar."

Riana's muscles protested at the ensuing workout they were about to endure. She held out her hand and Mr. Fraely dropped the pouch of coins into it. Riana stood there for half a second then turned. The doorbell chimed once again as she dragged her booted and screaming feet back outside. A slew of curses for Mr. Fraely crossed her mind, but the warm evening air promised comfort.

She hitched the mule to the cart and doted on the animal for a moment, rubbing the spot between its ears. Once they were ready to go, she led the mule and the cart out to the rock road. She looked at the sky to note that she had about three hours before sunset.

Despite the stress to her body as much as her soul, she found her smile as she rode along. She reached Landsend's docks and turned the mule down the walkway that led to the biggest quays. Rows of boards clunked rhythmically under the cart's wheels. The Dreavynan glittered in the evening sunlight through towering ship masts.

Riana inhaled the fragrant air. This side of the docks wasn't so bad. Not so fishy as the southern quays, closer to the market where the fishermen took their catch to sell.

The mule twitched its long ears and blew as they moved along the dock. Below, the sullen water lapped at the wooden planks. Riana purred and clucked her tongue and said some nonsense things in a soothing sort of voice to keep the mule calm. She turned the mule north and toward the Jade Lady.

It was a beautiful ship. The hull was vivid green, the boottop hovering at the surface of the water shone in golden yellow. White sails on oak masts were wrapped up tightly. on the bow of the ship, the lady herself was curled in a sensuous pose, hands tangled in wind-blown hair. The ornament was painstakingly painted in a golden hue, making her regal in a forbidden sort of way. Tethered and tied off at the dock, the moderately-sized merchant ship swayed restlessly, as if in anticipation of the next voyage.

The plank stretched from the ship to the dock. A sailor passed and after catching the man's attention, Riana asked for the Captain of the ship. While she waited, she patted the mule between the ears.

Riana turned at the sound of wood creaking. Captain Rustofo would have looked portly except for rippling forearms and bulging shoulder and neck muscles. His muscles were not the only formidable physical attribute; Riana guessed his height to be more than seven and a half feet. She goggled at him, not being able to fully take in the man's unnatural height nor the scale of his giant muscles and wide build.

Aside from his imposing size, the face of the captain emanated jovial warmth. The giant turned his dark beard-swathed face down to her to peer at her with gray eyes.

"Well..." the man said in a warm, gravelly voice. "The Fraely was correct. You are a beautiful young lady," he paused, appraising Riana's face only, never letting his gaze wander over the rest of her non-facial features.

Why would 'the Fraely' – she liked this new nickname for her guardian - be telling a sea merchant I'm beautiful?

"Truly, you flatter me without cause. Certainly, Mr. Fraely would not have complimented me so freely," Riana said.

The captain still stood at the top of the gangplank, looking down at Riana. "A proud father would have many wonderful things to say about a white rose such as you. Would you deny your father's generous opinion of you?"

Riana squirmed under the attention. "He's not my father," she noted without hesitation. "And he is certainly a proud man," she said.

The man crossed his impressive, dark arms over his equally impressive chest. He cocked his fur-covered face to one side. "Yes, proud indeed," he said in a knowing voice. "Well, Ms. Riana, fair rose of the northwestern port, would you be so kind as to let a poor old sailor have the pleasure of your company over a cup of tea?" the hulking captain made a bow in her direction, giving the appearance of humility with his long, dark whiskers touching his barrel chest.

Riana screwed up her face, her mouth opened before thinking.

"Do sailors drink tea?" she asked incredulously. A vision swam into Riana's imagination of that big, hulking man sitting at a properly laid table and clasping a fine porcelain cup in his meaty paws.

The captain's head jerked from his prostration, locking eyes with Riana. He burst into laughter. His laughter was as big as he was. Riana smiled at the good nature of the giant, feeling relieved for his sense of humor. "No, we don't sit much to tea while riding out to sea. But we procure some fine samples of the stuff. I only meant to offer you some tea, as I thought you might enjoy it."

Riana considered the offer, not sure why she would be invited to drink tea aboard a merchant ship from which she had been instructed to pick up sugar. Riana combed through her memories. When Grandmother had done business with merchants, they had often invited her onboard and spent time conversing about things outside of the transaction. She also thought she could talk up Starliss Wine while she was at it. Captain Rustofo was not in the ledger of customers with whom they traded. Judging by his thick, rolling accent and brown skin, she guessed he was from Idalfyn.

"Thank you for your gracious offer. I would be happy to join you," she said. Idalfyn was on the opposite side of the Aelos continent. Starliss Vineyard had no customers in that region. In her mind she was doing numbers to ensure they could support expansion to another region while maintaining their current customers.

Another towering figure appeared at the Captain's shoulder. The Captain tilted his head to peer at the arrival then shifted to wrap a massive arm around a young man who Riana could only assume was the Captain's son. While the young man was absent the paunch and grizzly facial hair, and his hair was long for a man, the large stature, set of his eyes and full pout of his mouth was his Captain's.

Riana's stomach dropped into her feet. She worked back a threatening blush. She cursed her fair complexion. If the Captain was handsome (for an older man), this younger version was divine.

There was something else, something just under the surface of what she saw with her eyes. A light shimmered green and incandescent around the young man. She stared at it, knowing she'd seen this before but couldn't place where. She blinked and the color faded.

The Captain's eyebrows retreated into his salt and pepper hairline while an all-too-knowing smile parted his face to reveal his yellowing teeth. The young man blushed in response, ducking his head and casting his gaze into the waves lapping against the boat. One corner of his mouth quirked upward as he wrapped a giant hand around the back of his neck.

"This young lady is Riana," he announced to the man whose shoulder he clasped and waved elaborately down the gangplank to Riana.

Riana looked down at her boots and leathers and wondered how much not like a young lady she looked.

"This is my son, Kristopher," the Captain introduced.

Kristopher cast furtive glances at Riana. "Pleasure," he mumbled, his voice rumbled with a deep bass. He rubbed at his nose. "I heard Father invite you to tea." He kept his head ducked but raised his eyebrows in question.

She nodded and steeled herself against her lack of graceful attire – Grandmother would be so disappointed. But, Grandmother, she thought, they're a bunch of sailors. I'm sure leathers aren't going to hurt my reputation. Maybe it will even help.

Keep your wits about you. Your attire is just one aspect of your business presentation. The other is your brain and your tongue. Use them wisely.

Riana could just hear her grandmother's voice in her head, coaching her in the art of business, of building relationships to sustain their viability as the only vineyard and winery in this corner of Aelos. Riana hoped she'd do her grandmother proud.

CHAPTER SIXTEEN

The Jade Lady bobbed and swayed in Landsend's harbor. Riana had been given the opportunity to speak of her apprenticeship, and that she did with zeal and fervor. Starliss Wine was the most exquisite, most delicious, most drinkable wine on Aelos. The vineyard produced eleven grape varieties, all of which thrived in the coastal mists of Landsend.

"But, surely this is the wrong sort of climate for grapes," Captain Rustofo pressed.

Riana wanted to kick herself. She wished she had a bottle on hand to show them how good their terroir was for producing wine-making fruit.

"I hear what you're saying. The latitude is much further north than Aelos's other prominent vineyards. A taste and you'll understand. Perhaps if you're staying in Landsend for a few days, I could invite you to visit the winery? It's not far from here."

"I'm not sure I'm in the market for wine," Captain Rustofo said, waving away Riana's invitation.

"Father, I'm sure we'll have time for a quick trip to Starliss Vineyard. We'll be here for several weeks. We're on the hook to attend the new Baron's Ball." He rolled his eyes at the mention of the ball.

"I have to go to the ball as well," she said and rolled her eyes back to Kristopher. And she meant it wholeheartedly. It was not the scene in which she wished to find herself. Business required certain adjustments to comfort. Riana was happy to do it. The Vineyard would, after all, be her responsibility in only a few short weeks.

Kristopher kept up the charade, nonchalantly leaning across the table. "Well... maybe we should attend the event in company? To lessen the awkwardness and suffering of attending?"

"You know," Riana said, leaning back in her chair and fixing him with a bored look while she regarded the state of her cuticles. "Misery does love company, I've heard. Sure, let's do it." Despite her playful banter and demeanor of aloofness, Riana's insides jangled.

"Then, it's all set!" Captain Rustofo suddenly boomed, startling Riana so she sat bolt upright, her eyes going shock blind for a moment while her heart thudded desperately in her chest. She jumped in her seat, her knees banging at the underside of the table and knocking her teacup over. She reached for it as it rolled off the table, mortified at the thought of breaking a piece of fine dishware. She wasn't sure how she'd done it, but the cup landed gently in the palm of her hand and she replaced it to its saucer.

"That was close!" she said and laughed nervously.

"Wow," Kristopher said.

"Nice save," Captain Rustofo noted, folding his formidable arms over his impressive chest and nodding in approval.

"Maker of Wine. Savior of Falling Cups," Riana said. "That's me."

Captain Rustofo laughed while Kristopher fixed her with a lopsided grin.

"And she's funny," Captain Rustofo noted.

"Oh, that's nothing," Riana said, waving away his comment. "You should meet my friend, Ribbit."

It was out of her mouth before she knew what she was saying. Once the words had flown, the fear and sadness crashed down on her. She sat soberly for a moment while Captain Rustofo and Kristopher asked about this friend whose name was the sound of an amphibian.

There was a story behind his nickname and Riana knew it well. The memories flooded her but crashed into her belly with a solid thump. These men couldn't possibly understand her plight, her sympathy – no, empathy – for her friend. They couldn't understand her need to find a way for Ribbit to make it free. Even if she had to break him out herself.

Her thoughts churned and folded in on themselves then circled back and chased its beginning with its end.

"What's wrong?" Kristopher asked, and gently took Riana's hand, which had been resting on the table near the saved teacup.

"Oh," Riana said, unaware how long she'd sat like that. "My friend Ribbit is in some trouble."

"What sort of trouble?" Kristopher asked.

"The sort you don't come back from," she blurted, then realized how much venom laced her words.

Kristopher looked at her with puzzlement.

"They say he's a Tyrmini, which I just can't believe." She was careful to bite her words short of: "and even if he was, I don't know why it's such a bad thing." That would be inciting the wrong sort of attention from these two men.

Captain Rustofo's chair scraped against the wooden boards and he walked toward the railing.

Kristopher pulled his hand from Riana's and clasped both hands in his lap, looking intently at them.

Riana looked between the two giants. "Did I say something wrong?" she asked.

"My mother was a Tyrmini," Kristopher said. "Dad managed to keep her hidden for a long time, but after I was born, the High King's Captain of the Guard caught up with her."

"Did they..." Riana couldn't bring herself to finish the question.

Kristopher nodded. "Yes, they executed her." His voice cracked. "Dad just can't handle talking about it."

Riana's mind raced. Her first emotional reaction was a deep sympathy for losing a mother. Riana had not had that happen once, but three times, in a sense. First her birth mother, leaving her an orphan, then her adopted mother and again with her adopted grandmother – and very likely by the hand of the very man who had dealt the fatal punishment to Kristopher's mother. Riana felt a certain satisfaction mixed with guilt that the man was dead and gone. Perhaps the next Captain would be less awful.

"I'm so sorry for your loss. I think you and I may have quite a bit in common. My grandmother was just murdered by Captain Luther, the High King's righthand man. Though the townsfolk believe she was murdered by a rover from another town."

Overhead a gull cried. The ocean swelled and receded. A breeze picked at Riana's hair and skin. She pulled her cloak tighter. Another set of thoughts churned in her mind. Captain Rustofo had protected his wife, hidden her, kept her safe for as long as he could. They had been able to keep the long reach of the High King at bay for a time. It was astonishing. And more than that, it offered Riana new hope. Maybe she could rescue her friend. Maybe she could stow him away, keep him safe somehow.

"I'm so sorry for your loss as well," Kristopher said.

Captain Rustofo lumbered back their way. "My deepest condolences, Riana."

Riana didn't cry. Not today. She'd failed to keep her grandmother safe, but maybe she could do something for her friend.

"How did you do it?" she asked.

"Do what?" Rustofo asked.

"Keep her safe and hidden for so long?"

Captain Rustofo's gray eyes were like liquid silver in the fading daylight, shiny with unshed tears. He nodded, not speaking right away. Riana counted three breaths before his inhale became large enough to fuel his words. "The sea is an easy place to get lost. My wife stayed aboard almost always. And we had the help of someone very dear to us, of whom we shan't speak of this eve."

"Can this person help my friend, Ribbit, maybe?" Riana asked, realizing there was desperation in her voice.

Captain Rustofo shook his head. "I don't think so. Our friend has not been heard from for a long time. I fear she's gotten caught up in trouble, as you said, she cannot come back from."

Riana was lost in thought, turning potential solutions over in her mind for how to get Ribbit free and keep him safe.

"So, when shall I pick you up for the Baron's Ball?" Kristopher asked.

"What?" Riana asked, having been too deep in thought to have heard him.

"I said, when would you like me to pick you up for the Baron's Ball? You still want to go with me?"

"Oh," Riana said. "Right. The ball." She was too busy trying to think of ways to rescue her friend. Thinking about the doldrum of the ball was the furthest thing from her mind.

And then an idea struck her. "Oh. The ball," she said, emphasizing the event. She straightened in her seat, placing both palms on the wooden table they sat at, looking intently into Kristopher's eyes. "The ball at the Baron's Keep. The ball we're all going to."

"Yes, the very one," Kristopher said, raising a dark eyebrow her direction. "Am I missing something?" he asked.

Riana nodded, eyes wandering from Kristopher's to stare into her mind's scheming, while one index finger tapped out an insistent rhythm. She plotted.

Captain Rustofo shuffled from one foot to another.

"Riana?" Kristopher asked.

Riana steepled her fingers and focused her gaze back to Kristopher. "Why don't you two come by the vineyard tomorrow and we'll discuss the ball."

In the meantime, Riana had some planning to do.

CHAPTER SEVENTEEN

The next morning, Riana sat in her usual school desk, rubbing a sore shoulder muscle, waiting for the teacher's appearance. She looked out the door and saw a Baron's Guard conversing in low notes with Mrs. Tomly. When their teacher entered the schoolhouse and made her way up the aisle to the raised platform at the front of the class, Riana heard her sob.

Mrs. Tomly turned to the class, snuffled and wiped vigorously at her already-red nose. "I'm so sorry to announce, children, that Robert Snow, Junior will not be returning to school."

Riana held her breath.

Elynda, who sat in the paired desk next to her grabbed at her hand and squeezed.

Riana endured the torture of her friend's need for reassurance. She waited for Mrs. Tomly to announce Ribbit had been executed. Worried the Baron's Guard had gone ahead with the sentencing without waiting, as was customary.

"Ribbit has been taken into custody by the Baron's Guard," Mrs. Tomly stuttered on a fresh wave of sobs.

Relief washed over Riana. He was still alive. Perhaps her plan could work.

"What for?"

"Why?"

"Ribbit?"

"How come?"

The questions shot through the classroom. Riana looked around. Donny was not there.

"Ribbit has been taken into custody for being Tyrmini," Mrs. Tomly answered.

The classroom erupted in gasps of fear, shouts of 'no' and from some children, silent shakes of their heads as the faces reflected open shock.

"But, Mrs. Tomly, Ribbit's a good boy. Nice. He can't be a Tyrmini." This was from a young, olive-skinned girl whose words were thick with accent.

"I know, I know," Mrs. Tomly said. "I don't understand it either."

Riana's stomach fell to her toes. People thought of Tyrmini in one sense: dangerous, evil, mean – to put it in the perspective of a child. If she were successful in getting Ribbit free, he'd have to live in exile, get lost somehow and never be found. What sort of life was that?

"What if he's not Tyrmini?" Riana asked, careful to keep her rage and frustration at bay.

Under the table, Elynda gripped her hand in a new position. As if to quiet her. A warm tingle spread from her hand and up her arm. Riana looked at Elynda. There was a vibrant green nimbus floating around her. Riana stared, but Mrs. Tomly's next words snapped her back to reality.

"Oh, they have confirmed," Mrs. Tomly stated. "He was in the company of an elemental."

Riana wanted to argue. They couldn't possibly know unless he'd displayed some power. Could they?

But then, maybe he really was Tyrmini. Maybe he'd accidently set off his power as Riana had. She kicked herself. If she'd clued Ribbit in on her secret, maybe she could have helped him before he'd gotten snagged by the guards.

"The High King's guards will be here by the end of this moon cycle. They will be searching for more Tyrmini. They say, where there is one, there are often more."

Riana sat stunned. Not only was Ribbit in danger, but any teen in Landsend could be at risk.

Panic set in to the tune of her pulsing heartbeat. Beside her, Elynda hooked her arm around Riana's.

Riana looked around the room. Anyone of her classmates could fall prey to the High King's specialized retinue of Tyrmini guards. Anyone of her classmates could be either executed or taken by the guard to prove their abilities were strong enough, and their loyalty stronger yet, to carry out the High King's bidding to eradicate the Tyrmini-born population. Or creatures with elemental power.

"Please be on your guard, children," Mrs. Tomly said. "Should you encounter a Tyrmini it is best to run straight to the authorities. Make sure you tell them everything you've seen. They'll keep you safe."

Riana banished the need to roll her eyes. She doubted the local Baron's Guard could manage a Tyrmini. In fact, she was banking on it.

Thinking of the Baron's Guard reminded her of the idea she'd had with Kristopher. She leaned toward her friend as Mrs. Tomly turned to the chalkboard.

"Elynda," Riana whispered.

Elynda looked at her, her face pale as moonlight, highlighting the greenness and largeness of her eyes.

"Do you have a dress I can borrow?"

CHAPTER EIGHTEEN

There was one thing Riana missed about dresses. Just one.

"If we can pull this off," began Donny, "we'll be able to slip Ribbit out with no one the wiser."

Riana hmphed her agreement. She folded the parchment she'd been sketching on as Donny and she worked out a plan. She searched her pants and cloak and found no pockets. Annoyed, she stuffed the paper into her boot.

She rose from her perch against the big oak and dusted herself off. She relished how easy that was and decided one day she'd design pants that had a multitude of pockets to solve all her attire problems.

"So, I'll meet you at the Baron's Ball. We just need to work out transport for him – some way to keep him concealed until we get him into the forest."

Donny rubbed his chin, eyebrows nettled. "Conceal Ribbit and ourselves as well."

"Let's meet up again and work through the last details. Maybe inspiration will strike later today," she suggested.

Donny nodded. "Be safe," he said to her. He gathered his Baron's Guard cloak from the ground, gripped it in one meaty paw, and strode away from her.

Riana gathered herself, her wheels still turning on her plan to rescue their friend as she headed onto the road and off to her apprenticeship at the winery. If they fouled up, she and Donny would be imprisoned with Ribbit. If they succeeded, Ribbit would be an outcast.

But, an alive outcast, she thought. Which was preferable. Warm, loving, bubbly Ribbit could simply not stay imprisoned. And the third potential reality was far worse: death, as she'd seen at Tomas, the baker's execution.

Her dark thoughts followed her onto the road. The blue sky overhead was littered with fast-moving clouds. The wind smelled of rain. As she walked, she pulled her cloak tighter against the chill that drove through her. Her hair whipped around her and the trees dotting the nearby fields bent and rattled their new green leaves. The sun was not warm but illuminated the sky in a distant sort of way.

Once out of sight of the schoolhouse, Riana was joined on the empty road. Tom leapt from the grasses where he'd been concealed. He butted his head against Riana's leg and purred loudly. Riana stopped, bent, and stroked his ear. When her hand fell away, Tom bounded forward down the road, tail flowing behind him. Riana watched her new companion with a smile, momentarily forgetting her worry.

When Riana drew near to the vineyard, Tom slunk into the outer fields, nose high as he sniffed out a trail away from other humans. His travel would lead him into the forest. Riana wondered if that was safe and wondered if she should be worried about potential encounters with other creatures or animals, but she couldn't conjure the feeling to go along with the question in her mind. She decided Tom was probably capable of protecting himself.

Riana made her way to the winery feeling a little less stressed than before Tom had appeared. Her companion's presence cheered and comforted her, and she was grateful for the gift of his presence. She was still hungry though. It had been another evening without food at the Fraely residence. She was getting skinny.

She wondered if her grandmother had left her any provisions she could access before her coming of age. She had an immediate moment of anger that her grandmother had been killed. She realized how irrational it was to be mad at someone who was dead, but she was mad at her grandmother. Mad and sad and desperate and lonely.

But, if she were these things, what must Ribbit be feeling, she wondered. How much darkness and dread could their bubbly, good-natured friend handle before it changed him forever?

She entered through the wide, arched wooden doorway of the winery, deep in thought. Her feet carried her automatically across gray and wine-stained floorboards, past the giant crushing vat and barrels. She was at the office door before she heard a throat clearing. She turned, wondering who was shaking her from her reverie. Her mentor stood at one of the wine presses next to two people.

Two people who happened to be seven and a half feet tall.

"Oh," Riana said dumbly. "Hello."

Ms. Hightower's smile turned rigid, her eyes bulging. "Is that any way to greet our guests?"

Riana did a double take at her mentor and Starliss Winery's cellar master. Ms. Hightower wore a dress. Riana raked her memories to find an image of the woman in anything but an unbuttoned tunic, leggings and a vest and returned nothing. She looked uncomfortable in the petticoats and plucked at the square neckline which barely concealed her bosom, as was the fashion. Riana decided the color – a washed out periwinkle – wasn't right, but overall, dresses suited the woman.

Riana broke her gaze from Ms. Hightower. "I mean – it's so good you could make it out to Starliss Vineyard and Winery. Welcome."

Kristopher smiled lopsidedly at her while Captain Rustofo surveyed the press room.

"Impressive," he said. "Though, it will take some convincing to prove this sodden soil will produce anything but the weakest swill."

"I accept your challenge," Riana said, a burn of determination filling her.

Ms. Hightower stomped toward Riana. Her gait ruined the effect of femininity. She pulled Riana away from the giants and whispered, "What do you think? Which should we serve?"

Riana stared at the giant, wondering what he normally drank. She recalled seeing his teeth, stained yellow and decided he probably drank a lot of chokraffe, a dark, hot drink that was both bitter and sweet. Usually, it was served with milk and sugar, but some took it "dirt". She had drunk the beverage. She had learned it was made by roasting the roots of the raffe bush, a plant that grew in mountainous regions of Idalfyn, where the giants hailed from. The roasted roots were then ground into powder and steeped in hot water. The drink was known to calm a person, while stimulating the intelligence. It also helped calm the stomach. Which was why it was usually stocked on sailing ships.

Riana had tasted it at Elynda's house. Her mother kept it on hand for stomach aches. Riana had once eaten too much chocolate cake and the dark drink soothed her aching belly. It was rich and warm, soothing and almost chewy with tannins.

"The mulgoveign," Riana decided. It was a dark, rich red wine that had a hint of cherry and had the same sort of tannin level as chokraffe. If she was right, he should like the wine for its similarities to the warm drink.

Ms. Hightower looked over her shoulder at the giants then back at Riana. "That's a lot of flavor for a first-time drinker of Starliss. Are you sure?"

"As sure as I can be," Riana said.

Ms. Hightower shrugged and stomped away. Riana returned to her guests. "How fares the Jade Lady and her crew today?"

"Very well," Captain Rustofo said. "And how fares the enigmatic Riana?"

"Well enough," Riana asserted.

Ms. Hightower came back with two glasses and a bottle. She pulled a corkscrew from an apron pocket and went to work. "So, Riana convinced you to come taste our wine?"

"She did," Captain Rustofo said. "At least, she convinced one of us," he grumbled. He looked down at his son who was looking down at Riana.

Riana was doing her best to not notice how much Kristopher was looking at her. She flushed, cleared her throat, straightened her back and dove into the introduction of the wine.

"Mulgoveign is a stone fruit produced here at Starliss Vineyard and nowhere else on Aelos," she began. She had loved listening to her grandmother speak about the wine. Silently, she sent up a prayer for her grandmother's aid. "The fruit grows on the twisted limbs of the mulgoveign tree. Its growth period spans nearly a full cycle of seasons: meriyu, tijiyu, ryliyu and the fruit finally ripens when its skin has been touched by dawiyu's first frost. This is one of the Baron's favorite wines."

"Is that so?" Captain Rustofo said, peering into the wine glass and swirling the dark liquid. He sniffed at it, looking as though he could be contaminated by it.

"Yes," Riana confirmed. "That is why we have named this wine, Frost Smitten."

Captain Rustofo sipped carefully at the wine, barely taking anything into his mouth. Kristopher tipped his up and emptied it with one swallow. Riana crossed her fingers as she watched the Captain swirl the liquid in his mouth before swallowing. He opened his mouth to speak, but a scream rent the air.

Riana's nerves fired into alertness. Mrs. Hightower looked around, caught by surprise.

"Where did that come from?" Kristopher asked.

"Outside," Riana said and was running to the side door before the word left her mouth. She reached the door and shoved it open. Riana searched around for the source of the scream. Vines waved in the chill wind. Clouds scudded overhead.

The scream ratcheted through the air again. Riana took off, Kristopher and his captain at her back. Rows of vines sat stalwart against the fear leaking out into the afternoon. An odd purplish cloud clung to the vegetation. Riana picked the row where the center of the cloud hung and beelined down it.

A young woman, not much younger than Riana, cowered in the dirt, vines and leaves arching over her. The light filtering in here was tinted in a purple haze. The girl crab crawled backward while the purple cloud matched her pace. She shrieked again.

Her plain dress was smudged in dirt and her apron was stained. Her bonnet had fallen off and lay forgotten. Riana ran up to the girl, skidding the last few feet to her side. She grabbed the girl's shoulders and attempted to pull her up on to her feet, at the same time trying to catch glimpses of what this mysterious cloud was.

Kristopher stooped, pulled the girl bodily from the ground and carried her away. Captain Rustofo lent his hand, allowing Riana to pull herself upright. She barely saw him. She was transfixed by this new phenomenon. Mrs. Hightower caught up to them and looked on while she panted.

"What is it?" Riana asked.

"By the Holy Mother and Father," breathed Mrs. Hightower. "I haven't seen haleosphere in ages. I thought we'd captured them all."

"Captured? Haleosphere?" Riana asked.

The swarming mass of clouds twisted in on themselves, like living threads of color. Riana reached for her sketch pad, then looked at Mrs. Hightower and thought better of it.

"I'll go fetch the Baron's Guard," Mrs. Hightower said.

"Yes, good idea," Captain Rustofo said. "Best to get the authorities."

Riana looked up at him. He looked at her over Mrs. Hightower's head and winked.

Mrs. Hightower nodded curtly. "Very well. And of all the days to wear this silly, nonsensical dress." She huffed and turned away.

Riana watched her exit the row of grapes before she turned back to Captain Rustofo. "So..."

"So, let's get this haleosphere to someplace safe," Captain Rustofo said.

"And why would I want to help what looks to be an elemental? That would be against the law," Riana said, nerves tying knots in her stomach.

"But you do want to help," the Captain said.

Kristopher walked up to the two of them. Riana saw him from her periphery and gave him a guarded glance, then shifted her gaze back to his father. Perhaps this was a trap. Maybe they were working for the Fraely and hoped to trick her into helping an elemental and then being arrested and imprisoned. But the Captain's own wife had been Tyrmini before she had been executed. Yet, if that was the case, maybe they were following the rules to stay out of trouble. Maybe they had learned their lesson.

"How do you know?" Riana asked, crossing her arms over her cloak and tunic.

"Let's just say we have a mutual friend."

"Um... guys," Kristopher said. Riana looked at him, but he was looking past her, his eyes wide with shock. Riana turned in the direction of his gaze and found herself face-to-face with the most beautiful creature she'd ever seen.

The creature's face was a mosaic of moving pastels. Its primary color shifted from white to teal to blue to purple then pink and back again. Every now and then Riana saw glimpses of gold and orange that mimicked the setting sun. Its large eyes were a captivating yellow-gold, set in rich black. Framing its eyes were wisps of white eyelashes so long they extended past the creature's face and ended in elliptical feathers that punctuated the lashes. The creature looked foxish in the shape of its face, the end of its nose ended in a black tip, lines tracing up its snout and over its vivid eyes. And yet the body of the creature was almost serpentine in shape and covered in what appeared to be clouds, rather than either scales or fur.

The creature's body twisted between the clouds gathered around it. Riana could barely distinguish where the creature's body ended, and the clouds began.

She involuntarily took a step forward and was midstride to take another step when two large hands wrapped around her shoulders.

"Do not dream of getting any closer," Kristopher breathed.

"Why?" Riana asked. She leaned into his grip.

"Because while that creature is certainly beautiful, it is also very dangerous." Kristopher whispered.

"What is it?" she asked.

"A haleosphere is an air creature. Air and water. It uses its ability to mimic weather. Once it's close enough, it shifts its form to what you see now. And lures you in."

"Then what?" Riana asked, still fascinated by the swirling pastels undulating through the form of the creature.

"You're distracted by the colors, aren't you? And those beautiful eyes," Kristopher said. "But look at its jawline, Riana."

Riana tore her gaze from the mesmerizing colors shifting and swaying over soft, cloud-like fur to the black-lined mouth of the haleosphere. Almost invisible, a pair of translucent, needle-like fangs dropped past either side of the lower jaw.

"What are those for?" Riana asked, but almost certainly knew the answer – or at least a version of it. Now that she had seen them, she couldn't tear her gaze away.

Kristopher breathed in slowly, carefully. "Those fangs are perfect instruments for piercing your arteries and drawing out the oxygen-rich blood. You have two arteries that are easily accessed from the soft spot near your collar bones. And the haleosphere is smelling, sensing their exact location. It mesmerizes you to give it time to search them out, and then when it is satisfied it knows the location, it will strike. It will strike quickly, wrapping you up in its body as it sinks its fangs into your arteries, and it will drink thoroughly until you are dry."

Riana swallowed, all too aware of her rich blood being pumped swiftly by her anxious heart.

The creature shifted, just the tiniest bit. Riana squeaked. Wind erupted around them, tossing up dirt and leaves, pushing Riana's hair into her eyes, whipping her cloak around. She threw her hands up as she was hauled backward by the giant boy behind her.

Riana fell to the dirt, pushing her hair from her face, shielding her eyes to see what was happening with Kristopher. Kristopher held a knife in his hand and before Riana could protest an attack on the creature, he raised the weapon. But, instead of slicing at the creature, he sliced at his other hand. Beside him, his father, had done the same thing. They stood like a wall in front of Riana with bloody hands held toward a blood-thirsty creature.

"What are you doing?" she shouted. She pushed herself up from the ground and launched herself at the two giants. She'd be damned if they sacrificed themselves to protect her. She pushed at the men, but they were solid and ungiving. She looked past them.

The creature hissed, its colors shifting from pale pinks and oranges to sickly green and purple. Its golden eyes looked more menacing with the shift in color and its fangs were prevalent against the black inside of its mouth. The creature looked from Kristopher to the Captain. It locked its gaze onto Kristopher, coiling back. Riana knew its next move would be to lunge at the giant. And she just couldn't allow that.

For the second time since her grandmother's death, she called on the secret she held deep within her. She called on Magloryn. It only took a moment to tap into the well of light within her and draw it up to protect these strange, kind giants. With hands full of light, she pushed aside the Captain and his son, who tripped and fell into the vegetation.

The power coursing through her was like liquid silver. It was cool and enthralling, gentle and steel-strong. She was light enough to float yet as protected as if she were wearing armor.

The creature recoiled, snapped its mouth closed and shifted back to its undulating pastels. Riana held out her hands and allowed the energy to flow from her to the creature in a soft ray of light. The light twisted and turned and finally connected to the creature, in the spot between its eyes. Riana gasped as the creature's intentions raced into her mind. She felt its hunger, its confusion, its need.

"He's just hungry," Riana said. "So hungry."

"Riana," Kristopher's voice came to her muffled, as if he were speaking through the cover of a blanket. "Can you speak back to it?"

Riana was bathed in the creature's need, but the question pulled her back to herself. Of course, she could. Magloryn was the savior of all creation on Aelos. Her love was a paramount connection. Riana didn't know how she knew this, but the realization shook her with a deep compassion.

"Yes," she said.

"Guide it into the forest," Captain Rustofo said. "Tell it there are animals to hunt there."

Riana nodded. There were animals to hunt there. Deer and wild boar, elk, and also elemental creatures. Creatures she'd saved. Riana's stomach squirmed at the idea of setting up an ecosystem of elementals all vying for the same resources. Was this sustainable or would they all wipe each other out? She wished life wasn't sustained by the consumption of other life, but it seemed that was the way of things.

Life is balance. The thought flowed through her like water. The deer and rabbit and mouse have their purpose. The antoli and fire nymph have theirs, as does this creature. It is always about balance, the give and take and the letting go and hanging on. Without the predator, the prey would consume too much vegetation. Without the prey, the vegetation would become overgrown. The world must operate in synchrony with all its elements. The world is out of sync and you must help to right it. The forest has plenty of prey to sustain another, many other, predators. The world is righting itself because you are here.

In Riana's mind, her perspective zoomed away from the predator before her. She saw the forest, the mice and mole, deer, rabbit and many other prey creatures. She saw the undergrowth being eaten away, the trees contracting disease which led to their death and diminishing of the forest. Then she saw the return of the antoli, berubula, fire nymphs, amatsu and haleosphere. The antoli hunted the rabbits. The amatsu hunted the fish. The berubula kept the crab population in check. The haleosphere would hunt the deer. The forest swelled and grew, gained vibrancy and health.

Riana sighed as the truth of balance settled into her. She opened her eyes to the creature. "We have a home for you. To keep you safe, you must stay in the forest. Eat the deer. Become comfortable in the trees. There is safety and food in the forest." Riana sent the picture of the forest to the mind of the creature, lacing her thoughts with feelings of comfort, showing the creature the deer that roamed the forest and the safety of the trees.

The creature stared at her, blinked then nodded. It turned its head away and ascended into its clouds. The clouds rose from the fruit vines and skidded toward the forest. Riana watched it until it was safely past the treeline before she allowed the connection with the creature to separate. Like a switch turning off, she allowed her access to the power to drop out.

Coming back to the mundane from the pure love of Magloryn felt like a letdown, yet the energy still flowed around and through her, lifting her mood, setting her power as a solid core within her. She rubbed her hands together to dispel the last of the tingling energy in her fingers and turned to face the Captain and Kristopher.

They were still on the ground and stared at her, mouths slightly open, eyes wide.

"What are you?" Kristopher finally uttered.

Riana's fear threatened to erase all the positive, loving energy she was basking in. "Are you going to take me in?"

"In?" the Captain asked.

"To the Baron's Guard? Or the High King's Guard?" Riana asked.

"Why would we do that? You're one of us," Kristopher said, and smiled.

CHAPTER NINETEEN

Riana stood at the barrel that served as a table and swirled the rich, dark wine in her glass, watching the way it caught the low light and greedily absorbed it. She couldn't shake the feeling someone was watching her and kept glancing into the dark recesses of the winery to catch whoever it was spying. No one was there. All the winery staff had gone home for the evening.

Even Mrs. Hightower, who offered to stop into Mr. Fraely's and give Riana's regrets she would be late this evening. She'd smiled wickedly at the prospect. Mrs. Hightower seemed to take any opportunity to jab at the General Store owner.

The conversation was unsafe for any ears besides her own. She only wished Elynda were here, to at least know she was allying herself and preparing to rescue their friend. She sipped her wine and let the familiar warmth spread through her. She hoped it would dispel the feeling of unease she had about the earlier rescue of the creature. She should be elated. Instead guilt and shame crept through her. And the nagging sensation she would soon be in trouble for using her power.

"So, this Baron of yours has a concealed entrance to his castle?" Captain Rustofo asked.

Riana shook herself from her thought process. Maybe she did have trouble on its way; not from what she'd done already, but what she was planning on doing. Perhaps it was just paranoia of their current conversation being overheard that sent her eyes darting around the room.

"Yes," she said. "One of the many perks of being a wine dealer to a local Baron who was maybe a bit too enthusiastic of a drinker." She dismissed any other questions on how she knew this to be true. In fact, she had learned about the secret entrance when she had stumbled on Captain Steph and Sela talking about the Baron's need for more elixir. Later her grandmother had confirmed the information, very shortly before she'd been killed, giving Riana the details of where to find it, both the inner entrance to the tunnels leading outside and the outer entrance leading inside. Sela had said the information may come in handy. She'd been right, it turned out. "Grandmother hated it because she had to walk past the prisoners in order to make special wine deliveries to the Baron's father."

She didn't know what kept her from revealing the story of the golden elixir. Perhaps it would come with time. For now, she only let out the secrets that would help their cause: release Ribbit.

Kristopher and Riana would enter the Baron's Ball together and meet up with Donny. The passage started in the library, which was open to party-goers and just adjacent to the ballroom. Riana knew how to access the entrance, thanks to her grandmother. She, Donny and Kristopher would spirit through the tunnels. Any guards they met along the way would be handled by Donny. They would be cuffed (or at least seemingly so). The story Donny and Riana had worked out earlier would inform guards Riana – and now Kristopher – had been caught attempting to steal items from the Baron's Keep.

"If things get physical, I can help," Kristopher said.

"How so?" she asked. She wondered if he would reveal he'd taken after his mother. It wasn't lost on Riana that the father-son duo were out on the sea, just as Kristopher's mother had been to keep her safe from harm.

He raised his eyebrows at her. When she returned his gaze, nonplussed, he walked over to her, standing close and towering above her. She craned her neck to peer into his face.

"I see your point," she said, swallowing against the sudden racing of her heart. Riana reminded herself being Tyrmini, or Magys, was only one form of power. Although, if the guard were attracted to men, his achingly handsome demeanor was more likely to knock them off their feet than a well-placed blow to the head. Riana backed away from the close contact so her head would clear, and her breath would even out.

"Once you've spirited your young friend from the prison, you'll escort him to the exit behind the castle, where I'll meet you with the carriage to take him away," Captain Rustofo said.

Riana shook herself and looked away from Kristopher to the Captain and nodded. "Perfect. Then, we're set." Riana could feel fire nymph wings fluttering in her stomach, her nervousness fueled by both fear and excitement.

CHAPTER TWENTY

Elynda and Riana headed to Elynda's home through a thick downpour. With hoods pulled low, they plodded along down the North Road of Landsend. They didn't speak because the heavy rain drowned out their words.

Riana was grateful for boots which kept her feet dry, but poor Elynda's dress skirts would be soaked by the time they reached her house. In the distance, Riana could make out the angry crash of the waves against the cliffs. The day was near night-black from the bulging and gray clouds overhead.

Riana wondered what Tom was up to. She wondered where he went in the awful weather. She hoped he was safe and dry somewhere, but not in her room. The last thing she wanted was Tom being caught by the Fraely. Even in his guise as a feline, she wasn't confident Fraely would leave him be.

They still had another mile or so. Riana was just sucking up her frustration with the weather, and the insistent pain in her gut that was a level of hunger she'd never endured before, when a cart rolled to a stop several feet ahead of them. Riana tried looking to see who it was, but the cart was covered and blocked her view. Riana strode up to the cart and peered in to identify the driver, automatically on edge without being sure why.

Donny Derringer looked down at them. His muscly mass took up the larger part of the bench and he gripped the reins like they were shoestrings. His cloak was still too small for him, but the plain tunic he sported revealed the muscles of his neck and top of his chest. Riana was stunned once again by the transformation she'd seen him go through in just a few short months as a Baron's Guard.

"Want a ride?" he shouted above the rain.

Elynda climbed into the seat before Riana could open her mouth to respond. She quickly climbed in after her, grateful for the rescue.

Lightning brightened the sky to the north, followed shortly by a crashing boom.

Elynda grabbed at Riana's arm and held on until the rumbling abated.

Riana stared out of the cart at the storm, tingling from the energy of the lightning. She was awestruck at the power of the elements.

Elynda turned to Donny. Yelling above the storm she said, "Thank you, Donny. It's a treacherous afternoon."

"Where are you headed?" he asked and looked over Elynda to peer at Riana, seemingly trying to catch her eye.

Riana looked at him and could swear there was some dangerous emotion playing out, just under the surface of Donny's expression, but she couldn't name it. She went on looking at him, analyzing what she was seeing on his face, when Elynda answered his question.

"My house, please, Donny," Elynda said.

"I'm glad you're here," Riana yelled around Elynda. "I've solved the transportation issue for Saturday's plans."

Donny gently flicked the reins and the cart rolled along the rocky road with jolting bounce. "That's fantastic. Whose cart were you able to commandeer?" Donny asked.

"The thing is," Riana said, "it comes with a driver and an additional pair of hands as well."

Donny turned his head, eyes still on the road before momentarily snapping a nervous gaze to Riana. "What?" he asked.

"You could say I've made some new friends," Riana shouted.

Donny didn't respond for three breaths, which Riana counted in her head.

"You told someone else our plan?" he shouted, and Riana didn't think it was to carry the message over the pounding rain.

"Listen, you have to trust me," Riana said.

"Are you new?" he asked.

"Rude," Riana pointed out, her anger stoked.

"You can't go running around telling people we're planning on rescuing our friend from the Baron's prison to save him from being sentenced as a Tyrmini."

Elynda leaned away from Donny, pushing herself into Riana, who had pushed herself to the edge of the bench. Riana adjusted her feet to bare the extra weight of Elynda against her so she could avoid falling out of the buggy.

"I didn't just tell anyone," Riana shouted. Lightning flashed and thunder immediately proceeded the flare of light. Riana waited for the rumble to cease before she continued. "They're Tyrmini in hiding. Well, the son is and the father is protecting him."

"How do we know they're not the High King's Tyrmini Guard tricking people into revealing themselves as sympathizers just to lop off their – our –," he corrected himself, "heads?"

"I know because they helped me rescue an elemental," Riana said.

"That could all be part of the ruse," Donny pointed out.

"Trust Riana," Elynda said. "She's a good judge of character."

"Riana is reckless," Donny told Elynda. "I don't like this. Not one little bit."

They had arrived at Elynda's house. Donny pulled the buggy to a stop near the porch. Riana jumped out, rounded the back of the cart, and faced Donny. "Then don't help us. We'll manage on our own," she said.

She was aware she was soaked to the bone, rain dripping down her face, her cloak's hood heavy against her head. Her anger throbbed inside her.

"I'm not saying I'm not going to help, Riana," Donny stated. "I just don't think it's wise to trust people we know nothing about."

"Fine," Riana said. "Don't trust them." She crossed her arms. "I'm moving forward. You can help us, or you can stay out of the way and let us proceed. Your choice."

And with that, Riana turned on her heel, marched past the sodden horse driving Donny's buggy, and fled up the porch stairs with Elynda on her heels. Riana listened through the pounding rain as Donny whistled to his horse and the cart rattled into movement. She didn't look back as he drove away.

Just as they stepped up the three short steps, Tom materialized in the lamplight and meowed at them. He was soaked, his ears drooping, and his tail wrapped around his feet.

"Oh, poor Tom," Elynda said and rushed toward the creature masquerading as a cat.

Tom looked up at Elynda with wide sapphire eyes. Riana got the feeling he was intentionally looking extra miserable to solicit Elynda's sympathy.

"Come on in and let's get you dry," Elynda said. She scooped him into her arms, and they proceeded into the Heilbee home.

CHAPTER TWENTY-ONE

Riana sat on the low mattress in the attic room of Elynda's house. Elynda dropped her soaking dress to the floor and reached for a towel to dry off. Riana followed suit, hanging her clothing on the line next to the small fireplace to dry.

Tom was doing a neat trick. Riana could feel the heat coming off him, and steam rose from his body. He stretched and rolled on the oval beige carpet covering the hardwood. A deep purr undulated through him. His orange fur was dry in moments.

"Jealous," Elynda said, watching Tom.

Tom rolled to a sitting position and eyed Elynda with regal blue eyes, almost as if he were looking down at her. His ears twitched back. He exhaled sharply through his nose and turned away from Elynda.

"I guess he told you," Riana said.

"What was that about?" Elynda asked.

"Well, he can't very well just change clothes, can he?" Riana asked.

"I suppose not," Elynda said.

"You have your tricks and he has his, I think is what sums up what he was thinking."

Elynda giggled, knelt to the floor, and stroked the fur on Tom's neck and behind his ears. Riana could swear he was smiling as purrs vibrated through the room.

Elynda wiggled into her night dress and turned to Riana. "Alright, then. Tell me everything."

"What do you mean?" Riana asked, lost in thought about Donny, his intentions both toward her and toward Tyrmini in general.

"I mean, who are you going to the ball with? Hm? When were you going to share that little morsel of a secret with your best friend?" Elynda asked. She folded her arms over her stomach and stared with her incredible jade eyes.

"Oh, that," Riana said. She launched into her story about the sugar run, meeting the Rustofos, their involvement with other Tyrmini and their participation in Riana's plan to help Ribbit escape from the Baron's dungeons.

"And where do I fit into this plan?" Elynda asked.

"Out of it," Riana said. "I'm committed to keeping you safe."

"Nope. I'm coming with you," she said.

"Elynda, it's bad enough one friend is in the dungeons, I don't want to tempt fate for two friends' imprisonment."

"Too bad. So, you better think of some way for me to help because I'm in."

Riana opened her mouth to argue more, but Elynda held up a hand, widened her eyes and stuck her other hand in a balled-up fist onto the curve of her hip.

Riana sighed. She thought about it. If she refused and didn't work Elynda into the plan, Elynda would not only feel betrayed, she'd rebel and potentially cause more trouble. She hung her head.

"Fine," she conceded. "You will go with Kristopher and I to find Ribbit and get him up through the tunnels to where Captain Rustofo will be waiting to take him back to their ship. Since Donny isn't going now, we can say you're the healer checking in on the prisoners and Kristopher and I are your helpers."

Elynda smiled. "That works well. I'll bring my bag to add to the ruse, and in case Ribbit is..." she choked on the next word, swallowed, then finished: "...hurt."

Riana's stomach rolled at the idea of their friend suffering. Tomorrow could not come fast enough.

CHAPTER TWENTY-TWO

Riana could not believe her situation. Elynda had made it clear: one did not wear a dress at her age without a corset. This meant Riana was stuffed into an unyielding, unforgiving, unmoving straight jacket some heinous person had devised to torture women. She gasped as Elynda yanked at the strings, drawing the ribbing tighter.

"Ouch," she breathed, but even her protest was breathy and weak.

"You'll be fine, Riana. I don't know how you've managed to get away with not having to wear a corset. It simply isn't fair that all other women should suffer but not you."

"I'm not making women wear these cursed contraptions. As soon as this evening is over, you won't catch me dead in one of these things."

"Oh? And what about when you marry?

"Marry?" Riana asked and her mind sprang to a certain giant young man whom she'd be meeting soon. Oddly, a second face sprang to mind after Kristopher's. Seeing Donny's visage in her thought stream of marriage startled her. Elynda yanked at the strings once more and Riana's temper flared. "If wearing ridiculous attire is required for the job, then no thank you. I'll be spinster in pants and boots for all time."

Elynda was quiet for a moment. "You know, I believe you could too. Especially when you inherit the winery and vineyard."

Elynda was only tying the strings now, but Riana felt as though she'd pinched her once again. Not just a fold of skin or a lump of muscle. The pain skewered her through the middle and clamped down on her throat. She wondered when the pain of her grandmother's absence would abate. It hurt so much, and while on one hand she hoped she could move on soon, she also relished the pain. As if her suffering could make up for her role in her grandmother's death.

Elynda seemed to sense her thought process. "That's what your grandmother would want. She was strong and independent. She'd want you to have the opportunity for that sort of livelihood as well."

"Yet, how much better to have her here as I learned her business?" Her words were weak by her lack of breath. "She was gone too soon and gone because of me. Because of my mistakes. Because I couldn't control this... whatever it is inside me."

Elynda pulled at her shoulder, turning Riana around to face her. She put a hand on either side of her face and stroked her thumbs across Riana's cheeks. Riana was surprised at the sudden sensation of wetness on her face. She was crying and had been unaware.

Elynda searched her eyes. "This was not your fault. If the art of the Tyrmini were not banned, we would know before we came of age if we had abilities. You told me this yourself. If we knew before the abilities manifested, we would be prepared for their arrival. And we'd be taught how to use them with care and accuracy. If this is anyone's fault, it's our High King's."

Riana hung her head. Elynda had a very good point. But, the point still didn't revive her grandmother.

"I won't let her die in vain," Riana said. "I'll save Ribbit. I'll keep others from the High King's control."

CHAPTER TWENTY-THREE

Riana had to admit she looked exquisite, thanks to Elynda's ministrations. The dress she'd lent her was royal blue, the same color as the Starliss sigil. She stood straight as an arrow and only mostly because the corset demanded it. While she detested wearing dresses, tonight she could see why her grandmother adored them. They had a way of demanding attention, and that would serve Riana well in taking over her grandmother's legacy.

Although, she had no idea how she would navigate the tunnels under the castle swathed in frills and furbelows. Her grandmother's role and her own were turning out to be slightly different.

Riana walked carefully to the cart, grateful for Kristopher's shaking hand which held her own in a sturdy embrace. If she fainted for lack of air, at least she was confident he would catch her.

When they got to the cart, Kristopher bent low, wrapped an arm around Riana's waist and hoisted her into the cart, pausing just before setting her down. He pressed his mouth close to her ear and whispered, "You look stunning."

Chills ran down her neck and spine. She bit her lip against the sudden response her body made and relished Kristopher's proximity, his smell and the strength of his arms around her. He set her down, so her feet touched the floorboard of the cart. Standing in the roofless cart, Riana was pleased to be at eye level with him for once. She took in his smooth face, his eyes, the curve of his mouth. And then she remembered to respond to his compliment.

"Thank you," she said. "You look dashing as well. I'll be the envy of every lady at the ball."

"Let them envy," he said. He smiled, revealing a perfect mouth of straight and shiny teeth.

Riana's heart thumped wildly as she imagined pressing her own mouth to his. He turned away from her and she slid into the farthest seat, making room. Kristopher helped Elynda into the cart beside her and then he joined his father in the front bench.

"They're even bigger than I imagined," Elynda whispered to Riana. Then she turned to them. "Are all of your countrymen are as large as you?" she asked Kristopher's back.

Kristopher looked at his father, who stonily looked back at his son. Riana saw a conversation pass between them unsaid. She imagined Kristopher asking his father how much he should say, and the Captain ordering Kristopher to use discretion.

Kristopher smiled as he glanced back at her. "Our family is slightly above average height," he said.

Riana wondered if 'slightly' was an understatement and had a tingling notion someday she might find out, though she couldn't say why. More than that, she stored away her curiosity to ask more pointed questions about Kristopher's lineage once they were alone again.

Captain Rustofo clucked his tongue at the horses and the cart rattled away.

To their left shoulders, only one of two moons had risen. It was a vivid golden globe rising on an azure eastern horizon. Toward their right the sun melted into the Dreavynan, casting the sky in reds, pinks and purples. They drove along the Western Road, accompanied by the crashing waves, the spring breeze and the sun and moon caught in each other's reflections.

Riana thought there couldn't be a more perfect evening for rebellion.

She was deep in thought when a warm hand clasped her own. She looked over to find Elynda grasping her hand, nerves painting her face in worry.

"It'll be okay. We'll get him out," Riana assured her.

"Okay, but can you do it without getting caught in the process?" Elynda asked.

"Absolutely," Riana said, although she wasn't entirely sure without Donny as an escort. Maybe they would get caught. Maybe tonight was the perfect night to relish the last bit of freedom.

I will not be caught and enslaved in this dragon-forsaken dress, she decided, contemplating how nightmarish it would be to spend time in a dungeon in evening wear. The corset is torture enough.

Captain Rustofo pulled the carriage into the wide semi-circle of the Keep's courtyard. Riana's stomach squirmed with nerves. Kristopher climbed from the seat and held out a hand for Elynda. Once Elynda made a smooth exit, Riana took his massive hand and allowed him to help her from the cart. The three of them huddled under Captain Rustofo.

"I'll see you later," he said meaningfully and raised his eyebrows high over his gray eyes. He winked at Riana and then at Elynda and nodded at Kristopher. Kristopher nodded back, his face a mask of determination.

They made their way through the courtyard to the Keep's main entrance. The impressive structure was built on a high hill and perched on a black, rocky cliff overlooking the crashing waves of the Dreavynan. Appointed by the Dragon Slayer turned High King after the campaign to exterminate the Tyrmini and elementals, the first Landsend's Baron had spared no expense.

The walls of the main building were made from glittering manestone scraped out of the Shadow Mountains and transported to Landsend by many horses and carts and a whole lot of strong people. Its milky white with a hint of blue shone in the night like a lamp against the dark sea behind it. Its namesake hung in the clear sky over four towers whose pinnacles were dressed in Landsend's pennants waving sea blue and silver with the sigil of the lighthouse. The curtain wall surrounding the courtyard and keep was made of more manestone.

Fires in black grates of iron sconces fashioned in the shape of giant lanterns lit the inside of the curtain wall. In the center of the courtyard a fountain shaped like ocean waves full of fish with glittering scales of opalescent greens and blues blossomed in the light of nearby oil-burning lamp posts. Along the outer ring of the circular courtyard were beautiful flowering bushes sprouting from luscious, green grass and evergreens.

The building was seven stories. Its parapets surrounded the main Keep. Through the crenelations, Riana could see guards marching up and down the walk in navy uniforms, brass buttons glinting in lamplight. The trio climbed the semi-circular stone stairway to the main entrance of the main keep. The foyer opened to marble floors. A chandelier of glittering crystals and silver dominated the center of the ceiling.

Elynda goggled at it as they passed a collection of busts depicting all the Tarbyrwin Barons. Once at the ballroom off to the right of the foyer, they encountered a young and beautiful man dressed in equally beautiful finery. His green and blue vest mimicked the waves of the Dreavynan, and he wore a velvet navy jacket. Between the perfection of his powdered and painted face, the cut of his jawline, and the plump curves of his lips, Riana thought the man was more lovely than many women. He opened his mouth to reveal the white pearls of his teeth and redness of his tongue.

"Riana Starliss of Starliss Vineyard and Winery, Kristopher Rustofo of the Jade Lady and Elynda Heilbee of Healer's Hall!"

Riana looked around, stomach fluttering, waiting to see one familiar face. Still hoping.

The ballroom was packed. Small groups of men and women gathered on the outskirts of the dance floor, chatting, and laughing. At the far end of the ballroom, on a small stage the orchestra played for the evening's event. Women in evening gowns with copious petticoats and bustles fanned their flushed faces as they sipped on Starliss Red and chatted over the noise of the music and dancing.

Elynda clasped Riana's hand with a sweaty grip. If Riana were nervous someone would question their being there, her fear subsided at a look at the revelers. She doubted anyone had even heard the announcer's voice above the swell of music, laughter and chatting.

Except for one attendee of the ball, who locked eyes on Kristopher and refused to release his gaze. And it was the very last person Riana wanted to notice them.

Ayrwin Tarbyrwin, the newly appointed Baron of Landsend was staring at Riana's escort.

CHAPTER TWENTY-FOUR

The Baron of Landsend was perched on the edge of an ornate throne. Riana wondered if the whole thing was made from silver. Carved on either side of the back were ocean waves so artistically rendered one could imagine hearing the crash and lull of the Dreavynan. Encrusted in the foam of the waves were aquamarine stones that caught the light of the many burning oil lamps and candles.

The Baron was a man past the middle of his life. His hair, which Riana guessed had once been blonde, was a shock of regal white – the same color as her grandmother's. And then it struck Riana that she was looking at her grandmother's brother. At least, her half-brother.

His eyes were even the same color of sea blue. Riana could not help the welling of sorrow in her gut. She wondered if the Baron mourned the loss of a sister, if he even knew he had a sister.

Aside from the uncanny resemblance in hair and eyes, the Baron was obviously the product of other parentage. Where Sela Starliss had high cheekbones and a smart, small nose and perfect chin, the Baron's features were what Riana thought of as hard. As if he'd been crudely carved from stone. His nose and chin and even his face had a squarish quality that made him an imposing figure.

Riana was so busy staring at this relation to her grandmother that when the Baron shifted his gaze from the giant to her, she simply stared back, lost in her thoughts. A sharp poke to her ribs brought her quickly out of her reverie. She darted a glance at Elynda who cleared her throat inconspicuously. Riana looked back at the Baron and dropped into a curtsy.

To her surprise, the Baron stood from his throne. The musicians stopped playing and the crowd went silent, turning toward the Baron. He slipped down the dais steps and walked toward Riana, Elynda and Kristopher. Riana held her breath. The crowd parted to make way for their royalty, dropping into bows and curtsies as he approached. From where Riana stood the crowd appeared to undulate like the waves of the Dreavynan.

Riana's insides quivered. Kristopher was statuesque beside her and Elynda had a death grip on her arm. When the Baron came within five feet of the trio, they bowed and curtsied in unison, and waited for the Baron to speak.

"Rise," he said lazily. When Riana could look again, she saw the Baron was darting glances between each of them. He pointed to Kristopher. "You hail from Idalfyn?"

"Yes, your lordship," Kristopher confirmed. "It is a great honor to meet the esteemed Baron of Landsend."

"Is it?" the Baron drawled.

Kristopher bowed his head.

"If you say so," the Baron said. He turned to Riana. "And you are none other than the adopted granddaughter of the late Sela Starliss of Starliss Vineyard and Winery. Riana, is it?"

Riana's nerves crackled. Her stomach lurched. She had to impress this Baron if she was to keep his loyalty to their brand, yet she was vastly aware her friend was currently somewhere beneath their feet in a dungeon because the Baron was keeping him prisoner.

How did grandmother do it? Riana wondered. Her father had killed her best friend. How did she remain civil with him?

Riana schooled her features, determined to do whatever she needed to do to rescue her friend. This man in front of her was an enemy, even if he was a paycheck. She had to act with care.

"Yes, your lordship, Sela Starliss was my grandmother."

"Mm..." he muttered. "And I understand you inherit Starliss vineyard upon your sixteenth summer."

Riana's mind reeled wildly. What was he getting at?

"Indeed, my grandmother left me to care for the production of Landsend's most prized winery."

"And are you up to the task?"

"Not on my own, sir," she said, trusting her gut on how to form the conversation. The Baron cocked an eyebrow high over his sea green eyes. "Fortunately, my mentorship is tended by the experts at the vineyard and winery."

The Baron nodded, seeming impressed with her answer. "That is good news. I have relied on Starliss Red for many decades to soothe the troubles royalty faces. I would be sorely disappointed if the quality suffered with the tragedy of your grandmother's passing."

"Murder," Riana said.

"Excuse me?"

"My grandmother did not pass, she was murdered."

The Baron waved a hand in front of his face as if to clear his nose of a bad scent. "Yes, of course. My condolences." He tacked the last part on, as if some internal mechanism had switched on to produce the appropriate response in the given situation. Riana realized if he knew Sela Starliss was his sister, he did not care about her passing past the point of whether or not it interrupted his joy in a glass.

"And mine for your father's passing," Riana said.

The Baron leaned in conspiratorially. "It was about damned time." The Baron brushed away a stray strand of white hair from his face, eyebrows raised.

Riana had no words. She simply stared, searching for a segue out of the morbid conversation.

The Baron waved down a nearby server. He took a glass of golden, bubbling champagne. Riana knew it was a Starliss vintage because she had helped coordinate the delivery.

The Baron handed Riana a glass. He raised his drink in the air. Riana mimicked him. "To a new generation!" he boomed and toasted Riana.

He turned to the crowd. "May the wine flow red, the champagne bubble brightly and the people of Landsend revel in its fruits!"

"Cheers!" the crowd shouted.

Riana sipped her champagne but did not smile. Yes, to a new generation, she thought, her resolve hardening and her nervousness about her plans for the evening fading in the face of the Baron's self-serving attitude.

The music resumed, and the partygoers went back to their conversations and dancing.

"Should you need anything, Ms. Starliss, please be sure to ask. Best of luck to the both of our inheritances." He nodded his head toward her in the mock of a bow. Riana curtsied.

The Baron turned away and crossed through the crowd, over the highly polished marble floors.

"Oh, I need something," Riana said, "but, I'm certainly not asking you for help."

Riana watched him stroll carelessly through the dancers in their fine dress. The Baron even deigned to saunter. Riana shook her head.

"Look at him," Riana said to Elynda. "It's so easy being him. He doesn't have to worry about being chained up and locked in a dungeon."

"Riana! Hush!" Elynda admonished.

"Oh, no one is listening," Riana said and waved away her chastisement.

"I was," said a voice behind her.

Startled, Riana wheeled around. Donny stood in front of her, his face serious.

"You're here," Riana said, a wave of relief crashing over her.

Donny nodded, looking down at his boots. He was dressed in an official Baron's Guard uniform. It was new, clean, buttons shining, white gloves gleaming. Donny had shaven his face so that it was smooth and hairless. He even smelled good. Riana had to admit, he looked good in that uniform.

"I couldn't let you have all the fun," he grumbled, looking up at her through dark lashes.

She grinned.

Kristopher cleared his throat, making his presence known. Riana shook herself.

"Donny, this is Kristopher Rustofo of the Jade Lady," Riana introduced.

Donny seemed to see Kristopher for the first time. His eyes went wide as he took in his full height, mouth falling open in surprise.

"Kristopher, this is Donny Derringer, our good friend (and ally)," she whispered the last two words, glancing around to ensure they were out of anyone else's earshot.

"You are a Baron's Guard," Kristopher stated, and to Riana it sounded like an accusation, or an insult.

"And you're a giant," Donny said.

"And I'm bored," Riana snapped. "Let's go."

Kristopher ground his jaw once toward Donny, then followed when she set out to skirt the ballroom.

It wasn't difficult. She smiled at familiar faces, accepted sincere and insincere condolences, promised to be a good vineyard owner and slipped into the library with no one being the wiser. Her friends followed her. Once they were all in, she looked out among the party and felt a smug sense of accomplishment. She would own Starliss Vineyard and protect Tyrmini. She would take the money from the Baron and she would smuggle his prisoners out from under his nose, while he drank his preferred Starliss Red and sauntered across the ballroom.

They entered the library just across the foyer from the ballroom. There were walls and balconies and pillars covered in books of all different shapes, colors and sizes. Oversized leather chairs were positioned near a fire and a table was laid out with a crystal decanter of some dark liquor and small drinking glasses.

Riana looked around the room, taking a moment to appreciate the collection of books amassed by the royal family. She wondered how many were like the books in her own small collection in the winery's secret room. Of course, royalty wouldn't have to hide them away; they could simply keep them on an open shelf with no consequences.

Across from the fire and armchairs, two large shelves sectioned off a small area of the library. Riana slipped between the shelves and entered the cave-like interior. She was surrounded by floor to ceiling shelves lined with books. Donny, Kristopher and Elynda joined her, making the small space feel even smaller.

Riana made her way to the corner her grandmother had told her about. She ran her fingertips over the canvas and leather spines of the books. There it was. Cave Dwelling Elementals. She pulled the book from its shelf and reached into the gap it made, searching with blind fingers. Her hand closed around cool metal. She wrapped her hand around it and pulled. The lever didn't budge.

Riana's heart sped. Doubts flooded her. What if the lever no longer worked? What if the new Baron had disabled it? They had no plan B. Ribbit would stay in the dungeon and face execution or recruitment.

Riana's panic pumped through her. She gripped the lever and yanked as hard as she could. It did not move.

"Here, let me try," Kristopher offered.

Riana moved out of the way. Kristopher squeezed his large hand into the hole. His eyes rolled toward the ceiling and then to the side, his lips pursed together as the tip of his tongue escaped his mouth. His biceps bulged as he pulled at the lever. Riana was convinced the secret entrance had been disabled, maybe even barricaded, and despaired for their friend.

Elynda found Riana and gripped her arm, tears welling in her eyes. Riana trembled.

Kristopher grunted with effort.

"Do you need some help, big guy?" Donny asked.

Kristopher paused to look over his shoulder and down at Donny, whose sarcastic grin slipped from his face. Kristopher returned to the work.

"It's no use," Riana said.

The sound of grating metal scraped through the small room, followed by a hollow pop. The bookshelf dislodged from the wall and hung ajar. Cool air washed over them, scented by dirt. Riana stared into the darkened hallway with an open mouth.

Kristopher flashed a smile at Riana, gave her a sweeping bow and said, "After you, my lady."

Riana caught Donny rolling his eyes.

Riana moved forward and Elynda moved with her, because Elynda was still grasping her arm. Once they were in the hallway, they blinked as their vision adjusted. Kristopher moved in behind them, carrying a lantern. Donny was invisible with the bulk of Kristopher in front of him.

"Where did that come from?" Riana asked.

Kristopher nodded back to the previous room. "In there," he said.

Donny shoved the door closed behind him.

Riana reached out a hand and said, "Don't -," but her protest was cut short by a clanging scrape.

"We couldn't leave it open," Donny said.

"Are you sure?" Elynda said and while Riana couldn't see the fine details of Elynda's porcelain face in the yellow circle of light cast by the lantern, Riana was sure Elynda scowled at Donny in disapproval.

"If we leave it open, someone who stumbles upon it could follow," Kristopher explained, seeming to agree with Donny's action.

Elynda shifted her gaze to Kristopher. "Everyone is dancing and drinking. The last thing they'll want to do is come to a library," Elynda countered. Riana could just make out her friend crossing her free arm over her middle and clapping her hand to Riana's arm.

"How many balls have you been to, fair friend?" Kristopher asked, crossing his arms over his chest.

"That's hardly the point. I'm a student of the human condition," Elynda said, and tilted her head back as she made strong eye contact with Kristopher.

"How many balls have you attended?" Riana interrupted their volley, curious about Kristopher's experiences.

"A few," he said defensively and shied away from Riana.

"We should get moving," Donny said. "There's no reason arguing now. The door is blocked, and it looks like you need a key to get back through."

Elynda opened her mouth to argue.

"We're getting closer to Ribbit. Let's just focus on why we're here," Riana said, before Elynda could launch a second attack.

Elynda shifted her emerald gaze onto Riana. She looked like she might argue with Riana, but then she snapped her mouth shut and nodded. "You're right. We're here for Ribbit." She looked at Kristopher and Donny with seemingly overwhelming distrust. She unlocked herself from Riana and walked toward the giant, then held out her hand.

"What?"

"The lamp," she said. "We'll lead the way."

He held the lamp for a moment, seeming to consider the small girl in front of him. At last the stalemate was over. He lowered the lamp to Elynda. "Fine," he said, "but, if I sense so much as a smidgeon of danger, I'm scooping the both of you up and out of its way."

Riana's scalp tingled at the thought.

"And I'll help," Donny added in a voice suspiciously deeper than normal.

Elynda gave them both a stern glance, which somehow did not lose its power with a height disadvantage.

What was going on between these three? Why did Elynda dislike Kristopher so much? Riana made mental notes to ask Elynda about her feelings when they were alone. She trudged forward in the limited light of the lamp, paying careful attention to the uneven stone floor beneath her soft slippered feet. She explored the walls of the tunnel with tentative fingers. The stone was cool, slightly wet and evenly spaced with dips Riana translated as mortar.

She scoured through memories of her grandmother's mental notes on the castle. Luckily, she had studied and made her own notes on the route to cement them in her mind.

From the library, the tunnel led down to a fork with two tines. Once there, their party would need to take the tine to the left. After they meandered a snaking trail of dirt hallways, they would need to search for a wooden doorway along the tunnel wall. They would take that doorway and follow it down a steeply sloping hill until it ended in a perpendicular hallway of gravel. Once in the gravel hallway, they would need to exit to the right. At that point is when it would get tricky with guards posted regularly and well-lit areas that allowed no shadows in which to lurk.

Riana paced down the hall, touching it regularly and looking intently ahead for the fork in the path. She worried. What if they'd added tunnels to the system recently? Or eliminated them?

When the fork appeared ahead of them, Riana breathed a sigh of relief. Her confidence swelled as she pointed to the left. She walked along the left wall, letting her fingers trail along. The walls were constructed of some sort of rough material, maybe clay. Her fingers looked for wood and when her hand met the distinct dip in the wall for a door, and her fingers ran over the grains of wood, she pulled Elynda to a stop while her heart sped along with rising hope.

Kristopher pushed an arm past her and Elynda and shoved the door open with a deep growl that set Riana's nerves on fire. She shivered in the darkness and Elynda looked at her from the corner of her emerald eyes.

The door rasped open, dust silting down from the threshold. Elynda peeked into the next tunnel, casting a small pool of light with the oil lamp she held. Here was the part Riana was nervous about. Her grandmother had missed one small detail: she hadn't said if they were to go right or left out of the door, or even straight ahead. She had said the hall would slope downhill.

"Alright, this is where we must test the incline. We need to be moving downhill."

Elynda and Kristopher nodded, their faces sallow in the glow of the lamplight.

Riana stepped through the door and took the lamp from Elynda. The light shivered along the wall and floor. To her left, the hallway ended behind the door. To her right, the hallway ran downhill. It seemed there was but one way to go. No wonder her grandmother had not said to go right or left.

"That simplifies things," Elynda said.

Kristopher and Donny followed along as Riana and Elynda led the way.

"This is easier than it should be," Kristopher whispered.

"We're almost there," she said, ignoring him.

"I see light," Elynda whispered.

At the end of the tunnel light flickered and swayed, illuminating the next hallway. Riana watched it intently as she lowered their lamp light and moved quietly forward. In the hallway, there were no guards. The torch on the wall burned brightly on the stone floor and showed the trio a row of prison cells.

"Something is amiss," Kristopher said.

Elynda bolted down the row, looking into each before charging to the next. "Ribbit!" she declared at last and threw herself against the black bars. Riana and Kristopher caught up with her. Ribbit hauled himself to the bars and gripped Elynda's hands.

"What are you doing here?" he asked frantically.

"Rescuing you, of course," Elynda said, tears streaming from her eyes.

"No, you can't," Ribbit said. "They'll be back any moment. You have to go. Quickly!"

Riana pulled the last trick literally from her sleeve. The twig in her hand would catch no one's eye as anything other than forest litter.

Kristopher hovered close to her, peering down over her shoulder between glances in either direction down the hall. Riana pushed the twig into the keyhole and prayed. The twig jiggled, then jumped and jerked. Sprouts of green appeared at its handle then spread down into the lock. A series of clicks echoed through the dungeon. Donny, Ribbit, Elynda, Kristopher and Riana watched intently as the plant life transformed itself.

The lock clicked, its gears squealed in protest and then the door popped open, swinging on ancient hinges. Kristopher, Riana and Elynda stared at Ribbit on the free side of the threshold. Ribbit stared back, just as open-mouthed and amazed.

"Am I dreaming?" he asked.

Elynda reached into the cell and dragged their friend over the threshold, gripping him in a tight embrace.

"Can't – breathe," he wheezed.

Riana took her turn embracing their small friend. She pulled back and looked him over as thoroughly as she could in the near darkness. He was bruised, his eyes were sunken, and he felt even smaller than ever. On the positive side, his limbs all seemed intact and he wasn't bloody or broken.

"I'm okay," he said and gave a weak smile. "Itching for some fresh air, if you can imagine that. Er – have you any to spare?"

Riana smiled at him, bemused by his ability for humor in such grim circumstances.

"I think we can arrange that."

"Let's get going," Donny said. "Wherever the guards are, they'll be back soon. It's odd not even one is stationed here."

"And who is this?" Ribbit asked, staring wide-eyed up at the giant before him.

"Ribbit, Kristopher. Kristopher, meet Ribbit."

"Pleasure. Let's get out of here."

"This way," Riana said and marched them down the aisle. The light from the torch died away. Riana gave their oil lamp more wick. Before they'd gone fifty paces, they faced the outer door. Riana shoved it aside, reeling from their success in freeing their friend.

The sound of the Dreavynan met them, along with a gust of wind and a soft patter of rain.

The Rustofos' cart was there. Riana searched for the Captain. The horses whinnied and tossed their heads. Behind Riana, Kristopher, Donny, Elynda and Ribbit all filed out of the dungeon and stood beside her. Kristopher gasped. Riana looked up at him, then followed his gaze back to the cart.

A man stepped out from behind the cart. A man Riana thought was dead.

Chapter Twenty-Five

"Well, well, darlin', it sure is a treat to see you again," Luther said.

The wind blew over the cliff side and knifed through the exposed skin on Riana's neck. She was instantly covered in gooseflesh. The roar of the ocean filled the twilit space between them.

"How-?" she started but found she didn't have the words to finish her question.

Kristopher stood like a statue next to her, his eyes darting around, in what Riana could only guess were his attempts to find his father.

Donny had slipped back into the dungeon. Riana met his eyes. Go, she thought. Just go and don't get caught. He seemed to understand her intention, but looked to be at war with himself. At last, he shook his head, turned and ran back through the dungeon.

Elynda stood rooted next to Riana, an arm around Ribbit's fragile form.

The sound of heavy feet filled the hillside. From around the corner of the keep came fifty soldiers, armed and ready. Riana looked at the Baron's Guard, all dressed in navy and silver, grateful Donny had ducked out.

"You underestimate who you're dealin' with, Sugar," Luther said in a deadly quiet voice. He wasn't threatening her. No, Riana caught the tang of regret in his voice. As if he had hoped Riana would have been smarter. Riana wished the same.

"Any thoughts?" she asked Kristopher.

"Yes," he said, "but, you're not going to like it."

Riana turned fully to him. "Why?"

He looked at her for a full breath. The wind ruffled his long, dark hair and the frills of his dress shirt. He unbuttoned his dress jacket. While he still held her gaze, he raised his arms in the air and took a step forward. "I surrender. You may take me. I will not fight or use my affinities."

"No!" Riana shouted, but that word was overwhelmed by Luther's gravelly laughter.

"Very well," Luther said and motioned to the guard. "We'll take you as well."

Kristopher dropped his hands, looking stunned. "You're not here for me?"

Riana grabbed Ribbit and put him behind her back. He wavered on weak legs. Elynda held him up.

"You can't have him back," Elynda said, tears boiling up and falling through her thick, dark lashes. "He's done nothing wrong."

Luther laughed some more, throwing his hands into the air and letting them fall to clap his knees.

"What is so funny to you?" Riana finally asked.

Luther pointed to Kristopher. "You're not why I'm here. And neither are you." He pointed to Ribbit. Then he pointed to Riana. "You're lucky I'm not here to kill you where you stand. Or take you back with me, but that's not a part of the plan."

"Plan?" Riana asked dumbly.

"Nope. Sure ain't, Sugar. I'm here for you." He pointed at Elynda. "But, I'll take you and you while I'm here." He pointed to Ribbit and Kristopher, but not Riana.

Riana, Kristopher and Ribbit turned their eyes to Elynda.

"Why?" Elynda asked.

"Well, hon', rumor has it when people come to see you with an ailment, you fix 'em up. Fix 'em up even when they ought to die. Even when other healers can't help them."

"And?" Riana asked.

"You still haven't put it together?" he asked, then clucked his tongue while he shook his head. "I figured you were smarter than all that."

Riana scrambled mentally to catch up to the man in front of her, mortified for being caught off guard. He was suggesting her friend was a Tyrmini? But she wielded no elements. And then she looked from Luther, to Elynda, to Ribbit and then thought about herself. None of them wielded elements. For all she knew, neither did Kristopher. She hadn't actually asked him about his power.

Something had shifted with her generation. They bore new gifts, new power that didn't look like their predecessors. They didn't look like Luther or Kristopher's mother or Kaely. She didn't use elements as weapons. No, something had been added to the mix and created a unique alchemy of magic specific to the user.

Ribbit calmed horses. Elynda healed. Riana... did what? She was stumped on herself.

And then it struck her. In the history she'd read, they hadn't used elements so specifically either. They hadn't even called magic-wielders Tyrmini. They'd been called Magyses. And the Magys channeled light energy combined with elemental power.

Tingles danced across her skin and caused a shiver. The imprisonment of Magloryn, the Dragon of Light was supposed to have deadened that source of magic to Tyrmini. Somehow it had reappeared. Had Magloryn escaped? Was there a new source of her energy the current generation was wielding?

Luther wasn't going to let her stand there and puzzle it all out. "Now, darlin', you know I'd love to stick around and chit-chat, but there's a High King waiting for his Captain to return. Guards, please apprehend the small one, the large one and the one with the raven hair."

"You aren't taking me?" Riana almost cried. She gripped onto Elynda, the friend whom she'd seen nearly every day through her entire youth.

"Out of the frying pan and into the fire," Ribbit said. He wobbled toward the oncoming guards, clearly weak from the time he'd spent imprisoned already.

Riana wasn't going to stand there and let everyone of her closest friends get taken. She'd fight. She felt the electric energy well up within her and clinched her fists to gather it into her hands.

"Riana," Elynda yanked Riana's shoulders around. "Listen, you have to find some way to track us down and help us escape. Do not start a fight."

The sizzling energy sputtered out. "But -," Riana started.

"No, you can't take them all, Riana. Look around you."

There were fifty guards closing in on the four of them. They were clearly outnumbered.

"But, if I fight and they imprison me, then we can try to break out together."

"You know it will be easier for someone to be on the outside."

Captain Luther had come close to them. Elynda let Riana's arms go and walked with Ribbit, holding him up for support. Riana watched a guard place manacles on Ribbit. Another approached Elynda and clapped the iron around her wrists.

"There'll be no need for that with these kiddies," Luther said. "Unless you think she's gonna heal ya to death. And you pose no threat to this other one, unless you're a horse. As for this one –," Luther looked up at Kristopher. "Put that one in irons."

The guard who had first put Elynda in irons looked up at Kristopher and paled.

Kristopher extended his wrists. "I won't fight," he said. He looked around again, searching the hillside. He seemed satisfied after he surveyed the area.

The guard hurriedly put the iron around his wrists. Half a dozen guards led her friends to a waiting cart that was covered and barred. Riana's stomach jumped into her throat as they closed the bars on Kristopher, Ribbit and Elynda. Tears stung her eyes. The wind whipped up from the Dreavynan and swept her tears away, leaving a trail over the bridge of her nose and into her temple and hair line.

"Now, darlin'," Luther said in a whisper over her shoulder, causing Riana to jump. "Don't cry now."

Riana whirled around and looked at him. "How are you even here?" she said, unable to help herself.

"Nevermind," he said. "Listen close, for I'll not repeat myself."

Riana mentally windmilled, caught off guard by his sudden serious tone.

"Your friends are not the only children trapped in the High King's custody." Luther stood there, whispering into Riana's face. "The High King wants you to chase after your friends. Wants you to jump through hoops so he can see just what you're made of. I'm going to give you a little head start. If you make it, and rescue your friends, I hope you'll have pity on me."

"Pity," Riana spat, recoiling from the man who had slain her one and only beloved family member. "Why would I have pity on you?"

"Very well," he said. "Not me, then, but the other children whom your friends will join. One who is very dear to me. Spare them for what I'm about to tell you. Rescue as many as you can. Do you agree?" His voice was urgent, his eyes pleading and desperate.

Riana mulled it over and decided it wasn't a hard decision. "Very well."

"The High King has several traps laid. You can skip at least three of them if you find the portal in this region. Find the portal and take it. When you arrive in the grasslands, you'll still have several traps to unravel, so be wary. There is another portal on the grounds of the High Keep. Get there and I will bring your friends and other children to the portal to make the escape."

"What would keep the High King from just following us through the portal?" Riana asked.

"He can't use the portals. He doesn't have enough light magic. No Tyrmini could use them. Only Magys kind and I believe that is what you and your friends are. Now, there's no more time to waste. Tell me you'll do this."

"I will," Riana said, sudden anxiety filling her. She was meant to chase her friends and she was meant to pass through several barriers for the testing of High King's curiosity. And doing this meant an inevitable exile from Landsend. Leaving now, before coming of age – which was so close – meant her inheritance would fall to Mr. Fraely if she were not back by her birthday.

All her dreams and hopes of making her own life, her own home and keeping the kind gift of stability her grandmother had bestowed upon her vanished with the slowly retreating cart imprisoning her three friends. She stood rooted to the spot and swallowed down her fear and disappointment.

Could she possibly wait? Her birthday was only days away. She looked at the bars on the cart. Elynda's face appeared against the cave of blackness. She gripped the bars and watched Riana as she went. If she was scared, she didn't show it. No, the only thing Riana could read on her best friend's face was determined trust. Trust in Riana.

Riana hung her head. She knew what she had to do.

Captain Luther limped away and soon Riana was alone on the hill with nothing but the Rustofos' horses for company. Where had Captain Rustofo gone? She searched around and finally saw Rustofo Senior's head appear over the crest of a nearby hill.

Donny appeared out of the dungeon, joining Riana in the wet grass. "I'm sorry, Riana," Donny said.

"There's no reason to apologize. I wanted you to hide," she said.

Riana turned to the approaching Captain and hung her head. "They took Kristopher. They took him along with Ribbit and Elynda."

Rustofo clapped a giant hand on Riana's shoulder. "We knew this was a risk. Kristopher wanted to take it. We will get him back."

Donny nodded emphatically. "Don't know how, but we'll rescue them," Donny said.

"I know how," Riana said. "Meet me at Lighthouse Hill at midnight."

CHAPTER TWENTY-SIX

She packed in the dead of night. Of course, that was after she had 'shopped'. Without qualms, she'd started her thieving binge of Mr. Fraely's General Store with the finest cloak he carried. It was brushed and treated lambskin. He'd tried to sell it on several occasions, pointing out it would neither let out heat nor let in rain and was the perfect cloak for a ship captain or sailor who would be regularly doused by rain and sea water. In the end, the price was too high, and Mr. Fraely was too stubborn to let it go at a lower rate.

Riana pulled it over her head and relished its lightweight and luxurious feel. It was one-of-a-kind. She also took a large rucksack which she then stuffed with food that would keep – jerky, grain that could be cooked with boiling water, dried fruits, extra socks, and a knife, to name just a few things that went into her pack.

Mr. Fraely would surely erupt in a tirade, but Riana wouldn't be there to see it. It wasn't the anger she wouldn't regret seeing most though. No, it was the careful watch she wanted to maintain on the Starliss Vineyard and Winery's profits. She now knew he was mucking around with their income – and had every right to as her sole guardian. Would he run her grandmother's business into the ground in Riana's absence?

She fought the welling anger and disappointment but failed completely. She couldn't bear the thought of him roaming through her winery, walking among the vines, and worst of all sitting in Sela's office chair. It felt like the biggest invasion of privacy. Mr. Fraely making decisions about the estate; about the business; about the people employed there.

He had power over the home as well. Riana could return with nowhere to live, no livelihood to rely on and no place of safety.

That was if she returned at all.

She stowed her extra cloak, tunics, and leathers in the rucksack as the hurt and anger and disappointment and fear threatened to overwhelm her. Then guilt sprang forward.

Her friends were imprisoned. They stood to lose their very lives, and here she was complaining about having her inheritance messed up. What utter selfishness. Chagrined by her own observations, Riana buttoned her rucksack closed and stood straight. She inhaled deeply and blew it out, careful to exhale quietly.

Her friends were counting on her. That was all that mattered right now.

Tom circled her before nudging at her elbow, as if to say, let's get going. Riana stroked his head and scratched behind one ear. He let out a soft purr.

Riana hugged the full rucksack close to her chest and belly, picked up her plundered oil lamp, and slowly moved out of the room on tiptoe, Tom close to her heels and moving silently. In the other room Mr. Fraely's snores wheezed through the sleeping house. So long, she thought toward him. Can't say that I'll miss you. Please don't mess up the vineyard while I'm gone. She felt the last thought was nothing more than a wish.

Once she was through the side door, the night greeted her with further darkness robed in cool mist. Particles of humidity clung to her face and hair. She set the rucksack and lamp down at her feet. She pulled the hood of her newly acquired cloak up over her wild silver hair and tucked away the escaping strands. There were no moons visible through the fog.

Riana pulled out a box of matches from one of the many pockets sewn into the cloak. She lit the lantern she'd taken. It was the only one she found in the store that was meant for carrying, with a wide metal loop over the top as a handle. The lamp was spherical in shape with a cage of sorts protecting the glass that appeared to have small bubbles blown into it here and there. It was beautiful, and judging by the tag she'd removed, Mr. Fraely would probably miss it from his inventory.

She held the lamp aloft and judged the size of the flame to be sufficient to cut through both the weather and the night. She set the now-lit lamp down and hoisted the large leather rucksack over her shoulders. It was heavy and she was grateful for it because it meant she had supplies for a while. She carefully bent and picked up the lamp and when she straightened, she made her way down the stairs and out onto the North Road, set on never returning to the General Store, for as long as her life should last.

She knew the North Road so well she hardly needed the lamp, but in the darkness the light was a welcome assurance. Tom was another source of comfort. Having a companion by her side made the darkness less imposing. Her ears strained around the hush and lull of the Dreavynan, the night birds and singing bugs and the crunch-crunch of her boots over the rock.

She tried to feel the realness of the moment, the moment she was leaving Landsend for the first time, with her inheritance in the hands of a man who hated her, her grandmother dead and her friends imprisoned, and her mind refused to soak it all in. She could only focus on the next step, which was to get to the Lighthouse Hill and meet Captain Rustofo and Donny.

She suffered a small thrill of excitement that sat weirdly against all the other emotions smashed inside her. With the letting go of her place in the community came an embracing of something new: adventure. She'd never been outside of Landsend and how she was meant to get to her next point of destination was by using an ancient magic she was eager to use again.

She scuffed down the road, mentally peeling away the layers of events and revelations that had happened earlier that evening. Ribbit was Magys. Elynda was Magys. Kristopher was presumably Magys. The High King was so stumped on what Riana was, he was willing to let her roam free, moving closer to her friends and risking their rescue in order to see what her power could do.

The stubborn part of her wanted to rebel. She didn't want to be a test subject. To be watched and prodded. The loyal friend part of her soul wouldn't back down from the chance to rescue them. Was it all a trap? Most likely, but Luther seemed to have some confidence in her being able to free her friends, and the others who were also imprisoned for possessing some form of power, whether elemental or elemental plus. So, perhaps she could do it.

She looked down at Tomas, walking along by her side in perfect step. He glanced over his shoulder, ginger hair rising slightly.

Every one of the elemental dragons had conspired to create Tomas. Perhaps they'd seen this journey coming and had intervened on her behalf. The High King might be setting a trap for her, but Riana clearly had powerful allies supporting her. If the High King didn't know that, she'd potentially have the advantage over him.

Tom slowed his steps, looking behind them again. Riana wondered how much the High King saw and knew and how he went about gathering the information he had. How did he know Elynda was a Magys? How had he known about Riana's plans for rescuing Ribbit?

Tom stopped in his tracks, turned fully around, and growled into the darkness. His body unraveled, expanding as the ginger cat at her side transformed from domesticated companion to wild elemental. His one tail split into three, scales erupted over fur, tracing its way along its back.

Tom lunged into the dark mist, scales fully erect along his spine, white fur around his neck luminescent in the darkness. Riana heard a distinct snapping click and saw a spark at his tail and then the creature was ablaze with blue flame which traced up his scales following the black lines striping down his body. Against the darkness Tom looked like a ghost of fire.

A menacing snarl ripped through the darkness followed by a yelp of terror. Riana recognized the voice.

"Tom, wait!" Riana shouted.

"Help!"

"Tomas!" Riana ran forward. The blue glow of Tomas afire and the yellow glow of the lamp mixed together and cast Tom's target in a white glow. "Tom, he's a friend!"

Tom chased Donny Derringer down the road. Donny pivoted and ran toward Riana. "Riana, call it off!"

"I don't know how!" Riana screamed, desperation fringing her voice. Frantically, she tapped into that light energy dwelling within her and cast her intention toward Tom. She reached a hand toward her companion. "Stop," she screamed.

Light surged from her palm in a single beam and struck Tomas between his eyes.

Tom yelped, missing a step and falling hard into the rock road. The flames dancing along his scales extinguished instantaneously. He panted, his black tongue hanging from his mouth, blue eyes wide and fearful.

Riana ran to him, sliding to her knees and pressing her hands into his side. Her fingers grazed the black scales. Her skin sizzled. She screamed with sudden pain and stuck her burned fingers into her mouth.

"I'm tho thowwy," she said around her fingers, guilt and shame filling her belly. She pulled her fingers from her mouth and stroked the fur over his eyes. Tom flinched, yipping in fear and pain. Riana's heart broke. She'd hurt him.

"Riana," Donny said, alarm clear in his voice. "Do you know this creature?"

"Yes," she said, anger rising toward Donny. "I thought we were meeting at Lighthouse Hill." There were tears standing in her eyes.

"Are you okay?"

"I'm fine, but Tom isn't. Why didn't you announce yourself? Why were you sneaking up on us?" she spat.

"I'm sorry, Riana."

"He's hurt. I hurt him," Riana said.

Donny bent down next to Riana. He peered at the creature, surveying him from the tip of his white snout to the scales on his tail. "I don't think so. I think he just got scared. You kinda blasted him with light."

Tom's breath slowed bit by bit, but his eyes remained wide as he peered at Riana.

"Look," Donny started. He lowered himself into a sitting position from his crouch. "It seems like you communicate with elementals through that light stuff. You moved too quick just now and basically yelled at him. He's scared. Now, maybe you can do the opposite?"

"What do you mean?" Riana asked, frustration evident in the growl of her words.

"Well, instead of yelling 'stop' to him, how do you comfort him with the same light stuff?" Donny asked.

Riana finally looked at Donny. His cheeks were flushed, and his dark eyes were round with concern. She took a deep breath. He was right. She could talk to him to calm him as much as she could alarm him. She more slowly tapped into the power before she cast it anywhere. When she had a clear connection in her mind's eye, she focused on her intention and emotion she wanted to convey to Tomas.

Calm, peace, warmth, gratitude flowed through her. She took out her guilt and anxiety; she didn't want Tom to feel those. She added an apology. I'm so sorry. Can you forgive me?

Tom took a stuttering, deep breath and with it his eyes relaxed, his panting slowed, and his head rose. His ears laid back, his tails low. He whimpered, nudged Riana's burnt hand and licked at the injured fingers. Riana ran the other hand around his ear, careful to not touch the scales.

"I'm so very sorry. I didn't mean to hurt you," she said.

"Me too," Donny said. He held out his hand and allowed Tom to take several tentative sniffs. Tom snorted and returned his affection to Riana. He rolled onto his back, showing his belly. Riana rubbed the soft white fur, relishing the warmth of his body. Tom purred in contentment.

Riana pulled her hand away from Tom and looked at Donny. He looked back at her. Anger rose, then was snuffed out by the realization the anger was a knee-jerk reaction to being in some form of interaction with Donny. And that just wasn't enough to warrant the same reaction any longer. The anger fizzled out.

"Thank you," she said. Warmth radiated within her and she was sure it showed on her face.

"What for?" Donny asked, looking confused.

"You really helped me with Tom. I wasn't thinking clearly, and you helped me see how I could do something different to soothe him."

"Well, if I hadn't startled you in the first place..." Donny trailed off.

"No," Riana said and stood up. Tom rolled and sprang to his feet. Riana held out a hand to Donny. "You're right. It's not your fault. We're both coming from the same direction. I should have guessed we'd meet on the road."

Donny took her hand. Riana pulled. Donny got to his feet, but Riana felt no effort on her part. She suspected he'd used his own force to keep her from having to work at it.

She secretly liked the way his hand felt on hers. His was strong and calloused. Hers were slender and small – strong and feminine.

Donny took a step closer to Riana and closed the space between them. Electricity snapped in the air around them. He held her hand even when it was clear he no longer needed her help. Riana squirmed uncomfortably.

Donny's eyes were fixed on hers. From Riana's vantage – a whole head shorter than Donny – she had a clear view of his pectoral muscles escaping the top button of his shirt and open jacket. She darted glances between his chest and his face. Donny cupped his other hand under Riana's, pulled her fingers to his lips and brushed her knuckles with a velvet kiss. A warm thrill raced through Riana's body in a way she'd never experienced before.

"Thank you," Donny said.

"For what?" Riana asked.

"Trusting me to help you on this journey ahead," he said.

Riana pulled away slightly, rubbed at her arms and mumbled words that didn't really make any sense but seemed to be an affirmation. She was still flustered by the kiss to the knuckles.

Donny turned his attention to Tom, holding out a hand, as if this were an automatic gesture he'd done for ages.

Tom sniffed his hand and then butted his head into Donny's hand. Donny scratched behind an ear.

"What is this Tom thing? And why did they take Elynda? I couldn't hear everyone properly from behind the hill."

"Tom is... a creature. I don't know exactly what he is. Elynda is apparently an old sort of Tyrmini, called a Magys, as is Ribbit and Kristopher. All three of them are being taken to the High King."

"You should know, this is going to be dangerous. The High King plans on testing me," Riana explained.

Donny pulled at his pack and motioned for them to move forward. Riana ducked her head in agreement and set the pace.

"Testing you how?" Donny asked.

"I really don't know. Perhaps against Tyrmini?" Riana guessed.

"And how does this work? We're meeting at Lighthouse Hill, but why?"

"Donny, you of all people should know things are not straightforward when it comes to all this Tyrmini and Magys stuff," Riana pointed out.

Donny straightened, pulling his face into a scowl, before it relaxed into resignation. "You got me there. So, what's at Lighthouse Hill?"

Riana eyed him nervously. Wondering how open he'd be to getting sucked through a magic portal to end up in another part of the country. "It's probably better if you just see it," she said.

CHAPTER TWENTY-SEVEN

Riana entered the cave-like structure, buried beneath a mound of Tyrinth and was welcomed by the cool blue glow of the lanterns springing to life. Donny entered after her. He looked at the floor as the blue energy filled the grooves in the maze-like pattern on the stone floor.

"Whoa," he said. "What's this blue stuff?"

Riana thought about it. She really couldn't say for sure what exactly it was, except – "I think it's the stuff that lives in Tyrmini and Magyses. The stuff that makes us different."

"So, if you aren't here -?" Donny asked.

"No blue lights," Riana confirmed. "No opening door, as a matter of fact."

"Wow," Donny breathed.

Rustofo barely squeezed through the opening. Once inside, he stretched to full height and just missed touching the ceiling with the top of his head.

"Serena would have loved to see this," Rustofo said. Riana's heart broke at the look on his face: full of sorrow and awe. She waited a moment while the blue energy fully expanded into every nook and cranny of the room, extending up to the wall sconces. The eerie blue flames wavered but did not make a sound, like normal fire did.

Tom crawled through the opening and bounded to the stone floor. He slunk over the maze carving, his mohawk raised slightly. He positioned himself just behind Riana's legs as she faced the center of the room and the device that would transport them from Landsend in the northwest corner of Aelos to the Shoqui plains in the southern-central portion of the continent.

Riana didn't want to waste any time. "Okay, Donny, you take up the western corner."

"The which?"

"West," she pointed to the corner to her right, having taken up the northern point of the golden tile that connected to the silver circle. Donny shuffled over and stood with his toes touching the western point of the square.

"Great. Tom, you need to stand on the south and Rustofo, you stand to the east." She wasn't entirely sure why she wanted them in that particular configuration, or that it mattered, but it felt right, and she figured that might be enough.

Donny stared at the clear stone suspended in the air at his eye level. His mouth gaped. "How's it doing that?" he asked.

Elynda had asked the same question. She had been here for the discovery, the wakening, the transport and the meeting of their new friend, Tom. Her heart ached and she wanted nothing more than to get to her friend in time to keep her from harm. She wondered if the High King would kill them before she could rescue them. She decided he would not do that with Elynda. He needed her healing abilities. If Elynda did heal him, how much more darkness would the High King be capable of?

Riana swallowed back her worry, both for her friend and for Magys and Tyrmini kind across Aelos who were doomed to another annihilation should the High King recover his strength.

Riana waved away his question. "I'm really not sure. This is all new to me," Riana said, fighting the urge to tell him to stay focused and quit asking so many questions. As she said it, an idea formed in her mind so suddenly she felt it couldn't have been the fabrication of her imagination.

"Oh," she said. The information appearing in her mind took over her senses. She peered into the crystal's depths. It turned, casting rainbows across her face. She inhaled sharply. Sudden meaning sent an electric charge from the crown of her head through her body and to the tips of her toes.

"That is the Light," Riana said. "The Light is supported by all other elements." She pointed to the stones. "Air, fire, water, Tyrinth, and this –," she pointed to the stone hidden in the depths of the well in the center of the square. "This is shadow. All these things work in conjunction with each other in perfect balance. The Light is buoyant, weightless but not independently powerful without the other elements to support it."

Riana shivered. There were wells of knowledge to be accessed from this short explanation. "I can't do this alone. I might be the one leading the charge, but I can't do this without each of you. You can't do this without me, or each other. We must rely on one another through this journey, support and care for one another as if our lives depend on it, because they do."

Riana took turns looking at first Donny, then Tom and then Rustofo. Rustofo nodded. "I will do my part."

Riana turned to Donny. "I will happily serve my role."

When Riana turned to Tom – who was sitting on his assigned elemental crystal – Tom put a paw forward and dipped his head to Riana.

Riana nodded in satisfaction. "Good. Then let's get going." She pulled at the memory of the incantation she and Elynda had performed using the notes from her grandmother's journal. She pointed to the stone in the west direction. "Tyrinth," she spoke, then pointed to the south. "Fire." East was "Water" and north was "Air". "Creation," she evoked, looking into the depths of the well in the center of the tile. Finally, she looked back into the rainbow-hued crystal floating above the others and said, "Love."

The clear stone hovering in the space above the tile sparkled, casting far-reaching rainbows to dance across the stone walls. Each of the gems grew luminescent, to the point Riana shielded her eyes from the light. The floor beneath them vibrated. Riana stood firm in her position. Tom braced himself, his black scales rising in a defensive gesture. Donny looked as if he might take a step backward.

"Stay exactly where you are!" Riana shouted at him.

Captain Rustofo saw this interchange, widened his stance to maintain his position, and gritted his teeth. A deep rhythm started to pulse through the air and wind sprang up around them. Fog rolled around them as sparks of fire flashed. The room grew dark. Standing on the transport was a different experience then standing to its side. Stars blossomed around them. In the distance Riana marveled at a blooming pink, blue and purple cluster. Riana wasn't sure what it was, but it was vast and beautiful, and she had a feeling she was witnessing a hugely powerful event. The floor dropped away from underneath them and was replaced by space.

Riana screamed in surprise and exhilaration. Donny looked as though he'd lost all ability to speak. Rustofo had squeezed his eyes shut and appeared to be frozen. Tom flicked his tails and looked around as if this were a normal, everyday occurrence that mildly irritated him.

The air was cold, but not unbearable. There was a stillness Riana couldn't qualify against any other experience she'd had. While the space that surrounded them seemed real, there was also the sense of dreaminess that wrapped around them. Riana peered around her, marveling at the expanse. Over her right shoulder a throng of translucent shapes ghosted through the stars and darkness in a loosely formed group. Riana stared in wonder and curiosity. They floated closer to the group and Riana's breath caught. They were beautiful.

They skidded through the ether on wide wings. Their elongated bodies shimmered in shifting colors of blue, purple and green. A long tail stretched away behind them, following their bodies' movements with grace. Riana looked closer and could not see an actual body, only the light that outlined a form.

She wanted a closer look, but Riana felt a shift that seemed to be pulling them out of the ether. The air grew scented with grass. The darkness faded while the stars disappeared. The space beneath their feet was replaced by solid ground. Riana found herself facing the bark of a large oak tree.

"Oh," she said in surprise. She was certain on the other end of the transport tile would be another just like it. Instead they stood in an open field of tall, waving grasses, surrounding a tree. Yet, the veins in the bark of the tree shimmered in pulsing blue energy, as the maze in the stone had on the portal. Donny and Rustofo were to her right and left, forming a circle around the tree, just as they had done on the portal in Landsend.

Donny turned on his heel, bent over and vomited noisily. Rustofo spilled to the ground, holding his head as though it were a spinning top.

Riana bent to the tree's base and carefully poked through the dirt. The loam wafted up to her nose. Her fingers explored the cool Tyrinth, pushing through grass roots and buried acorn shells. Her hand was fully submerged in soil when her fingers brushed the rough, ungiving surface of stone. She pulled the dirt away, and her eyes took in what her fingers had discovered: the stone maze tablet was there, but the tree had grown around it. Or perhaps that was the way the Magyses who built this portal had concealed it. Her mind wandered to Kaely. Perhaps a Magys back then had been like Kaely, able to grow vegetation with intention.

Tom slunk around the tree toward Riana, as though nothing had happened. Something was clenched in his teeth.

He half-chirped around the mouthful before depositing the object at Riana's feet.

CHAPTER TWENTY-EIGHT

Riana scooped up the object and held it tightly to her chest. Tom sat down beside her, bumping his head against her arm. Riana wrapped him up and kissed him on the face. When she let him go, Tom bounded away, sat down, snorted, and began to bathe himself.

The journal was somewhat damp. A corner looked as though it'd been nibbled on, but otherwise it was in good shape. She dusted it off and flipped through its pages. She could still read the writing, even if it was now slightly blurred from exposure to the elements. Riana pulled the rucksack off her shoulders and pushed the journal inside, determined to keep it safe from further harm, or loss.

It was only then she surveyed her surroundings. She was most impressed by the need to remove her very warm cloak. Once she'd done that, she took in the sights and sounds. It was still nighttime. In the distance a bird cried out, a pinpoint of heartbreak in an otherwise beautiful evening. The sky was alit with the vast expanse of stars. Stars that somehow felt a little closer since she'd been through the transport portal, among them. The two moons overhead lit the landscape in a white glow, painting the world in a monochromatic blue.

The hush of the wind rustled the tall, silver grasses punctuated by a variety of animal sounds. Riana could not name many of them. There were high-pitched trills, deep squawks, and low rumbles.

As much noise as Riana heard, she saw little aside from the grass and sky. This nighttime chorus remained invisible.

Content with his cleaning job, Tom looked out into the fields and with only a minor shift of his whiskers to indicate his intention, he bounded into the grasses. He was immediately lost to sight and sound.

She pushed her overly warm cloak into her expanding rucksack and pulled it onto her shoulders once more. Donny took a swig from his canteen, swished and spit.

"You okay?" Riana asked.

"Fine," Donny said, "just got a little motion sickness is all. I do that on ships as well."

"Really?" Riana asked.

"Yeah. Sailor blood does not run in my family."

"Speaking of sailors..." Riana trailed. She turned from Donny and went to Rustofo. "Are you doing alright?" she asked him.

"Just a little dizzy. It will pass, my dear."

"So, these are the Shoqui Plains," Riana said.

Donny shuffled over to Riana. "What do we do now?" he asked.

Riana thought about it. "When Captain Luther took Elynda, Kristopher and Ribbit, he said if I took a transport I'd skip three of the hurdles, but there would be more puzzles to unravel. He also said we needed to go to the High King's castle."

"Into the castle?" Rustofo asked.

"Yes," Riana said, sure that's what Luther had said.

"That's gonna be tough."

"Why?" Riana asked.

"Because the entire castle perimeter is guarded by the Tyrmini Guard. And only those personally invited to the castle are allowed entrance."

"Well," Riana said, "there must be a way. Luther seemed to think we'd be able to get in." Riana pulled Grandmother Sela's journal from her rucksack and held it up to them. "Hopefully, this will help us."

Rustofo nodded. "I'll build a fire."

"I'll help gather wood," Donny offered.

"I'll see what I can learn," Riana said. She sank to the ground, set down the journal and rummaged through her rucksack for matches. Once located, she relit her lantern and sat it next to her. She leaned against the tree and began to read, starting at the beginning again. A knot formed in her gut at the thought of reading the pages where she'd left off. She had to read them now. There may be information there that could help them recover their friends.

She re-read the pieces in the beginning to make sure there was nothing she'd missed before when she hadn't been looking for the particular information about entering the heavily guarded castle of the High King.

As to who your mother is,

Sela had written. Riana closed her eyes and counted to ten as she inhaled and exhaled to calm her shaking body and wheezing breath. It was odd because it seemed her breath had not stilled her own nerves, but the cacophony of nature had quieted. She looked around but saw nothing. In the distance, the grass rustled as if stirred by a breeze. The breeze never reached her. Riana strained her ears, heard nothing and so turned back to her grandmother's journal.

... your mother is, she is none other than the High King's sister.

Riana gasped.

For years now I've wanted to share this with you, sure it will help you identify yourself among all the lack of belonging you must feel as an orphan, though I have come to think of you as my own.

Something rustled in the grasses. Riana thought it might be Donny or Rustofo returned from their hunt for firewood. She glanced up but saw nothing. She returned to her reading.

However, it is not who your mother is that has kept me from divulging. Rather, it is your paternal parentage that poses the most threat.

A low growl rumbled through the air. Riana bolted upright, dropping the journal to the ground and knocking the lantern over. The lantern rolled away from her. The light wobbled, illuminating the grass in a golden glow. A black shadow cut through the lantern light, rising above the uniform curtain of stalks.

The hair on Riana's arms and neck sprang upright. The night went dead silent. Riana stared, unable to move. The black shape disappeared.

"Riana!" Donny screamed.

A snarl overlapped his cry.

Donny yelped. A solid thump and hush of grasses followed the sound.

Riana's heart gained speed. The silence stretched away. She strained her ears to listen and heard nothing.

"Donny? Donny! Captain Rustofo!"

The creature burst into the opening and lunged for her. It had been crouching, Riana realized. It had crouched in the grasses and sneaked through the fields to approach her in stealth. When it rose to its full height, its head nearly brushed the bottommost limbs of the ancient and tall oak. Limbs that Riana would not even be able to jump and reach.

Instinctively, Riana backed up and met the rough bark of the tree, stumbling when her boots tangled in roots. She fell hard to the dusty ground. The creature towered over her. Light from the lamp cast one side of its black body in a yellow glow.

The creature of legend's lower half was encrusted in scales. Along the top of his back blackened fur shot out of gaps in its scaly armor. The face of the animal was covered by shorter versions of quill-like fur, absorbing light and reflecting nothing, save the deep glow of its wild, yellow eyes. All around the beast an ever-shifting shadow curled in tendrils like smoke from a flame.

The beast coiled, the light barely touching its shoulders through the shifting cloak of shade. It tipped its massive, snarling head forward and took another step closer. The tail thrashed back and forth. The yellow eyes of the dyrnai caught Riana in a death stare and refused to release her. Frozen, Riana watched as the wolf lunged, mouth gaping. It toppled her, its weight crushing her into the ground.

Paws on her shoulders, she wriggled to break free, but barely moved. The dyrnai caught her gaze. Riana fell into the pools of gold, suspended, and stripped bare. Air wheezed in and out of her lungs under the weight of the creature atop her. The wolf's head reared back, mouth stretched wide to reveal massive canines. A disembodied growl rolled over her. Drool dribbled onto the bare skin of her neck, thick and warm. It lunged.

Pain erupted through her shoulder. She screamed as Shadow swallowed her.

Everything in her mind emptied. She was lost, wandering in darkness. The world woke in her mind again.

Riana inhaled sharply as Mr. Fraely's rough hand caught the line of her jaw. Pain exploded through her face. Another crashing blow landed on her nose. Tears sprang to her eyes.

Why had she tried to run away? She knew she wouldn't be able to escape.

"You return every last matchstick you stole," Fraely shouted at her.

Riana pushed her torso from the floor of the General Store. Blood dripped from her face, splatting on the wooden slats and mixing with a thin layer of dust. Riana stared at it. Elynda would want to murder Mr. Fraely for this. She felt a warm relief wash over her at the thought of her friend.

Fraely grunted, which was the only warning before his shoe landed in her ribs. She heard the crack of bones. The air in her lungs was forced out in a violent exhale. She rolled on the floor, unable to breathe. Pain splintered through her side. She wrapped her arms around her injured ribs. He kicked again, this time finding her soft belly. The force of his blow knocked her into a nearby shelf. She curled in on herself and vomited. The taste of bile filled her mouth.

Fraely closed the gap with one step, lifted his leg and hammered his foot onto her leg. Another crack resounded through her body as a scream escaped her mouth. He bent down and pummeled her face with heavy fists.

He's going to kill me. I'm going to die, Riana thought.

A soft chirp whispered into her ear. She couldn't focus on it because *Mr. Fraely had handed off the beating to his apprentice, Treyor. Treyor knelt beside her and pulled a dagger from a sheath fashioned in the shape of a shadow wolf.*

"Do you know what the bite from a shadow wolf does?" Treyor asked her. He sliced viciously at her, catching the skin on her arms as she guarded her body. Blood welled and spilled. He was on top of her then. Underneath her, the forest floor crinkled with a layer of leaves and debris.

Treyor sliced again, making his way past her flailing arms and cutting open her belly. Hot, searing pain spilled through her like ink from its bottle.

"One bite from a shadow wolf –," Treyor started and sliced again, cutting into the soft flesh of breast, "– and you'll be lost in a river of fear forever."

Riana sobbed. She would die in the TyrMinHai. Beaten, broken and cut wide open. Treyor aimed the knife again, but a soft chirp caught his attention and he stopped mid-thrust. Perhaps that thrust would have been the killing blow. The one he meant to plunge into her heart. He looked around through the trees, searching for the source of the noise. It sounded again. Riana's head had gone muzzy. Weakness stole over her. She would die. She knew the feeling of it. She'd done this before.

The chirp sounded again.

In another life, long ago, there'd been another Treyor. He'd hunted her down as she'd hiked through her favorite forest. He'd sliced her and cut her and she'd nearly bled to death.

A soft rumbling growl reverberated in her ears, then a wicked hiss. Something tickled at her bruised face.

Treyor lurched off her body and took a step backward, fear suddenly replacing the murder in his eyes. "No," he said.

A vicious yowl cut through the air. It was right next to Riana, right in her ear. She didn't remember that yowl from the last time she'd been here. The last time Treyor had almost killed her. No, it had been fire nymphs who'd attacked Treyor.

Riana's mind reeled. The last time Treyor had attacked? Confusion swept over her.

Fraely approached her through the trees. He opened his mouth and yelled but the words were jumbled nonsense. He swung at her, but the punch only landed an ineffective blow against her face. She closed her eyes tightly and waited for the next attack.

Hot breath warmed her neck. She opened her eyes, not sure if she'd see Mr. Fraely or Treyor and was surprised to see the even more frightening face of a shadow wolf. But he was backing away from her.

Riana was sitting with her back against a giant oak. She was not in the TyrMinHai. Her legs were stretched out in front of her and she had the odd sensation of detachment from them. An awful throbbing ache spread through her right shoulder. Straddled over the legs she knew to be hers was the creature she'd named Tomas.

"Tomas," she wheezed, and wished she hadn't spoken. The throb in her neck grabbed hold of her throat and squeezed. Her head responded in blinding pain that pushed against the back of her eyes as though they would pop from her sockets. She closed her lids to keep her eyes in.

Seeing Tomas had sparked the chain of memories momentarily wiped from her mind. With her eyes closed, time and logic caught up with her. Feeling spread down her body and into her legs. Warmth turned to uncomfortable heat. She opened her eyes.

Tom's spiked plates were raised, and blue flame danced along them. In the glow of the blue fire, his fur looked as black as the shadow wolf's.

Tom snarled and swiped in the shadow wolf's direction. The wolf backed away; eyes wide.

Tom took two steps forward. His tails whipped around him. A barb on the end of one tail slashed, catching Riana's leg. She hissed through tight teeth. Tom glanced behind him, ears turning back and scaly mohawk lowering. As if to say, 'oops'.

The shadow wolf saw his opportunity and lunged.

"Tom!" Riana shouted.

Tom turned. The wolf opened his maw wide. In the creature's mouth Riana saw a blackness so complete she could compare it to no other memory in her life thus far. The wolf meant to bite Tom.

Fury burst within her. Without knowing what she was doing, she found herself crouched on the balls of her feet next to Tom. She placed a hand delicately on the creature's shoulder, ignoring the flames licking at her fingers. She wrapped her other arm around Tom, turning her head into his face. She was intent on protecting him. No one would hurt Tom.

The wolf bared down on them. Tom extinguished his fire, pressing his face against Riana's collar bone. Light burned through Riana's veins, into every muscle, tendon and joint. Nothing mattered more than protecting the creature who'd come so unwittingly into her life.

The crack of broken bones and a yelp echoed through the clearing. Riana opened her eyes and looked at the shadow wolf. All around her danced figures of light, dispelling the darkness. Sparks of blue fell like rain to the Tyrinth, touching the spikes and scales on the shadow wolf. The wolf snarled and cried, a pitiful sound stuck between pain and anger.

Riana had a moment of compassion for the creature. In response the blue light beings danced and flowed toward the shadow wolf. They touched its face, danced across its scales and fur, stroked its ears. The creature's whines slowed then abated. It looked at Riana with a grateful stare, then closed its golden eyes. It exhaled deeply as if falling asleep and then the shadow wisped away. The wolf grew lighter, becoming transparent as strips of darkness caught the wind and floated away. Eventually, there was nothing left of the creature.

The dancing figures of light twisted and twirled over the ground where the wolf had lain and then they too caught the breeze. They followed a line over the fields, illuminating the sky in a soft glow.

Tom chirped. Riana felt the sound through the hold she had on him, a vibration from his chest into her ear where she pressed her face into him. She straightened, holding his shoulders.

"Are you okay?" she asked him.

In response Tom nuzzled his face into hers and purred. She scratched at his cheeks, her fingers running over the small line of scales in his fur. And then she realized the shadow wolf and Tom had some similar traits. They both shared those dark scales. Riana wondered if it meant something. Riana also wondered what happened to the shadow wolf. Was it dead?

"That was a dyrnai," Rustofo exclaimed, his voice booming into the clearing, making Riana jump.

"Yes, a shadow wolf," Riana agreed. She stood and looked out into the field. "Donny?" she called.

Donny crept out of the grass and into the circle of light cast by the forgotten lamp. "That was..." he shook his head. Sweat rolled from his temples. He swiped at the trickle. "I couldn't move. Riana, I'm so sorry."

Riana moved closer to him, bent and took hold of the lamp. She held it up to him. On his neck were bloodless pricks, like deep shadows with veins of gray. As she surveyed the wound the veins lightened, pulling back into the bite marks until all that were left were four punctures like tattoos.

"You got bitten," Riana confirmed.

Donny's eyes flashed wide and he grabbed at his neck in surprise. "I didn't feel a bite," he said.

Riana moved her hair off her neck and pulled her tunic down to expose her own bite. "I didn't feel it either, but it's there, isn't it?"

"Yes, like four black spots," he confirmed. "But, where did the wolf go?" Fear painted his face white.

"It's gone," Riana said.

"Yes, indeed." A disembodied voice echoed overhead. "You've managed to pass the first several of my tests and this one too. That was some display of power."

Tom who had been glued to her side, hissed at the sky.

CHAPTER TWENTY-NINE

Riana looked skyward, searching among the constellations for the source of the voice. When she saw nothing there, she searched the limbs of the giant oak. In the dark, it was nearly invisible tangled among twigs and leaves, save for a reflection of the lamp's light. She held the lamp aloft to get a better look.

Captain Rustofo stumped toward Riana and rooted himself behind her. Riana felt his body heat, and maybe it was the energy of his intention to protect her, but she was grateful for the sense of safety in his presence.

"What is that?" Donny said, looking the direction Riana pointed the lamp.

Riana's heart somersaulted. She was looking at a giant version of her own eye. The multicolored iris set in the white globe was all encased in what appeared to be a glass ball filled with fluid. Riana's mouth hung open in horror as she had an immediate recognition of the mirror image of her own feature. Sizzling energy ran through her. Her hands shook. Her mouth went dry and her throat stuck together.

Beside her, Captain Rustofo inhaled sharply.

"Magloryn," Riana breathed, unable to speak anything else.

"Well, not all of her," the disembodied voice drawled.

"It's the High King," Rustofo whispered to Riana.

"Acute observation, Captain," High King Achyla said. "Was it the color of my eye that gave it away?"

Magloryn's eye descended, surrounded by a mass of shadow. Once it reached Riana's eye level, the shadows collected in a singular pillar that formed a humanoid shape, with the giant eye resting at the head. The colors in the iris shifted in quick succession: violet, sapphire, emerald, aquamarine, topaz, diamond and then deep black opal with flecks of every color Riana could imagine, plus some she had no name or identity for.

A deep rumbling quaked her core. Rich sorrow welled within her, pain seared her senses, fire sparked at her nerves, indignation rose on its heels and finally a hope so profound she was sure she would be swallowed whole by it.

"That eye does not belong to you," Riana spoke to the shadow encompassing the eye. Every hair on her body stood on end as she crackled with energy. Her body grew light. She stepped toward the eye, meaning to pluck it from the shadows and reclaim it. She was consumed by the sense of having found something that had long been lost to her. She needed it back. If she could get it back, she would feel whole for the first time in her life.

The shadow backed away. "Now, now," High King Achyla spoke. "This eye has been mine for some time. And I won't be parting with it anytime soon. I mean, it's so handy to have around for spying on Tyrmini.

"I thought my little tool wouldn't work now that you have none of your special friends around. Seems like there's one other I didn't account for." The eye turned and looked down. Riana followed the gaze. Tom snarled, scales high. He swiped at the shadow, which disbursed only to regather its form once again.

"So, it's elemental magic you can see," Riana said, more speaking to Magloryn than to the High King. And if the eye did not work on her, that meant she had no elemental magic. What she had was something immune to the gaze of the dragon of light.

"Just the four main elements, dear," High King Achyla noted. "Water, Fire, Tyrinth, Air. Shadow and Light – apparently – are undetectable by sweet Magloryn. Funny, isn't it? Mother of all magic and she couldn't sniff out the two major sources of it.

170

That's not true, a voice said in Riana's head. He just doesn't know how I sense those two elements. This time the voice was laced with smug satisfaction. Riana recognized the voice and was awash in comfort by its appearance.

"Now, then," the High King resumed. "You've passed – we'll just call this – the first test. Well done, my dear. Well done." His tone sounded as if he were praising a pet for a trick well executed. It turned sour with his next words. "You've still got two more."

"Bring it on," Riana challenged.

The cloud laughed. "Spunky. But, I'm not ready for the next test. No. I think you'll just have to wait, oh fair and strange child." The voice giggled. "Oh, the next will be such a wicked treat!"

The cloud slipped away, carrying the eye with it. It wisped through the tree branches, ascended into the sky and then winked out of sight.

Tom shook himself and mewled at the sky. Riana took that as good riddance.

"I couldn't agree more," she told the creature. "I would have liked a little more out of him. Like what he learned about me from this little test of his."

"So, am I to understand," Donny said, "that you are not a Tyrmini?"

Riana nodded, still puzzling through the pieces of information herself. "It seems so. Grandmother talked about two different sorts of magic wielders. Prior to the capture of Magloryn and the commencement of the reign of High King Achyla, the first, there were only Magyses."

"Hold a moment," Captain Rustofo said, holding an impressively large hand up. "This sounds as though it will require a fire. I think we'll be safe here now with the dyrnai gone. Let me just bring back the wood I found, and we'll make camp." He stumped away.

Riana felt the vibration of his movement through her feet.

Donny looked at her expectantly. She looked back nonplussed.

"Don't you think you should go help him?" she asked.

"Oh," Donny said, "oh, yes, you're probably right." In the lamp glow he burned crimson, turned and hastened away.

Riana held the lamp closer to the ground and searched for the journal. She found it and lowered herself down again. She held it in her lap with a hand protectively clutched over the cover and looked out into the grasslands.

Crickets began to sing. The sweet, long song of a heartbroken night bird joined the nighttime concert. Frogs chirped. Way off in the distance a howl cut through the air. Riana shivered. Tom sat beside her, pushing his body against hers as he too looked out into the night, into the danger and into the darkness.

CHAPTER THIRTY

"According to Grandmother, there are two sorts of magic. The first wielded by Magyses is etyr. The second is Tyrmini magic," Riana explained. The fire crackled, casting a flurry of sparks into the air. Riana held out her hands and warmed them near the flames. Tom lay next to her side and looked out at the surrounding landscape. Donny sat across the fire, his olive-skinned face and black hair bathed in the ruddy glow of the campfire. To her left, Rustofo squatted near the fire, poking at the embers and staring into the flames.

"There were always Magyses," Riana continued. "A Magys wielded all elements in varying degrees, including Light and Shadow. But, when Magloryn was captured, the amount of Light magic available to those who wielded magic diminished. That's what led to the birth of Tyrmini. It's very similar, but Tyrmini powers are raw and rough, explosive, harder to control and more powerful in the tangible elements. When High King Achyla, the First, enslaved the Dragon of Light, he turned all Magys kind into volatile power containers.

"This was not what he intended. He intended to snuff their power altogether. His theory had been that Magloryn was the source of magical power, and without her in play, magical power would die. Instead, he thrust the Tyrinth into chaos. Power structures of all sorts, the economy and even the source of food growing, and production halted as the people on Aelos grappled with their new identity and a king who was out for the blood of any magic born.

"Aelos spiraled into chaos, depression and famine," she said.

"This is the great age of darkness Mrs. Tomlin taught us about," Donny said. "She told us the Tyrmini magic was new, but she left out the part where it was caused by the High King enslaving the Light Dragon."

Riana nodded.

"High King Achyla saved the day in the seventh year of the famine," Donny said. "By exterminating Tyrmini."

Riana stroked Tom's scales and furs. He purred contentedly. "High King Achyla, did indeed exterminate Tyrmini, but it looked a lot different than saving the day. He turned people against these Magys-born-turned-Tyrmini first. Where there were too many or too powerful Tyrmini for the citizens to overthrow, he recruited even stronger Tyrmini and wiped out the opposing forces.

"Back in those days, many of the positions of power were held by Magyses. By wiping them out, turning the people against their leaders, he left positions open to fill with non-magical citizens who were all too grateful. It looked a lot like revolution and freedom from a very dangerous population of magic-wielders."

"Meanwhile, the magic-wielders now termed Tyrmini were battling their own power, outcast, on the run, homeless, hunted and killed," Captain Rustofo added.

"You know this?" Riana asked.

"I am of the few who are in possession of texts that record the true history," he said vaguely, his accent making hard edges around the consonants and rolling the r on 'record'.

"And why is that?" Riana asked, tired of the mystery Rustofo cloaked himself in.

Rustofo watched the fire crackle, a grim look on his face. His jaw ground one way and then the other. He'd been crouching, his forearms rested on his knees. He stood to all of his hulking height. The sky was lightening with approaching dawn and the gleam of his eyes in his square features shone.

Riana craned her neck to look at him. Tom stopped purring and mimicked Riana's gesture; his head cocked to one side. Donny was silent next to Riana. The fire burned without a crackle. Even the tree seemed to be holding its breath.

"I am Captain Rustofo," he finally said, "but, I am also King Svelt Rustofo of Idalfyn, third king since the dark age."

"You -," Donny started. He stood up, bent his head, closed his eyes and held out a hand in a stop gesture. "Wait. So... that's a lot to unpack. You're the King of Idalfyn?"

"Yes," Rustofo said.

"You have access to original, untainted history about Tyrmini and Magyses," Donny counted this truth on a second finger.

Riana was still craning her neck as she sat on the ground. She watched Donny, grateful he was taking the lead on this conversation, and somehow not entirely surprised by the truth Rustofo shared.

"And, you're the third in the line of kings appointed since the dark ages," Donny pointed to a third finger.

"Yes," Rustofo said. He ducked his head a bit, turning one cheek toward Donny.

"But that means -," Donny started, then cast a gaze up to the right corner of his mind.

Riana stood up. She was following what Donny was getting at.

Donny looked at her. "Help me out with the math. You said it's been about five hundred years since all the Tyrmini killings, right?"

"Only three kings in five hundred years?" Riana asked. "That would make you around -,"

Rustofo crossed his arms and looked down his considerable height at Donny and Riana. "Don't you know it's very rude to assume a person's age," he said.

Riana turned to Donny. "Wait. Let's think about this. Let's assume both his father and grandfather are passed."

Rustofo uttered something guttural, kissed the back of his hand and flipped it into the sky. Donny watched this with rapt fascination. Riana assumed this was some respect for the dead custom.

"Okay, so they're gone. His son is around our age," Riana said.

"Says you," Donny said. "Do you actually know how old he is? I mean, he could be fifty and just reaching puberty."

"Oh," Riana said. "That's a good point. Okay, well, what do we know? Have you heard anyone talk about Idalfyn and a new ruler?"

Donny looked into the dirt, his eyebrows squished together.

Rustofo crossed his arms, a quirk of a smile hiding in his beard.

"Only the rumors that he's been missing the last ten years and the King regent, his brother, has given up on finding him."

Rustofo snorted. "Like he could find his own arse with both his hands."

Riana glanced at him but kept her focus on Donny. "Ten years?"

"Yes, ten. I'm sure of that."

"Okay, why would he do that? Why would he run away from his seat on the throne?"

"You know him better than I do," Donny pointed out.

"Apparently not," Riana said and frowned at Rustofo.

"True," Donny conceded.

Riana wrapped fingers around her chin, folded her other arm over her belly and kicked out a leg. "Rustofo told me he kept his wife safe by being out at sea. But then they found her."

Rustofo dropped his hands to his sides and balled his fists.

Donny didn't see this. "How did they find her?"

Riana glanced at Rustofo. She was probably pushing her luck, but if he wasn't going to just come out and tell her the whole story, he could simmer in anger all he wanted. "He told me they had kept her safe by keeping her at sea. At the time, I assumed it was because he had been with her."

"Stop," Rustofo whispered.

"What brought her back from the sea?" Donny asked.

"Please -," Rustofo said.

Riana interrupted him. "Kristopher said they found her after he was born."

"It was my fault!" Rustofo shouted.

176

Riana was expecting that. Donny jumped, but Riana simply turned toward him, hoping he was finally ready to tell them the whole story.

"I ordered her back to the castle. She was pregnant with our son. I couldn't have her risking the safety of the heir. I thought we had protected her. Thought we'd done everything to keep her identity hidden." He sobbed. "I loved her. I loved her so much. And I killed her."

"What do you mean?" Donny asked.

Rustofo inhaled deeply. He looked up; his eyes shiny with tears. Riana watched him struggle to find his voice.

"I ordered her home. But, I was careful. The people of the Aestyrah provided us with a piece of stone that blocks the view of the dragon's eye. The kingdom was ecstatic for the return of their queen. But she was so unhappy on land. After the months of her pregnancy, she slipped into a depression. It made her careless. I thought Kristopher's birth would enliven her, give her something to keep her busy and keep her mind from the sea. It only worsened. What was a mild depression before birth was a treacherous black hole afterward."

Riana held her breath. She was sure what she would hear next was not the version of the story she'd heard before from Kristopher. Which begged the question: which version of the story did Kristopher know as truth?

"She wouldn't nurse. She wouldn't hold Kristopher. She wouldn't even look at him. She begged me to let her return to the Jade Lady. It was her home before she became my wife. She didn't even want to take her son with her. She wanted to leave him. And me.

"We fought. Or, at least, I chastised her, and she sat silently during my tirades. She stopped eating, stopped speaking, and stayed in bed. One day, I brought Kristopher to her. She took him. It was the first time holding her son. Three months and she finally held her son. She smiled at him. I'll never forget the look on her face. I thought, finally, finally she was coming out of her depression. She held her boy, kissed his face and told him she loved him. I was so pleased. She gave Kristopher back to me and said she wanted a bath. I took our boy, my hopes swelling. I called for the bath to be drawn.

"I spoke with the chef about preparing a special meal for my wife. When it was ready and enough time had passed for her bath to be done, I brought the food up to her quarters myself, carrying our son as well.

"She had taken a bath. And she'd taken off the talisman. By the time I put it on her again it was too late. I don't know how they got there so quickly. By the time I had called for the Jade Lady to be readied, the High King's Tyrmini guard were beating at the draw bridge gate. I managed to get my queen on board, but they had anticipated our move and ambushed her and her crew after they set out to sea. The Jade Lady was returned to me with Idalfyn's queen tied to the mast, her throat slit and her dress black with blood."

Donny hung his head.

Riana clutched her tunic at the chest.

"I should have let her go. She was never happy on land. I knew that. But, selfishly I kept her with me."

Riana wanted to argue, but maybe he was right. Maybe he should have at least been more caring and understanding about what she was going through.

"No. She was selfish. How can you be a mother and not want anything to do with your son?" Donny asked.

Rustofo's bent head whipped up to glare at Donny. "Don't you dare speak of my wife that way. It was the land that made her sick. If she'd been on the sea she would still be alive."

Donny snapped his mouth closed. "Sorry," he managed.

"Does Kristopher know?"

"He knows his mother was murdered by the High King," Rustofo said.

"But, not the part where you kept her on land and she suffered with a depressed mind," Riana said, careful to speak softly.

"Not that part," Rustofo said.

"Well, I won't be the one to tell him."

"Thank you, fair Riana," he said. "After she was gone, I raised Kristopher with a watchful eye. As soon as I caught scent of his abilities, we headed for the high sea."

"And that was ten years ago," Donny said.

"Which makes me one-hundred and forty years old. And Kristopher is a young thirty-seven. The giant blood means we live a bit longer than human races."

Riana had the information out of him, but she felt too sick with sympathy to take any joy in knowing it.

"So, you've been on the run to protect Kristopher and the first time you take a risk to help someone on land your son is captured by the High King's guard. I'm so sorry," Riana said.

"We'll get him back," Donny said. "We'll get them all back."

"This is bigger than just my son, or Elynda or Ribbit. There is an entire nation of young ones who are regularly murdered by order of the High King. I think we've been out to sea for too long, protecting only me and my own. Kristopher is a man's age now. He must learn to fight his own fight. I help in honor of my wife. In honor of the generations of Tyrmini who've been slaughtered. We need a change."

"Well. Let's start with our three and see where we go from there," Riana said.

CHAPTER THIRTY-ONE

Riana unrolled the map on the ground and set the oil lamp on one side to keep it flat. She set her grandmother's journal, or as she was coming to think of it, her rebellion handbook, on the other side of the map.

Rustofo knelt on her left and Donny hovered close at her right shoulder. Rustofo pointed. "We are here."

Beneath the label, 'Shoqui' was a smaller label reading 'Midlun'.

"We need to go here," Riana pointed to the small image in the center of the map depicting the High King's castle.

Donny pulled a compass from an inner pocket of his navy-blue Baron's Guard cloak and clicked it open with the push of a silver button. The intricately carved cover flipped open and revealed a wobbling plate with a large N that settled to the left.

Riana looked up at the sky. The sun rose in front of them. "Seems right," she confirmed. "The castle is northeast of us, so we need to head in that direction," she said, pointing between her left shoulder and the sun.

"Great. Let's do it," Donny said.

"Hold on," Rustofo said. "It's not so easy. Look." He pointed to the map again. A giant line cut around Udari city on both the east and west sides. Riana, Rustofo and Donny found themselves on the west side of that western line.

"What is that?" Donny asked.

"Boy, have you never looked at a map before?"

Donny scowled at him but said nothing.

"It's a river," Riana said.

"Well, I mean, obviously it's a river. I knew that," Donny said, but his dark cheeks burned a little crimson. "I meant, which river is it. That's what I meant. 'What is that river?'"

"Right," Rustofo said.

"That is the Ogelvein," Riana said, "and it is a very wide river. We can only cross at a bridge or by barge."

"So, we board a barge and get across," Donny said.

"Don't you think so close to Udari City there'll be people looking for us?" Riana said.

"Why would they be looking for us?"

"Probably to capture us on behalf of the High King. I think he means to throw every blockade possible into our path."

"I agree with Riana. We should cross further south of the city and avoid as much interaction with people as possible."

"So, we're going south first, then northeast?" Donny asked.

Riana nodded. "I think so. Look at this." She opened her handbook to a page outlining transport portals. "Luther said there's a portal into the castle. Right onto the grounds. But, it's located down here, in Ogelith."

"Ugh," Donny said.

"Yes. What the Donny has said. Ugh," Rustofo agreed.

Riana was pointing to a map in her handbook that mirrored the map she'd rolled out, except the rebellion handbook map had several illustrations the conventional map lacked. The circular symbols with a six-pointed star was noted on the side as meaning portal. The only problem was there was no way to know in what shape the portal was in. If it would work, if it was buried or demolished or overgrown. "It'll be a risk, but if the portal is functional, it'll be worth it."

"If it's functional," Donny said.

"Either way we risk something," Riana noted.

"Go northeast and risk discovery," Rustofo said.

"Go south and risk time," Riana said.

"And danger," Donny added. "Do you even understand the nastiness of the Ogelith swamps?"

"Do you?" Riana asked, an eyebrow cocked high over one eye. Donny had never been outside of Landsend before last night as far as she knew.

"I've heard the stories," Donny muttered. "And they aren't pretty."

"Well, we've already faced a berubula. I mean, what worse is there?"

"Lots," Donny said, "and some of it from the two-legged species, also known as people." He leveled Riana with a serious gaze.

"Unfortunately, people populate all areas of the known expanse of Aelos, my friend. They're unavoidable. But, maybe the people in the swamps are less loyal to the High King."

"They do tend to be true to only themselves," Rustofo noted.

"Do you have experience with the Ogeliths?" Donny asked.

Rustofo stood up and wrapped a hand around his neck. "You could say that," he said.

Riana thought about pushing him to explain, but decided he'd divulged enough mysteries for one morning. "I've only had the pleasure -," Riana's tone didn't match her words, "- of meeting Captain Luther, who hails from Ogelith. This is all new to me."

"Listen," Donny started. "Can I just say, I've got a bad feeling about this. I vote we head northeast and risk discovery."

"And I vote we risk Ogelith and the transport stone that would take us immediately into the castle," Riana said, stubborn that was the right choice.

Rustofo looked between the two. He folded his arms and looked out into the field. "Dyrnai are known to inhabit pockets of land all over Aelos. They're rooted in shadow. As I recall, there are more shadow-rooted creatures in the swamps of Ogelith than any other region on Aelos. If the High King is using shadow creatures to do his bidding, we could be walking into an ambush."

"And if we head northeast, we could be walking into an ambush of Tyrmini Guards," Riana noted.

"That is true," Rustofo agreed.

"I'd rather face creatures than a set of Captain Luthers," Riana said.

"I see your point," Rustofo said.

"Well, I don't. We can keep hidden, keep on the side roads, where there are plenty of roads, and cross the river by barge to Udari," Donny said.

"And then how do you suggest we get into the castle?" Riana asked.

"I'm sure there's some sneaky entrance somewhere. Some secret tunnel or concealed door. All castles have them."

"But we don't know those secrets," Riana pointed out. "We know this one." She thrust a finger into the map in her handbook. Her insides coiled into a knot. Her grandmother had laid out the information for her. She was sure they should go to the portal in Ogelith. It was the only way.

"I have a bad feeling," Donny asserted.

"Well, I don't," Riana countered. At which point both Donny and Riana whipped their heads to look at Rustofo.

He stared back with suddenly wide eyes. "What?" he asked, alarmed.

"You're the tiebreaker," Riana said, "what you say, we'll do."

"Whoa, whoa," Rustofo said, gesturing with a stop motion using both hands. "Let's just reason this out as a group."

"We've tried that and it's not working. You tell us which direction to choose."

"Come on, you two. We can figure this out together. There's no need to get overly stuck on one action or the other."

"Yes, there is. It's either Riana's path or mine," Donny asserted.

"Now, listen, I think there may be another way. A third option."

Donny opened his mouth to argue but Riana shooshed him. "Let him speak."

Donny clamped his mouth closed with an audible snap.

Rustofo knelt again and looked over both the guidebook map and the conventional map, which had more detail. "If we head north across the plains and into The Sleeping Mountains, we can take the portal there to the Inilu Forest. That portal can take us to the Ogelith portal, which is a one-way ticket into the castle."

Donny scratched his head, eyes squinted as he stared at the map where Rustofo pointed. Finally, he said, "That is a lot of portal hopping." He seemed to turn green as he said it.

"It's only three hops," Riana said, trying to minimize his distress. "And we'll be traveling by foot to the next portal, which should be enough time for us to shake off the effects from our first hop." Admittedly, Riana had no symptoms of portal hopping as Donny and Rustofo did.

"What I don't understand is how they work at all," Rustofo said. "They haven't worked in over five hundred years."

Tom chirped and butted his head against Riana's arm.

Rustofo nodded, as if he understood what Tom were saying. "True," Rustofo said. "Riana is altogether a different sort of magic."

Riana ducked her head. She still had so much to learn, but the one thing she did understand. "It takes a certain level of Light element to operate the portals. And we haven't had that available on Aelos in five hundred years," she said

"So, why now? We know Magloryn is still enslaved. How is there suddenly more Light accessible?" Rustofo asked.

Riana's insides squirmed with the answer while Tom butted his head against her, rubbing his cheek against her shoulder. He seemed to know the answer too. Riana picked up the journal, putting a finger between the pages that mapped out the portals, and held the book to her chest. "I think I can answer that question as soon as I finish reading this."

Meanwhile the slow chant thrummed inside her. Magloryn. I am Magloryn.

CHAPTER THIRTY-TWO

Elynda was hustled through the damp stone hallways by Captain Luther and two Tyrmini guards. One was a ravishingly beautiful woman with dark skin and dark eyes who had a hard edge to her beauty, the crop of her hair, the glint in her eyes, the structure of her physique. The other was a man Elynda would describe as oafy, if it weren't for the fact he terrified her. There was danger in the gazes he cast her way, an empty darkness in his brown eyes and an energy Elynda could sense around him that made her want to run and hide.

Captain Luther held a secure but gentle hand around Elynda's upper arm as they approached a split in the hall. He steered her right before he released her arm once again.

Elynda did not like his touch on her. She despised this tool of the High King and his treachery. However, the first and only time she'd mouthed off to him, the ravishing beauty had backhanded her. Captain Luther had admonished her, but Elynda got the idea he really hadn't meant it, and if she were to mouth off again, there was no reason the guard wouldn't repeat the action – or worse. Elynda decided to pick her battles.

They reached the end of the long hall, passing through globes of light cast by low burning oil lamps. Their shoes on the stone echoed in an arrhythmic clatter. In front of them a heavy wooden door hinged in wrought iron scroll work blocked their passage.

Luther swiftly knocked at the door. A frail voice muttered something unintelligible. Luther seemed to understand the meaning and pushed the door open. He ushered Elynda through, followed before turning to the two guards. "Guard the door," he told them.

The dark beauty folded her arms over her center and leaned heavily on one leg. The oaf glowered at Elynda before he turned his back to the door. The face of the beautiful guard disappeared behind the closing door.

Elynda's hands grew warm. Tingles chased from her crown to the tips of her fingers. She knew that feeling. Whoever was in this chamber was very ill. She turned away from the door and faced a bed chamber larger than any she'd ever seen. A large bed dominated the center. It was drenched in hues of scarlet. A fire crackled and warmed the chamber to near suffocating degrees. The flames cast dancing ribbons of light and shadow over the bed linens and walls. Large oil lamps ensconced on the walls burned with a soft hiss. Despite the lamps and fire, the chamber felt cavernous – dank and unwelcoming. Elynda decided it was due to the lack of windows and felt in danger of catching fire.

Propped on the bed was a man so withered and drawn he looked as though he were made of wax. Elynda was unsure how the body remained animated. Most she'd seen like that had been corpses. She was filled with repugnant horror and while her hands had the idea she needed to heal this man, the rest of her wanted out of the suffocating room.

"Your majesty," Luther said, his thick drawl oily on the open vowels.

Elynda stared at the living corpse on the bed. The living corpse who had countless people executed, maybe even murdering many himself. Thick disgust sat in her belly as her hatred toward the man filled the room.

"Curtsy to your King, girl," Luther hissed.

Elynda crossed her arms and glared at the man. "You're no King of mine," she declared.

Luther jumped up and reached for Elynda. He wrapped a hand around the back of her neck and grasped her elbow with the other. Pressure mounted against her body, but the king began to chuckle.

"Wait," he said, between laughter, his voice barely a whisper. Luther seemed to feel the command more than hear it. He dropped his hands from her as though he'd been burned. "Don't damage the girl, no matter how willful she is."

Elynda never felt more like a precious instrument than she did in that moment. An object without a name. She'd healed dozens of men, women, children and babes and they had all looked on at her in adoring fashion. Stunned, surprised, grateful and always with her name on their lips. They respected her to a level that made Elynda uncomfortable. To have the opposite sort of sentiment stunned her.

"Come here, child, and touch me," the King said. "I've been too long in this form and the flesh has grown weak."

"You think I can cure you?" Elynda asked, wondering if she could refuse the power coursing through her, ready to transfer itself into the monarch.

King Achyla regarded her, a half smirk playing on his mouth. He lifted his hands from his sides and folded them atop his sunken stomach. "Oh my dear, I think you better," he said.

"Or else...?" Elynda asked.

He looked at Luther, his smirk twisting to a scowl. "Show her," he said.

Luther bowed his head and moved away from Elynda. He knelt in front of a large bureau and rapidly moved his hands over the drawers. Elynda tried looking over or around him, but his body blocked her view. Eventually, the drawers swung out and Elynda recoiled from the object he drew from the dark interior.

Captain Luther carried what looked like a crystal ball, except inside the crystal a giant eye was suspended in a clear liquid. She had seen eyeballs; she'd even had to put one back into someone's socket. This eye was removed, severed at the optic nerve which dangled in the fluid – yet it still animatedly looked around the room. It seemed to be searching and then at last it fell on Elynda. Elynda audibly gasped. The eye shifted from the multicolor hue of a rainbow to blue and then to emerald green, as if mimicking her own eye color. She had seen multicolored eyes like this before; they belonged to her best friend.

Yet, this eye was much too large to belong to a human. Elynda mentally scaled the size of the eye. It was at least twenty times the size of a human eye. She reeled as she calculated the size of the creature the eye belonged to. On the heels of that imagination, she wondered just why this creature's eye had the same color and shifting ability as her best friend.

His majesty propped himself up against a bank of pillows and then Luther placed the eye gently into his lap. "Come here, child," the king said.

Elynda wanted to refuse but was too curious. She stalked over to the High King, working to keep her nose from wrinkling at the stench of his decaying body. The king muttered something foreign to Elynda's ears. A dark shadow accumulated in the center of the room and snaked its way to the bed. The king tilted his head back, opening his mouth and the shadow plunged in. The king's eyes rolled up in his head, revealing the whites before they filled with blackness.

Elynda's heart hammered in her chest. Fear squeezed her throat and rooted her in place. She was frozen as the High King gripped the eye. Shadowy tendrils twisted through the sphere of ambient fluid until they drove into the eye. The eye shivered, as if in pain. Elynda wanted to cry out against the thing that was clearly hurting the eye, but her throat tissues were glued together.

"Look into the eye, dear," the king said.

Elynda's gaze was drawn as if by force to the eye. Reflected on the glass an image wavered, first translucent and then gaining solid form and color. Elynda saw Ribbit and Kristopher. They were huddled together in the corner of a dark room. Ribbit looked worse than she'd seen him when they'd brought them here. His eyes were sunken and haunted by blue shadows. His cheekbones were prominent. His color was pale as moonlight. There was no sound to the vision, but as Ribbit coughed, his body spasmed with the effort. Kristopher wrapped an arm around Ribbit. His face was tortured. He yelled out, looking past Elynda into some unseen reality.

Forms appeared in the vision. Two guards grabbed at Kristopher, wrenching him from Ribbit. Ribbit fell to the floor, no longer supported by the giant. He lay on the ground, struggling to breathe. He rolled himself enough to look in the direction Kristopher had been taken. He lifted a hand weakly, his face drawn and worried, and cried out.

The perspective of the eye shifted from Ribbit to Kristopher where the two guards hammered him with blows. Elynda wrapped her hand over her mouth as tears spilled from her eyes. One guard kicked Kristopher in the face and blood sprayed from his mouth. Kristopher raised his arm to cover his face. The other guard swung a heavy baton, striking the giant in the exposed ribs. A punch landed in his eye and then a boot in his groin, then stomach. Kristopher vomited. His face was dragged through the bile as a guard pulled his hair to expose his face to punch him again.

Kristopher was a bloodied mass of swelling skin within moments. Elynda knew all too well he would have broken ribs, possibly a punctured lung, maybe missing or broken teeth, nose, cheekbone, and he'd probably be peeing blood for a couple of days.

"Now, I don't need to tell you, dear, that your friends appear to be in need of healing, wouldn't you say?"

Elynda sobbed, her gut turning into a solid mass of anguish. She could help her friends. She could heal them. She knew it. "Please take me to them. I'll do whatever you want," she said.

"Perhaps we'll take you to your friends," the king said. "Perhaps. If you heal me sufficiently, I promise to release you to your friends so you can do the same favor for them. But not until I am healthy." The king's voice rose as he shouted the last sentence. Spit flew from his mouth and his eyes watered and reddened with the effort.

Elynda hung her head. Tears streamed down her face. They could die. Ribbit was no doubt starving. If they didn't give them food, water, and healing attention her friends would expire. But, to help the very man who'd put them in this position was a vile thought. What he could do with poor health was heinous. What would he do with his health fully restored?

Elynda wondered if she could sacrifice her friends. If she could watch them suffer and do nothing to save them. She knew it was the right thing to do. A sick High King was better than a healthy High King. Living in a world without Ribbit in it was an unbearable thought.

Elynda crumpled to the ground under the weight of the decision she had to make.

What would you do, Riana? What choice would you make? She thought, beseeching wisdom and strength.

She glanced up at the eye again and this time through the vision of her friends' suffering, she saw the multicolored iris. The eye stared at her. Warm peace filled her, from the crown of her head, like molten light pouring through her body.

Tell him you will help him but tell him it will take a while.

This was the voice of Magloryn, the elemental dragon of light. Riana had told her what it had felt like, describing the peaceful, loving quality.

He does not know the full extent of your power. You are a daughter of Light, and anything reflecting light is outside of his understanding.

"I'll help you," she said, trusting the voice. She looked up from the floor and into the shadow-filled eyes of the king. "I'll heal you. But it will take time."

A smile curved in sinister angles across the king's face. "It behooves you to take as little time as possible, my dear, or else your friends may expire."

Elynda had no words, just frantic thoughts and more than enough worry to cause a pinch in her chest and a knot in her stomach. Then it occurred to her, this High King was not the only person in the room with power. He could threaten her, but so could she. She straightened her body and balled her hands into fists.

"By the smell, I'd say without my help you're only days from death. You're rotting from the inside," she told him. She didn't need to make it up; the truth was evident. "Furthermore, it appears your extremities are necrotizing. If I come back here and my friends haven't been given food and water and a place to wash their wounds with clean water and clean bandages, I will not heal you. Your fates are tied, your majesty. Deal death to them and I will do the same to you."

The king gritted his teeth, his shadow filled eyes gone wide. A low groan escaped his clenched teeth. His head began to shake in a no gesture, then gathered speed until Elynda thought for sure his neck would snap. The groan grew into a deep growl, an inhuman noise that vibrated through the room. Accompanying the deep other-worldly growl was a cacophony of screeches and wails, as if she were hearing a crowd of people being burned alive.

Elynda grabbed her ears, but the sound permeated through her hands. She added her own scream into the mix. She could not wrench her eyes from the king. His body was a mass of tensed wiry muscles and bones, the tendons in his neck erect and protruding. No, no, no – his head shook at an alarming speed.

Suddenly, his head stopped. His body went rigid, his mouth stretching open farther than humanly possible. Shadow erupted from his mouth. He violently vomited a mass of darkness, thick and tar-like. And he was aiming it right at her. Elynda gasped in fear before she was consumed by darkness.

Her world became an open expanse of emptiness. The thick, black void rolled away from her on all sides, underneath and above her as well. She was suspended, caught up in a visceral darkness, as if it gripped her.

You think the worst thing that can happen to you is seeing your friends' deaths? A voice spoke. *I always thought his imagination was lacking. But, you. What do you fear?*

Elynda instinctually recoiled from the sensation of prying eyes inside her mind, squirming away from the invasion.

Don't be silly, dear. You cannot keep me out.

Help, Elynda cried. Somewhere her physical eyes dripped tears, but she couldn't say where those eyes were. And she was unaware of a body attached to those eyes.

She is a daughter of Light. You have been perverted. Begone from her! The loving voice of Magloryn opposed the power consuming Elynda.

A rich animal cackle bounced around inside Elynda's head. Now, somewhere, a mouth said, 'stop', weakly. Elynda wasn't sure who the mouth belonged to, but she thought it seemed familiar.

You're so weak. What do you think you'll do?

Elynda, Magloryn said. *I want you to try something.*

As the Dragon of Light spoke to her, Elynda began to feel her intention. A head nodded her understanding. She dug deeply into that well of healing she'd recently discovered. Warm, heady love filled her. She channeled the feeling from her gut and heart to her hands. Hands. Somewhere there were hands that belonged to her. After her hands burned with the healing energy and the scent of ozone filled her nose, she let the energy cascade off her palms, fingers, then wrists and arms, shoulders, chest, neck. She let the healing energy fill her entire being and then cast it into the gripping darkness.

The darkness wriggled, loosening her a hair. She inhaled and focused the energy with more power. It flowed through her.

This is me, Magloryn spoke. *It is me, and it is all the elements. Allow the energy to find the heart of darkness and heal it.*

Elynda exhaled with lungs that were hers. She remembered now. She had a body.

Your body is an amalgamation of all the elements working to house your spirit. In this lifetime, you are one: body holding spirit; spirit animating body. Breathe again.

Elynda obeyed. She continued to funnel healing energy through her, aiming it at the darkness. She knew it was meeting its goal because the darkness reacted.

Stop, it demanded.

You are love, Elynda told it.

No.

You are compassion.

I am destruction, it countered.

You are inspiration, Elynda said.

I am chaos.

You are creation.

I am Death.

You are wrong, Maglorgyn said.

Heal, Elynda willed.

The darkness growled, released and surrendered.

Elynda fell to the ground and gasped for air. Stars blossomed in her vision. Her head swam. The room tilted around her.

"You should not tempt the Shadow," the High King whispered weakly and worriedly.

Elynda looked into his eyes and saw real fear.

CHAPTER THIRTY-THREE

They traveled north and slightly west for three days across the expansive Shoqui plains. It was hot. Riana and her companions stripped away all unnecessary layers of clothing, but this led to Riana's fair skin turning bright red by the end of the first day. At night, she lay atop her blankets, her skin throbbing and on fire while she froze inside. Yet, she couldn't bare the touch of a blanket on her skin.

On the second day she wore her light cloak to cover her skin. She sweltered and sweated, but she did not burn further. Rustofo and Donny both had skin of deep shades of brown and were unaffected by the beating sun, save for a deep rosy hue that passed overnight.

Tom was in his element.

The terrain changed over the third day, shifting from wide, open expanses of grasses, dotted with copses of short trees to rolling hills with red dirt. The countryside swapped grasses for wildflowers. Riana marveled at the variety. Bright blue stalks swept across one hillside while another valley was filled with oranges, reds and yellows. She had no name for any of them and she wished for a book to help her identify the flora and fauna of the area they traversed. The end of the third day found Riana brimming with the sights and smells of the day.

Rustofo stoked the fire while Donny prepared the deer Tom had hunted and returned to camp. Riana yanked her boots from her feet and sighed in relief.

Over her left shoulder the sun was setting, lighting the sky in vivid oranges, pinks and golden yellow. It was beautiful here. She pulled a notepad from her cloak pocket and the accompanying pencil. She sketched the hillside but grieved the fact she had no paint or chalk or dye of any sort to mimic the rich colors of the evening.

Donny was skilled with preparing meat, his father being a pig farmer and his mother a butcher. Before Riana had finished her sketch, the meat was skewered and stacked over the fire to cook. Juices sizzled on the logs and smoke rose into the evening sky as the nightly chorus of nocturnal animals started up.

Riana pulled the journal from her bag, and picked up reading, as she did every night. She flipped to the pages she'd been so careful to avoid. Her mother had been the High King's sister and she was about to read the truth of her father's identity. She continued.

However, it is not who your mother is that has kept me from divulging. Rather, it is your paternal parentage that poses the most threat.

That much she had read.

So much so that I feel I cannot even reveal it here on these pages, lest this book fall into the wrong hands. I am so sorry, my child. I hate to leave this burden upon you. And I entrust that Mylah will find you in Landsend and divulge this truth in person.

Riana dropped the book in her lap, stunned. She'd waited weeks for the revelation, had built up the courage to know the truth, and still her grandmother had chosen to keep the truth from her. Anger swept through her. She ground her jaw, fighting against a growl. She wanted to throw the journal into the fire, but she needed its other helpful information. Tears streamed from her eyes as her stomach squeezed in on itself. So, it was up to this Mylah person. The anonymous and absent Mylah. The infamous savior who'd deigned to reveal herself.

Well, she couldn't count on that. She couldn't count on her grandmother even to give her the truth she sought. Riana clenched a fist over the cover of the journal and vowed to find her own truth.

Still emotional, she determined the only thing she could do at present was to glean as much information as she could from her rebellion handbook. Heart still thrumming, she flipped the journal open once more and turned to the section dog-eared to mark the explanation of the portals. She pored over the information on how they worked to prepare for the next hop. She rubbed at her sore thighs and tight calves, carefully stowing her anger, as she reviewed the mapped-out paths.

"We should reach the portal early tomorrow. I don't think it's far away," Rustofo told her.

"What a relief. I'm not looking forward to the hop, but all this walking is making me worry a lot less about it," Donny said.

Rustofo chuckled.

Riana had a squirm of nerves as they talked about using the portal. It appeared there was more than one type of portal. The portal they'd taken from Landsend operated to and from the Shoqui plans and back, but there were other portals you could jump from to land in Landsend, but not the other way around. The portal in the Inilu forest had the ability to go to two different locations, depending on where one stood on the portal. The incantation was slightly different too. As was the incantation for portals that were built to go to three different locations.

While Sela Starliss's notes about these portals were clearly outlined, she had borrowed from other texts when it came to the science of the portals and noted some of it was unclear. The language they used five-hundred years ago was different than it was now. She was interpreting as best she could.

Two-location portals should be used with the regular incantation; however, the text seems to indicate one must position oneself facing the direction one wants to head. If I understand through the archaic language, if you're at the The Sleeping Mountains portal and you want to go to the portal in the Tyrminhai Forest, near the edge of The Waste, you must stand in the southwestern position along the tile's perimeter, so that you're facing northeast, the direction of the destination.

Furthermore, the text indicates an addition to the incantation. After you've called the elements in, you must also call out the destination name.

Riana had read the passage several times over the last few days, but found the information, as simple as it was, wouldn't stick in her brain. During the day as she walked, she found herself questioning, where was she to stand, what was the name of the location where they were going, was she supposed to face the direction they were heading, or stand in the direction they were heading? She scoured the words and confirmed again what she'd read last night and the night before.

Riana closed the book and looked out over the fire to the vista of wildflowers turning gray in the oncoming twilight. She thought she'd heard something. The fire crackled and deer meat sizzled and spat as juice dripped into the flames. Tom was out on patrol, roaming around the perimeter of the camp. She looked around but didn't immediately spot him. A single insect's whisper was joined by another, and then a third. Riana relaxed into the curve of the boulder she leaned against and breathed in the cooling air. It was fragrant and clean. It was unlike the salty air of Landsend, and it missed the pinch of ozone she'd grown up with, but the scent of dirt and sunshine was delicious in her lungs.

She marveled at her situation. She'd never been outside of Landsend and now, she had been to the Shoqui Plains, headed into the Sleeping Mountains and then they would soon see the Inilu Forest and the Ogelith Swamps. She wanted to relish the travel, the experience of being in different parts of the world, but her wanderlust was dampened by Elynda's absence, and their imprisonment. Not for the first time, Riana sent a silent prayer up to Magloryn to keep her friends safe.

The next morning, Riana and company scoured the landscape for the next portal.

"So, where is it?" Donny asked.

Riana growled. They'd been up for less than an hour and he was already grinding on her nerves. "I don't know, Donny. The map points to somewhere around here, from what I can tell."

"Well, then, what are we looking for?" Donny asked.

Riana ground her teeth. He might not be bullying her any longer, but his questions rubbed her nerves raw. "As I've mentioned, you aren't looking for anything. I am looking for a shimmer."

"A shimmer?"

"Donny, unless you're a Magys, you won't be able to see it. And it's not easy for me to spot. So, could you... shhhh!"

"Sor-ry," Donny said, and then mumbled, "-just trying to help. Goddess. So sensitive."

Riana stalked away, hoping the portal was not in Donny's vicinity.

Over the crest of a nearby hill, Rustofo and Tom searched through a field of violet wildflowers. A bird flitted over Tom's head and away. Tom bounded in its direction. The bird was fast. It quickly flitted up into the air out of Tom's reach. Tom slowed. Riana thought he was about to give up the chase, but then he launched himself into the air.

Riana gaped. Was he flying? Tom's tails twisted wildly behind him. A blast of wind exploded away from Tom. The air shot through flowers and grasses. Rustofo shielded his face as the wind caught him full force. Dirt and bits of flowers, sticks, pebbles and other debris caught up into a whirling cloud of wind that encircled the creature. Tom ran, his giant paws catching wind.

It was clumsy, but it accomplished his goal. Within several lunges, Tom caught up to the bird, and gave one quick snap of his jaws to capture it behind a prison of canines. He dropped to the ground, his mouth full, wings flapping wildly until a final crunch stilled the bird. Tom chomped several times and then swallowed the bird. He sat on his haunches and cleaned his face. Seemingly satisfied, he turned toward Rustofo and bounded in his direction.

Rustofo yelled in exhilarated shock, hoisting his hands into the air as if in celebration of this new trick. Encouraged, Tom launched himself into the air once more, circled the giant's head before landing a sloppy lick on his face.

"Argh!" Rustofo growled. "Get down from there and don't you lick me with your bird breath."

Tom loped away from the giant, playfully looking over his shoulder, then charged back to attack again. But, Rustofo was ready and ducked Tom's kiss. As the creature passed the giant, the giant snatched one of Tom's three tails and yanked. Tom yowled and lurched back around; paws stretched out to capture Rustofo.

Rustofo yelped before Tom toppled him over. Booming laughter echoed across the hill country as the two rolled on the ground. If it were not for the laughing, the interchange would appear savage.

"Ow," Rustofo said.

Riana ran toward him. "What happened? Did Tom hurt you?"

"No, something's sticking in my back," Rustofo yelled toward her. He stood and investigated the scrubby grasses.

Tom looked too, his tails undulating in turn. He turned toward Riana as she approached the two and chirped.

Rock and dirt crunched underfoot. Sunshine bathed them all in warm light. The sky overhead was a vibrant blue. Clouds skidded through the expanse. A breeze picked through the vegetation and fingered through Riana's wild, silver hair.

Rustofo knelt and brushed his hand over a section of grass and dirt. Riana drew close enough to peer down. Her shadow stretched over a section of stone with regular grooves.

Footsteps sounded behind her. Riana recognized Donny's gait.

"That looks like the stone carving in the Landsend portal," Donny noted.

"Only miniaturized," Rustofo noted.

There was more than just the tell-tale maze carvings in stone too. A shimmering line started in the center of the maze and led away through a line of shrubs and grass. Riana followed the shimmer, Tom on her heels. The bluish light disappeared into the slope of a hill. It didn't go up the hill but stopped at its base.

Riana stood in front of the hill, where the shimmer ended. She ran a hand across the jagged, dark rock. Greenery clung in cracks, growing from collected soil. Close up, she saw nothing, but the striations formed by layers of mineral and stone. She backed away from the rock face.

"Where is the opening?" she whispered.

Tom purred as he stalked in front of the rock. He paced several times while Riana looked far up, at the foot of the hill, to the left and then the right.

"How do we get in, Tom?" she asked the creature.

Tom sat on his haunches directly in the path of the shimmer. His tails drummed against the ground. He looked over his shoulder at Riana and chirped. Then stood and stalked directly into the hill.

CHAPTER THIRTY-FOUR

Getting in had been easy. Once they were in, Riana faced the larger stone maze and portal mechanism with rising panic.

There was no crystal in its center.

"What do we do now?" Donny asked. "It's busted."

"Do you always ask the obvious?" Riana asked. "I can see it's busted. I don't know what we do now. Why do I always have to have the answers? Why don't you think of something?"

"You're so cranky. Why are girls always so angry?"

"There you go again," Riana said.

"What?"

"Donny, if all the girls you hang out with are angry, and you're the common denominator, perhaps it's your infuriating presence."

Donny was silent for a moment and Riana wondered if she'd hurt his feelings enough to force his mouth to stay shut.

"Well, I don't think that's true," Donny finally rebutted. "Girls are just bossy, boring, hot heads."

Riana was holding Sela's journal and staring at the tile, sans crystal. She snapped the book shut. "I'll show you hot head," she said as she marched toward him, wanting nothing more than to clobber him over the head with the book in her hand.

"Now, now," Rustofo said and stepped between Riana and Donny. "Fighting won't solve anything. Let's put our heads together and see what we can figure out. And let's do it over a bit of food. I think we've all been going since dawn without a bite to eat. It's no wonder we're out of sorts."

"I'm not out of sorts," Donny mumbled, "she is."

"You're about to be out of sorts," Riana growled.

"That's enough," Rustofo said. He didn't shout, but the power of his voice still boomed and echoed in the cave.

Riana backed away, still angry, but also silenced.

She sat on the ground and leaned against a nearby stalagmite. Rustofo lowered himself to the ground near her and pulled his pack close to him. He pulled jerky and apples out and passed pieces of the salty meat to Riana first. She took it and thanked him for the sustenance.

They chewed in silence in the semi-dark of the cave. The entry was nearby and cast the otherwise dark world in a wash of blue light. Riana looked at the entry with wonder. From the inside of the cave, the entry was clearly there. From the outside there was nothing but a rock wall.

She looked at the maze engraving on the stone tablet on the ground. It didn't shimmer in blue energy like the Landsend tablet had. She chewed at her jerky and looked back at the entrance where she could clearly see the shimmer that had led them inside.

She followed the line of shimmer where it would be if it continued into the cave. Her eyes traced the invisible beam through the yawning entrance, across the cavern room, over the tile and into a collection of stalagmites. Tom lounged in front of the formations, bathing himself.

Riana pushed herself up from the cavern floor and crossed the dead transport tile.

Rustofo paused mid-bite, his mouth hanging open as he watched Riana cross the cave.

Donny flicked a gaze her way, but feigned disinterest and took a large bite of his apple.

As Riana drew near, Tom chirped at her. He leaned back as she stood over him and rolled to expose his soft belly – and rolled right through the stalagmites. The image of what should have been solid minerals wavered like a reflection on water.

Riana stepped over Tom and into the mirage. She tested the floor with one foot before pulling her back foot through and setting it on the solid ground. If the mirage had been real, at this point she would have hit her head on a rock ledge. As she pulled herself through, the cave unfolded in front of her. She gasped. It was gorgeous.

"Riana!" Donny shouted.

Riana turned and saw her two companions clearly, but they looked her direction with dismay. She stepped toward them and they startled.

"They used the same stuff here as they did on the cave entrance," she explained.

"So," Donny gestured to the stone in the middle of the cave.

"That's a decoy," she said.

"The real one is in there?" Rustofo asked.

Riana nodded. "Come on. Let's go." She turned and walked through the fake wall with more confidence. She turned. Donny stared at the wall, clearly unsure. Riana grabbed his coat and pulled him through. He winced as he went through the illusion. Riana giggled.

Rustofo stumped through as though he could see the path clearly.

Tom lazily strode through. Riana got the feeling he was not feigning confidence but saw through the disguise.

The ceiling of the cavern stretched far away above them. A small hole in the ceiling let through a spear of sunlight. The cave was illuminated by numerous energy lamps scattered throughout the cavern. The stone tile was situated in the center and the grooves shone with the ethereal blue glow. The crystal in the center glittered as though it winked at Riana.

She sighed in relief. "Okay, let's get going," she said, ready to move on to the next jump. Ready to move closer to freeing her friends.

"Whoa, wait. Right this second?" Donny asked. He turned a pale shade of grayish green as he spoke.

"There's no time like the present," Rustofo said, his r's rolling with his accent. His voice echoed off the high cave walls.

"It's already been three days since they were captured. Goddess knows what they're going through right now," Riana said. "Donny, you're to stand on the southern gem."

"I so wish I hadn't eaten that jerky," Donny said, but obeyed Riana's instruction.

"Tom, you stand in the west. Rustofo, you stand in the north. I'll be on the east, facing west, the direction we're to end up."

As soon as she stood on the eastern tile, the power swelled within her. The incantation came quickly this time and she added their destination to the final verse. The energy squeezed around them, and they were launched into the ether. The vista of stars was slightly different. In the distance, Riana could see a glowing orb much bigger and brighter than the rest and wondered if that was their sun. It was here, walking in the cosmos that she considered what other worlds were in the vast dusting of celestial bodies, and if there were others who used this space as a highway between destinations.

Her hair floated around her, and the cool nothingness wrapped her in a slightly suffocating calm. A deep rumble reverberated through the ether, disrupting the weird silence. Riana cast around for the source.

She didn't have to look far. The light-formed creature she'd seen on her last journey through the ether appeared over her right shoulder. She gasped. Its glittering form pulsed with orbs of white light over pathways of electric blue, deep pinkish purple and sunset orange. The eye of the creature, as large as Riana regarded her as it skidded along next to their group, just behind Donny. It was a beautiful eye too. The structure was constructed of light and color. The orb was lined with strands of deep violet and gold. The pattern it created was like a twisting funnel that tightened into a pupil of sorts. The pupil was pure white light with a thin horizontal line of black and a pinprick of blackness in the center only slightly larger than the slit.

The creature blinked once and nodded its giant head. Riana felt a warm homecoming from the creature, a hailing of familiarity, but a question in its greeting.

I am Riana, she thought to the creature.

The creature bellowed in Riana's mind, its black pupil suddenly springing wide. A wave of energy visible to Riana as an expanding circle of red rolled away from the creature. It struck Donny first, slicing through his center like a blade. He yelled, or he would have if verbal speech were capable in this star-strewn terrain. His arms and legs splayed out and his body convulsed. His eyes rolled up in their sockets.

The red ring moved slowly toward Tom. Tom pivoted in his position in the group's circle. His scales rose, his mouth opened to reveal his dark tongue and white canines. His mouth hissed while no sound came from it. He swiped at the oncoming ring. The red energy sparked; small golden triangles burst away from the ring where Tom struck it. The ring dissipated, golden energy skittering away into the ether.

The creature bellowed. Its voice was so loud, Riana wanted to cover her ears, except the sound was solely in her mind. It pulled away from them and Riana wondered if it would float away. It retreated until its size was half of what it had appeared up close. Riana breathed a sigh of relief.

Tom crouched in his position, scales on end, tails whipping around him. His eyes were trained on the creature. Tom hissed, noiseless in the forever. Riana looked at this space animal once more and found its size growing larger. Its triangular shaped and wing-like appendages flapped leaving trails of color spinning away behind it. It undulated toward them.

Rustofo tried yelling, gesturing in panic. Donny still convulsed. The creature belched out a deep growl, a sound that set Riana's heart racing. She had told the creature she was Riana and the creature had not liked that answer. It had recognized her though, but what did it recognize about her?

Riana thought of the strange mimic her eyes were to Magloryn's.

She closed her eyes and focused, hoping beyond hope she could contact the Dragon of Light. Hoping Magloryn could help them.

Magloryn, she cried out with her mind, with her heart. *Please help us!*

There was no answer.

Riana's eyes sprung open. An answer came, but it was not from Magloryn.

Get out! Thought the creature. *You do not belong here.*

Please, Riana argued, *we are just passing through.*

Get out! Your foul practices are not welcome.

What foul practices? Riana asked.

You pervert the Shadow. You pervert the Light. I will not allow it any longer. Stay out!

What do you mean? Do you know who I am?

I know you have the blood of my enemy in your veins. I can sense it.

I don't know what you mean. Riana was frantic. The creature bore down on them. Donny shivered. Rustofo gesticulated wildly. Tom was hunched and ready for the attack. Riana drew on the well of energy within her. She didn't want to have to fight the creature, but she had to protect her companions. The shimmering light and warmth spread through her body. She gathered it into her hands.

The creature bellowed, quaked and another red ring exploded from its body. The shock wave shook Riana. She drew the light energy from her hands and cast it out around her and her companions, willing it to wrap them in a protective cloak. The angry red wave shot toward them. The light energy Riana created shimmered through the circle they formed. It expanded through their bodies and formed an egg of blue light. The pod of protection barely squeezed over Rustofo's massive height when the red energy smashed into it.

The cocoon of safety rocked wildly, tilting them away from the attacking creature. The red energy exploded back, sparks of golden light showering the open expanse of the universe.

The creature halted its forward momentum.

Magloryn? It asked.

THE DRAGON'S EYE

The familiar pull yanked at her and they hurtled through the ether. The four were blasted back to Tyrinth. Their arrival in the other portal was harsh. They somersaulted toward the ground, spit out of the universe and bounced against the stone tile. Riana rolled away from the tile's center. She inhaled deeply, filling her lungs with much needed air.

Rustofo gagged and wheezed.

Donny lay flat and lifeless on the ground.

CHAPTER THIRTY-FIVE

Riana pushed herself up and launched toward Donny. Vertigo threatened to knock her flat.

"Donny," Riana said.

He was no longer convulsing, but he was limp and lifeless. His skin was pale and cold.

Rustofo knelt beside them, his breath ragged.

"Give him breath, Riana. He's not breathing," Rustofo instructed.

Elynda had taught her and the rest of the class how to administer breath when they had studied first aid in school. That had been years ago. Riana's heart drummed wildly. She tilted Donny's head to the right angle to allow the breath in, then pulled his chin down to open his mouth. She placed her own mouth on his, pinching his nose and blew.

She wished Elynda were with them. She'd know exactly what to do and how to do it. Riana was no healer. She did not possess the gentle strength her friend had, nor the vast knowledge of the workings of the body. Riana breathed and blew and prayed for the best. Had she killed this bully-turned-friend by insisting on her own way of doing things? He hadn't wanted to go through another portal. She should have listened to him and gone the other route. Then, this wouldn't have happened.

She breathed into his lungs again. A small quiver within Donny's chest initiated a deep inhale. Donny bolted upright so quickly Riana had to pull away or get hit by him. He coughed and spluttered. Riana rubbed his back awkwardly. Tears sprang to her eyes.

Donny recovered and looked at her. "Don't cry. I'm not dead yet." He groaned and laid back on the ground. "Kinda wish I were though."

Tom loped toward them, bent his face to Donny's, sniffed and then licked.

"Hey," Donny said.

Tom sneezed.

"Are you alright?" Rustofo asked.

"My insides are sore," Donny said, "but, I think I'll be okay. What was that thing?"

Riana didn't have a clue. She looked at Rustofo. "Do you know?"

He nodded slowly, then shook his head. "Only a guess," he said, eyebrows raised. He rubbed the back of his neck with his large hand then scratched at his chin and beard. He looked around them, as if cementing reality again by taking in their surroundings.

Riana did the same, looking at where they'd ended up.

Donny followed suit.

Tom ruffled his scales, drummed his tails and then set to the task of cleaning his face.

"Are we in a tree?" Donny asked, shock vibrating his words.

Riana couldn't take it in at first. The walls surrounding them did indeed appear to be made of tree bark. Blue light lit the maze pattern in the tile, but instead of sconces lining the walls, this portal room's perimeter was lined with arching miniature trees whose leaves and fruit were luminescent with neon green. The crystal in the center of the transport tile glowed white. Riana could have done with more light. The room was subdued, and she could make out little of their surroundings.

She pulled the lantern from her pack and lit the wick. She was running low on oil. She held the lamp aloft, rising to her feet. It seemed Donny was right. They were inside the largest tree Riana had ever seen.

Rustofo walked the perimeter of the maze tablet, stopping to peer at the strange luminescent plant life. "It would seem we have made it to the Inilu Forest indeed. These plants are native, as are the giant trees. When Idalfyn was in its prime, the reign of land extended south to this

214

forest. My ancestors used wood from these trees to build their ships and extracted the material in these plants for a non-burning light source."

"Yeah, but what about that creature that nearly killed me?" Donny asked.

Tom growled at the mention of the creature.

Rustofo turned away from the plant he surveyed and toward Donny, who was still sitting on the stone tablet, running his fingers over his temples and grimacing.

"I was worried we'd see one."

"You knew about them and didn't warn us?" Riana asked, anger bubbling to the surface.

"I couldn't be sure of their existence. I only have stories of them, but based on what we saw today, I'm sure it was one of the fabled fierystwhiel."

"Bless you," Donny said.

"I didn't sneeze," Rustofo said.

"Could have fooled me."

"Fier- what?" Riana asked.

"Fierystwhiel," Rustofo said more slowly, sounding out each syllable. "No doubt, you have another name for them. They are creatures made of energy without the flesh and bone of creatures on Tyrinth. And they are ancient guardians of the ether. From the stories of my people, Magyses who traveled by portal had to be accompanied by a creature speaker, one who had the talent to speak with creatures. Even so, the guardians on occasion judged travelers as unworthy of passing through the ether. And, well, we saw what they do in response."

"Creature speakers?" Riana asked. She stepped closer to Rustofo, excitement trilling inside her. Maybe that's what she was. She could speak with creatures. Tom sauntered toward her and nudged her leg with his head.

"Yes," Rustofo said and nodded. "And I do believe you may have such a gift, Riana. Tell me, did you speak with the fierystwhiel?"

Riana shied away, wanting to keep the conversation she had with the creature secret from her companions. The fierystwhiel had said some things she was still sorting out. Like how it had sensed the blood of her enemy. And that the enemy was a pervert to the ether. She shivered.

"I did," Riana finally admitted.

"And what did it have to say?" Rustofo asked.

"Yeah. Why on Tyrinth did it attack me?" Donny asked.

Riana rubbed at a growing knot in her neck. "It seems there may be someone out there using the ether for perverse purposes. The fierystwhiel was on the defensive to protect its domain from that person and didn't realize we were someone else." Riana danced around the heart of the intention of the creature.

"So, who is this other person using the ether?" Rustofo wondered aloud.

"I'll give you three guesses," Donny said.

Riana thought she knew too, but what the fierystwhiel said... it couldn't be.

And yet...

"I'll bet a pound of gold that's how he zooms that eye of his place to place. How else does it find us in the middle of nowhere?" Donny noted.

"But, he can't use the portals," Riana argued. "Even if he could use them, the fierystwhiel would quickly end him."

"Well, maybe his majesty has some other means of getting into the ether to travel," Donny suggested. "It is magic. I can't imagine we know its every application."

"Oh," Rustofo said, his eyes wide in surprise. "You may have a point, young Mister Derringer."

"Since we've survived the journey, I say we move on," Riana said.

"But, the next part of the journey requires yet another leap through that damnable portal," Donny erupted. "And, uh, no thanks! I've nearly died enough for one day."

Riana didn't want to admit he was right. Turning around to leap through the portal once more, especially so soon after coming through safely, was probably inadvisable. She paced the grooved floor and thought, twisting a wisp of silver hair as she concentrated.

"Rustofo, it seems you know this area," Riana noted. "What's in this Inilu forest? If we traverse through here to the eastern edge of the city, will we be safe?"

Rustofo crossed his massive arms over his chest. His face frowned in concentration. "I was young when last I journeyed through the forest to the High King's keep. Then there was seldom danger, but we were guided by natives to the trees. Natives that have since been exterminated by the High King."

Riana wrapped her cloak around her, embracing herself in the warmth of its folds. The air was chilly inside the massive tree. "So, we really have no idea what dangers lie outside this portal."

"But we do know there's a giant space beast just waiting to blast us with weird red stuff," Donny pointed out. "Which, by the way, really hurts."

Riana huffed and pressed her fingertips into her eyebrows, bending her head and closing her eyes to the dilemma. "Rustofo, what should we do?" she asked.

"This is your call, Riana. If we go through the portal we risk being attacked by a very powerful fierystwhiel, whom may expect our return and seems set against our presence in the ether."

"Or we chance the unknown with little knowledge of what's outside the safety of this portal, and – let's not forget – delay our arrival to the castle. And have to formulate a new plan to get into the castle."

Donny raised his hand, as if he were in class and were seeking permission to speak.

"Yes, Donny," Riana said, voice dripping with irritation.

"Why don't we just take a peek outside, first? Just see what's out there. If there's no beasty waiting to kill us, then we can move forward," he said.

"This seems good," Rustofo said. "What say you, Riana?"

"I say, I hate delaying. Who knows what danger our friends are in."

Rustofo stumped over to Riana. He took her shoulders gently in his hands. "I want Kristopher back just as badly as you want your friends back. If we die in the process of trying to rescue them, we do them no good."

His hands trembled just the slightest. His eyes were glossy with tears, the gray irises vivid in the murky light.

"Very well," she said. "Let us go meet this new, strange forest."

CHAPTER THIRTY-SIX

"Great," Donny said, rubbing his hands together in anticipation. "How do we get out of here?"

Riana looked around. She hadn't planned on exiting the portal, so she hadn't looked for a door. The circular room, which was the inside of the tree, boasted nothing but a wall of bark. Riana walked along the perimeter, running her fingers carefully over the wall. She expected it to be fibrous, splintery; but, instead there were smooth with grooves matching the pattern of bark. She stopped and put both hands against the wall. "It's so solid, like stone. Is this a tree or a fashioning of one?"

Rustofo walked over to the wall and ran a hand over its surface, then nodded knowingly.

"What?" Riana asked.

"This is petrified wood," Rustofo said.

Donny wandered over and mimicked them, passing a hand over the wall and looking at the two of them with a questioning gaze. Tom sauntered up next to Donny and licked the wall. "What does that mean?" Donny asked.

"Turned to stone," Rustofo said.

"Why?" Donny asked.

"How?" Riana added. "It's a complete, upright tree." And then sudden realization dawned on her. She'd been thinking the tree was standing atop the ground. "We must be underground," she said.

"Maybe," Rustofo said. "And it could be this was petrified by the Inilu natives long gone now."

"Wait. But, how?" Riana asked.

Donny looked around and then wandered away from Riana and Rustofo.

"The Inilus were a tribe of people who had considerable elemental power. They used a magical process of petrification for trees as large as this one in order to use them as housing or gathering spaces. When Magyses lived, the Inilus had a seat among governing leaders. Naturally, they would have had a portal in their region to travel to meetings of the government. Or host them."

"I see," Riana said. "So, if the tree is above-ground, it seems the exit would be along the floor level here, but I'm not seeing one."

"Oh, hey, guys," Donny said.

Rustofo and Riana turned to follow his voice. Donny pulled a lever. Grinding gears squealed and dust exploded from a sudden crack in the wall. Tom jumped away from Donny, flipped around to face the new crack and hissed.

"How did you -," Riana started.

"Just a little investigative work," Donny said, crossing his arms and grinning in satisfaction.

Stairs formed, one after another in an ascending staircase on the outside perimeter of the tree. "Well, done, Mister Derringer," Rustofo said.

Donny swelled, then strutted to the opening. "I'll lead the way," he said. He jogged up the steps and out of sight.

"Donny," Riana said, a twinge of panic grabbing at her chest. She rushed to the stairs and up them. Her footsteps were softened by the complete enclosure of the petrified wood around her. Iridescent blue mushrooms bloomed along the walls she dashed past. She could hear Rustofo's grunts behind her and the clicking of Tom's nails against the petrified wood stairs. She climbed around a bend and saw light filtering down to her. "The exit must be ahead," she told Rustofo. "Donny?"

Donny didn't answer.

Riana rushed up the last several steps, her heart pounding from the exercise and worry.

She burst through an opening, ready to charge after Donny, wondering what danger he'd found. Her feet landed on air and she tripped forward. Below her the ground was obscured through a thick mass of giant branches. She screamed as she plummeted forward. Her momentum yanked to a halt, her cloak pulling at her shoulders. She wrapped her arms around herself to keep herself in the covering.

"Where ya goin'?" said an unfamiliar voice.

CHAPTER THIRTY-SEVEN

Donny pulled her left hand while the hand that had yanked at her cloak, saving her from a deathly fall, released its grip. She pressed her hands into Donny's muscular chest and fought to catch her breath. Donny did not seem to mind the touch. She leaned her head into his chest as the world swam around her.

"You're shaking like a leaf, ya are," said the unfamiliar voice again.

"Riana isn't much of a fan of heights," Donny said.

How did he know? Riana wondered but couldn't speak because she was too busy trying not to throw up. Or pass out. Or maybe both at once, she wasn't sure.

"Not a fan of heights?" the voice said.

Riana was dying to see this stranger. Donny's voice sounded on guard. Riana assumed it was because of who had just saved her skin.

"Yes, as in being up this high – or nearly plummeting to her death from this height – tends to scare her."

"Ooooohhhh," the stranger said. "You're ground-dwellin' folks, are ya? What'r'ya doin' up in this mighty tree then?"

"We could ask you the same thing," Donny said.

"Dear boy, nothin' in this forest happens without my knowin' of it. The forest is in me as much as I am in the forest."

Riana's curiosity finally overwhelmed her phobia. She slowly turned around, grasping onto petrified bark. Donny held her arm, wrapping her in a protective embrace. It didn't feel bad, but it wasn't the look she was going for. She gently removed his arm.

She stood as tall as her twisted guts would allow and pulled her hand from the tree. The world tipped slightly, but she stayed upright.

Rustofo, wiser than Riana, stuck his head out of the entrance looking first to his left at Donny and Riana. When he saw them looking around him, he turned his head to the right.

"Greetings, friend," he began. "I am King Svelt Rustofo of Idalfyn, third king since the dark age. Whom do I have the pleasure of meeting, small friend?"

Riana wished he would move so she could get a good look at this new fellow. She leaned uncomfortably toward the platform's railing and peered at him.

"You are well met," began the stranger.

Tom poked his head out of the entrance next to Rustofo, spotted Riana and chirped, as if to ask if she was okay. Riana nodded, but then turned her attention back to the being who'd saved her from certain death.

Riana marveled at his tiny frame. He was about half her height with mossy green skin. Atop his head he wore what Riana could swear was an overly large mushroom, dusted with forest dirt. He bowed, flourishing his arm grandly, pointing his left toe forward and doubling himself over it.

His apparel was as if finery had been sewn of thick leaves. Riana could make out leaf veins in the leathery brown material. As he bent his head low, Riana could make out vines flowing from a back seam that stretched across his shoulder blades. His shirt was a white, fluffy material and he wore stockings the same white that ended in short pants rendered from the same material as his jacket. His shoes were black and shiny, like the backs of beetles. From fingers like twigs sprouted green leaves.

When the Inilu native rose again, it was his eyes that captured Riana the most. They were the richest, warmest cocoa brown. They were soft around the edges with laughter lines. The large nose in the center of his face, however, could not obscure the kindly smile that crinkled his eyes.

224

"I am Effan-ilu, last surviving King of the Inilu, since the beginning of the dark age," he said, his words laced with old sorrow. He pronounced his name ay-fawn-eel-oow, with an emphasis on the fawn and the oow.

Riana practiced it in her head until she realized she would most certainly be addressing him as His Highness and chided herself for thinking otherwise. And yet, she was also dying to sketch this strange person.

"I knew your father's grandfather well, young one," King Effan told Rustofo and Riana boggled at the words.

Rustofo bowed his head and put a fist to his heart.

"So," Donny interrupted the two kings' introductions to each other. "That means you're like five-hundred years old?"

King Effan bowed his head to Donny. "I am, in fact, much older than that, youngling. A fact you'll want to remember in my presence." He didn't force his words to sound overly authoritative and as kindly as he said it, they seemed all the more powerful.

"Oh," Donny said, and that was that out of him.

King Effan regarded Riana. Riana felt as though his chocolate gaze stripped her bare, bore all her vulnerabilities and weaknesses. She was naked under his scrutiny, and she waited for his judgment. The thoughts of the fierystwhiel echoed through her. Was she something horrible or wonderful? She hardly knew.

"You, my dear, and your companions shall come with me," the Inilu said. He did not smile. Riana's chest twinged with a pang of rejection.

They descended steadily down and around the giant petrified tree. Riana took in the forest from every angle multiple times, until she felt she had strong visual footing for what lay around the portal. She was never happier than when her boots touched solid ground. Or solid-ish. It was soaked and muddy and they sloshed between the pillars of gargantuan trees with difficulty, none more than Rustofo who cursed in a low voice as he unstuck himself over and over again.

Sunlight was scarce along the forest floor, filtered by layers of emerald tree roofing. Where spears of light reached the forest floor, small circles of vegetation sprang to life. Here a pool of white flowers, there a copse of tall mushrooms, over there a patch of clover. There was never a lack of things to feast their eyes on as they traversed the Inilu to the throne of its King.

And after they had hiked for long enough that Riana's calves ached from pulling her feet from the mud, she began to catch glimpses of other inhabitants. The ghost of a silver face with wide ice blue eyes peeking around a tree trunk. A collection of tiny beings on a log who disappeared as soon as she focused on them. Above her in the canopy, twisting creatures of brightly colored feathers who peered down behind the concealment of giant leaves.

Riana wondered if the others saw them. Or if she was alone in her delight.

Hello, she thought to the creatures. It's very nice to meet you.

She grinned as she walked along, catching a glimpse of a shy, winged creature very much resembling the fire nymphs she'd left in Landsend.

She turned to catch another look and tumbled over something in her path. She pulled herself upright and found the obstacle to be Effan-ilu.

"My apologies, your Highness! I wasn't paying attention."

"On the contrary, my dear," the King said. "You seem to be paying great attention." He smiled up at her from over a staff he clutched between his two gnarled and tree-like hands.

Riana stepped away from him, not sure what to make of this small man creature of the giant forest.

Before she could form a question, the King whistled a sweet, trilling tune that tripped over several octaves before fluttering to a soft stop. Riana instinctively looked to her right, holding out an arm for the oncoming flock of nymphs.

They cheered in their sing-song voices and launched themselves onto Riana's arm. A contagious laughter filled the air. Riana was the first to break and giggle. Then Donny and Rustofo. Tom sniffed at the flying creatures, sneezed and sat down, as if waiting for these new shenanigans to end.

Effan-ilu was the final to burst open in laughter, and when he did it was big and bold, much larger than his size and much merrier than even his eyes and smile. The infectious laughter built as the nymphs danced and laughed around Riana, swinging from her silver hair and lighting the sunset evening with a rainbow of luminescence.

When they had laughed until their bellies were sore from the effort, Riana turned to Effan-ilu. "What sort of nymphs are these?" she asked. She watched them as she walked along under the hulking canopy of darkened trees and in the cover of night, their way lit by the cheerful and mischievous nymphs.

"Can you not tell, my child?" he said, turning his chocolate gaze up to her and smiling patiently.

Riana watched them twist and dance, light and fly, laugh and twirl. "It's like they're happiness encapsulated in a creature," she said. "Like pure joy."

"Yes, so you know what they are," Effan-ilu said.

"Wait, I don't understand. What are they called? What element are they associated with?" Riana asked.

"My dear," Effan-ilu said, stopping in his tracks and turning a very sad gaze up to her. "Do you not understand all the elements? Can you not tell which element is associated with their behavior?"

Riana had been thinking of fire, Tyrinth, water and air. As the King of the Inilu forest spoke, though, she realized she had been missing two other elements. She turned away from him and watched the nymphs once more. Pure joy. That could only be one element, couldn't it?

"Light," she finally said. "They're Light creatures."

"There you have it," Effan-ilu said. "Well done, my dear."

"It's just that I haven't encountered any Light creatures yet. I'm so used to thinking of the Tyrmini elements I forget about the other two."

"The other two?" Effan-ilu asked, distracted by the antics of a particularly energetic nymph cartwheeling through the air and shifting through every color of the rainbow.

"Well, yes," she said, befuddled by his question. "Are there not six elements?"

"Five, child. Five," he submitted, rather sternly, Riana thought.

"What do you mean?" she asked, finally stopping dead in her tracks as she asked this ancient about the meaning of the fundamentals of the universe, as she knew it, as it had been explained to her by Magloryn.

He turned and placed his hands atop the staff he held. "Water, Air, Tyrinth, Fire and Light." He counted. "What other element do you think is missing."

"Well, Shadow, obviously," she said, puzzled.

The nymphs continued to dance and twirl, gliding through the evening air without a care. The King of the giant forest, however, was a solid wall of disappointed rejection.

"Shadow," he hissed. "You dare speak of it in my land."

"I don't understand," Riana started, "is Shadow not that which we all come from?"

"We come from the Light. Perhaps there are some creatures who are born of shadow but that is not Effan-ilu, nor the Light nymphs, nor any who are worthy of life. So, that is what I sense in you. That is what taints you. You are of the shadow." He pointed his staff at her with final judgment, as if catching her in a trap he'd laid a century ago, and was finally, at last, able to spring it.

"We are all of shadow and light," Riana said. Her guts had turned to solid stone.

"You speak of shadow as though it is something worthy and beautiful. There is one other who speaks this way, and he has been banished from this forest since he slaughtered my people five hundred years ago." His voice boomed through the forest. The trees quaked around them, groaning as if waking from a deep slumber.

The light nymphs scattered into the growing darkness.

"And none shall trespass here again and taint my home with darkness." Effan-ilu drove his staff into the ground in front of him. His eyes shifted from beautiful chocolate brown to muddy yellow and then to neon green. An outline of the same neon green formed around his person, casting the forest around them in eerie light. A deep murmur echoed through the Tyrinth, as if something were rending itself free from the depths of the ground beneath them.

And it wasn't happy about it.

"I call on the ancient, the unforgiving, the powerful. I call on the forest incarnate. I call on the Inilu!" A scraping metallic sound scratched across the evening sky.

Tom hissed at the ground around him, clicking his tails together to set himself alight with fire. Rustofo was wide-eyed as he held onto a nearby tree for support. The ground bucked beneath them. Riana stumbled, but maintained her feet. Donny fell hard on his knees. He rolled to his side and pulled himself up with the help of a nearby vine.

"Riana!" Donny shouted. "What's an Inilu?"

"Beats me!" she shouted over the cacophony. "I thought it was a forest! Rustofo?"

"I thought it was a people!" he answered. He crawled over the rolling ground toward Riana.

Tom seemed to be the only one who looked at ease with the entire Tyrinth wildly thrashing. He took off at a run toward the green-eyed forest king. The king swept a gnarled hand in his direction and a wall of trees sprang from the ground, twisting and bending as they grew to Riana's height in a breath and to Rustofo's height in the next. Tom was undeterred. He launched himself with the next quake and flew over the tree wall, his body a stream of fire.

Effan-ilu's face went slack for a moment before turning steely in determination. He swept his arms around himself in a dance-like gesture. As he did so, a circle tore up the soil around the King. He positioned his body squarely facing Tom and thrust his hands toward Riana's companion creature. Snake-like roots shot out of the ground, spraying the King in dark soil and moss. The roots seemed alive as they snaked through the clearing and aimed themselves at Tom.

Tom hissed and dodged the first root, then clamped him mouth around the second. A squeal of pain ratcheted out of the root and a nearby tree shivered. The root yanked away from Tom and retreated underground.

Effan-ilu barked in surprise. "What sort of creature are you?" he asked.

Riana spread her stance and rolled with the waves of shaking ground.

"Riana, do the thing!" Donny said, still clinging to the ground, his head smacking into the Tyrinth as it bucked beneath him. "With the light, Riana. Do the thing with the light!"

She summoned the light within her in a moment, feeling its coursing power slide through her being like rivers of silver and ice. She held her hands at her side and gathered the power there. She meant to fling it at Effan-ilu, but before she could focus her intention, the ground between herself and the king and Tom began to boil. The dirt bubbled as it formed a mound. Ear-piercing cries shredded the forest air. The mound grew higher, the smell of turned soil and moss filled Riana's nose.

She took a step back. The ground stilled. Donny and Rustofo flanked Riana, both breathing heavily. Across from them, across from the mound of Tyrinth, the roots had retreated and Effan-ilu was staring in rapt adoration at the mound. Tom was all hackles and flames, growling at the turned soil.

Overhead the last of the day's light faded away, pitching the forest to a deeper shade of evening. Riana could still make out the general shapes of things, but the details were lost to shadow.

"Now you'll know why the High King dares not set a foot in the Inilu Forest," Effan-ilu said.

"Please," Riana said. "I am not like the High King. I wield no power for the purpose of harming others."

"You may not mean it, but eventually Shadow will take you over. Even the High King himself believes emphatically that his tactics are for the good."

"You're not listening. I don't wield Shadow; I just believe it is one of the elements."

"And if you've tapped into that knowledge, you're open to its influence."

"That doesn't make any sense. Because I don't know a thing means I'm insusceptible to it as an influence?"

"You cannot tell me all your deeds have been pure and of the light," Effan-ilu said. "I can see the stain on you. I can see your heart hides a truth of shame."

"Everybody does things wrong from time to time," Rustofo noted. "I'd even wager you have. From one monarch to another, under the treaties that make us allies, I implore you to call off the beast who you mean to harm us. We pass in peace through your kingdom."

"It is too late," Effan-ilu said, his face a lined mask of defiance.

The ground vibrated at first, then shook wildly. Riana had only one thought, one hope for the safety of herself and her companions.

"Run!" she shouted. "Tom, come!"

Tom ran toward her, then bound over the mound just as its top erupted. Riana was frozen for a moment, showered in mud and forest debris. The creature clawed its massive body out of the ground with paws as big as shovels and claws just as long.

"Holy -," Donny said.

They craned their necks as the beast towered above them. Riana had never seen such a creature. Its eyes glowed the same eerie green as Effan-ilu. Its massive body was covered in long hair that was coated in lichen. Its face was lined in stripes the same glowing hue as its eyes, its nose tipped in a collection of strange appendages which shifted and twitched as if they each had their own mind.

The creature tipped its head back and howled. Spittle flew from its mouth, which was lined in pointy teeth. Riana buckled, falling to her knees as she clapped her hands over her ears. Rustofo grabbed her and hauled her to her feet. He twirled her around. Donny was ahead of them, running into the forest. Riana found her legs and pumped them hard. Rustofo kept pace with her. Tom exploded past them. Behind them, the ground shook with the pounding of the Inilu's steps.

The chase was on. Riana let out a scream as she pushed her muscles to drive her ahead. Muddy Tyrinth sucked at her boots as if grasping on to slow her down. She chanced a glance behind her to find the creature, eyes a weird neon green, closing the gap between them. Her nerves were alight and painted the dark forest in a tunnel. How they would get through the mud and muck, Riana didn't know. And then an idea occurred to her.

"Tom, can you make the ground ahead of us hard?" she asked.

Tom dipped his head and ran ahead of them until he passed Donny, who was already slowed with heavy, muddy steps. Riana kept running, pulling her feet out of the muck as quickly as she could. Eventually, her feet landed on more solid footing and she whooped in victory. Their pace sped as they traversed the sturdier ground Tom made for them.

Donny slowed enough to run next to Riana. "Where are we going?"

"We don't have a choice. We have to jump the portal again," Riana said.

Donny made a noise of exasperation, but if he was about to say something, the words were lost in a sudden booming explosion. Donny yelped, threw up his hands, but was thrown sideways into Riana. They hurtled through the air before crashing into a nearby tree.

Pain seared Riana's head and her eyes stung. She swiped at her brow and found her hand soaked in blood.

"What was that?" Donny asked, looking out into the forest. The Inilu was nowhere to be seen. Further up the path, Rustofo and Tom turned and ran toward Donny and Riana.

"What hit you?" Rustofo asked.

"Where's the Inilu?" Donny countered.

Riana's head spun and ached. She pulled a handkerchief from her pocket and pressed it to the cut on her forehead, trying to staunch the bleeding.

"Let's go," Rustofo said, not waiting for them to answer.

Riana pushed herself away from the tree, took two steps and fell hard onto her knees.

Rustofo bent down, scooped her up into his arms and began to run. Riana was jostled in the worst way. She fought against the urge to vomit and won, but just barely.

Tom ran slightly ahead of them. Riana was astounded by the beautiful way his steps left a shimmering golden glow in the ground. She was lost in the paw prints until the Inilu sprang from behind a tree and tackled Tom off the path of his making. Tom yowled, hissed then growled.

The Inilu, lit from nose to hind legs with lines of glowing green, swiped at Tom, Tom evaded, dealing his own blow. In an instant he was alight with fire, but at the touch of the flames, the Inilu extinguished them. Tom's fire went out as he circled the massive, mossy forest creature. The Inilu reared up, displaying giant feet like trunks of trees and smashed them into the ground.

Tyrinth quaked. Donny lost his footing and fell while Rustofo braced himself and Riana until the shuddering had stopped. Riana couldn't hold back. She bent her head as far as she could and vomited from her perch in Rustofo's arms.

Rustofo spoke some guttural word Riana was sure was a curse, and she didn't blame him. She was pretty sure she'd just splashed the giant's shins and feet in a spray of partially digested lunch.

" – so sorry –," she managed. Her head was spinning and aching. She tried to make out what was going on with the creatures, but the world shifted, and she couldn't grasp hold of the reality and make it sit still long enough to decide what it meant. It was all flashes of neon green, and sparks of electric blue, then blazes of fire.

The pain in Riana's head climbed a steady crescendo. Her world jounced and shook. She tried to call out to make the world stop what it was doing, but all that came out was jostled grunt. An explosion of pain splintered her eyesight.

Overhead a wild cackle ratcheted through the sky. Riana opened one eye to see the shadow-wrapped form of the dragon's eye floating above them.

Stars exploded in her vision. She gave one final gasp as the maniacal laughter echoed around them, and then the world vanished.

CHAPTER THIRTY-EIGHT

Elynda sat on the edge of the soft bed and chewed on warm bread. At any other time in her life she would have savored the bite. Bread was one of her favorite foods. She took a bite of cheese and stuffed a few grapes in her mouth as well, hoping their juices would help to moisten her dry mouth.

The butter for the bread was delicious. Everything was of the highest quality. She'd been allowed a bath, been given new clothes that fit her perfectly, a homey room and fed three times a day. She looked out the window set in the wooden walls. The gardens below were green and lush, providing a beautiful view for her.

She'd even slept well last night. She woke in an excellent mood until she remembered her friends were sitting in a dungeon on cold stone floors after being beaten and starved. The bread in her mouth tasted dry, the grapes flat, the cheese waxy. She swigged a large gulp of water and let it wash down the remnants of her meal. At least she would be strong enough to help her friends as soon as they were able to make their escape.

She prayed Riana was on her way, but even if she was it was too late for today's scheduled healing.

Elynda stood from the bed, smoothing the white down blankets where she'd sat. She paced the length of the room, her boots making soft clacks against the wooden floor. She had been practicing scaling back the amount of power being transferred from herself to another. It was difficult, though, without someone to practice on. Still, she'd felt the quality of the emanation was less. She hoped it was enough.

A knock at the door roused her from her reflection. She waited without answering. The door swung open and a ravishing beauty marched inside. Without a word, she grasped Elynda's arm and pulled her out of the haven of the bedchamber.

Captain Luther waited in the hall and when he saw Elynda he nodded. "I trust you are indeed ready?"

Elynda, desperate to be anything but ready, nodded.

They marched down corridors with wooden walls and floors, then turned down brick-laid floors with white-washed stone, then entered the very heart of the castle, which was comprised of slats of flat gray stone. There were no windows in this part of the castle and the only light came from the hissing oil lamps burning, filling the air with an acrid aroma.

At last they stood in front of the large wooden door with wrought-iron hinges. Elynda's heart sped in sudden panic. A healthy High King. What would he do with his returned stamina and strength? She hoped she could withhold the power, lessen its efficacy somehow. But she still wasn't entirely sure how it worked and if she'd be able to rein it in. She cast a prayer into the universe, to the Great Mother and Father, before she was hustled through the widening door.

CHAPTER THIRTY-NINE

Riana was consumed with fascination of her own death. She'd always wondered what it would be like after she died. If a piece of her would go on, if she would have an identity and if that identity would sync up with the one she'd worn on Tyrinth. She floated in the ether, stunned to finally have her curiosity sated.

This must be the afterlife, she thought.

Somewhere in her head, Tom mewled.

She looked around. *No! Did Tom die too? I'll never forgive myself.*

She must be in heaven, and Tom must have taken his spiritual form here in the ether, because he was resplendent. A word she could never ascribe to anything she'd ever seen in her life.

Tom? Are we dead together? You look so beautiful! What happened to you?

I am not dead, Companion. I am just as alive as you.

You're mistaken, Tomas. I've died. I think I hit my head too hard on that tree. So, either I'm a ghost talking to you in this strange place, or we're both dead. Riana was surprised she felt no sadness at the discovery of her own death.

Tom walked toward her on a path of nothing, yet every step he took left a deep golden impression that reverberated out like ripples in a pond after a pebble is thrown. His scales had grown to be not just the mohawk Riana was so used to seeing, but to a flowing metallic mane of glittering strands. His fur, which had once been golden yellow striped with his unusual scales, had turned a shimmering black that sparkled with its own lights in colors of green, blue, magenta, crimson, gold and white.

He stood in front of Riana – at least in front of her awareness. She had no sense of a body in this place.

We must find our pack. You must call to them.

Why can't you call for them? I don't know their names.

You do know their names. They've come with you on this journey to save your friends. Do you remember?

No, Riana said, and she got the feeling she didn't want to remember anything any longer. That remembering was much more painful than floating in this never.

Tom lowered his head and leveled her with his sapphire eyes. His long mane of scale-like hair shifted forward. Riana leaned toward him, drawn to him, comforted by his presence. She reached for him. Her hand appeared and touched the soft white fur along his neck and cheek. A low purr reverberated through Tom and through her with their shared touch.

In the distance a pink cloud floated in the starfield.

What is that, Tom? Riana asked her companion.

It is where we must go.

Why? She asked.

It will all make sense soon, Riana. Come with me. All will be well.

Riana held on to Tom's soft fur and smooth scales as they walked through the empty darkness sparked with dying suns and radiant stars. Comets zipped around them and over their left shoulders a meteor shower stormed over an icy planet too far from its sun for anyone but Tom and Riana to notice.

She turned her attention to their destination. *What's in the pink cloud, Tom?*

Tom hung his head a little and for the first time since she'd met him here, she thought he looked very tired, and maybe even a little sad.

What's wrong, Tomas?

He turned soft blue eyes to her. She looked deeply into them as though she fell down a well. The free fall took her breath away. Tom's eyes reflected everything that had transpired since she'd passed out from a head wound. It was as though she could watch the events play picture after picture in his eyes.

Tears welled and spilled and repeated over again. She shook her head in denial. *No,* she said. *No, I won't believe it.*

Tom turned away, hastily stowing the pictures back into his mind. *Come. We must hurry.*

Riana gripped his fur more tightly. Tom bunched his muscles and launched them through space. The pink cloud sparked with lightning. Thunder rattled the universe.

It had seemed like such a small thing when they'd been so far away. Now that they were entering it, the storm was massive. It towered over them and below them as they floated.

Riana pulled at Tom. *We'll really be killed if we go in there,* she said.

But your companions will most certainly die if we do not. Which do you choose?

Riana's breath caught somewhere in moving lungs that seemed disconnected to this awareness floating through the universe. She cast about within herself, looking for the answer, looking, it seemed, for the essence of herself that would reveal what she thought was right or true – if right and true were even things she believed in.

Something squirmed inside her, first in her center and then in her heart. Heat steadily built until she was overwhelmed by this new feeling. She grasped for the word, knowing it was there somewhere in her mind.

Urgency swooped in where complacency had lived moments before, accompanied by the new feeling for which she searched for a name, a label, a word.

And then it came to her.

She inhaled sharply, air catching in lazy lungs. Tears stung her eyes with sudden ferocity. Her friends were in danger. And that elusive, demanding feeling burning her chest and squeezing her guts: that was love.

Heart speeding, she turned to Tom. *I choose love*, she told him.

He smiled and nodded, then crouched low and faced the waiting storm. *I was hoping you'd say that.* His three tails thrashed wildly behind him, sparking together and lighting his scales on fire.

Tears streaming down her face, Riana gathered this new emotion in her mental hands and pulled it tightly into herself. White light expanded from them, overtaking the darkness of nothing with powerful brightness. Riana looked at her hands, the details of which were lost in the brightness of the power surrounding her, filling her, making her alive and electric with purpose and will.

Who am I? she wondered. The power that answered back was insistent, loud, sure.

I am love.

Energy shot through her, from above her head – which she could somehow feel – to past her toes. She faced the pink cloud ahead, the lightning cracking open chinks in the clouds to reveal a world inside.

Riana watched as the clouds lit over and over again, wondering how they would enter without receiving such a shocking blow as to kill them instantly.

I have an idea, Tom, she told her companion. She realized she was still touching her creature friend, even while he was on fire. Somehow one piece of her awareness was stunned she was not hurt by the flames while another piece of her was apathetic about this fact of her ability to endure the application of elements.

Please tell me how I may help, Tom said.

You are a creature of all the elements, are you not?

I am. I am made by all the dragons of creation. Each has bestowed upon me the gifts of their elements.

Which element is lightning?

Fire. And of course light and shadow. As all things are.

Tom's statement brought a flood of memories to Riana's awareness, including the struggle with the king of the Inilu Forest. And the Inilu creature. The conversation of the nature of shadow is what had sparked the conflict with Effan-ilu. She remembered nothing after passing out. She had no idea why they were where they were, and she didn't have time to consider. The most important thing had already been relayed to her: her friends were in danger, and she needed to act swiftly if there was any hope of saving them.

Yes, she answered, willing to sort through the memories later when her friends were safe. *Are you able to manipulate elements outside of yourself?* She knew the answer as she asked the question; she'd seen him do it.

I am, but I am young. I can only harness so much now, though I know in the future I will be better. Does this disappoint you?

Riana caressed his face with a radiant hand. A purr of contentment echoed away from him. *Of course not. You are not my servant; you are my friend. Can you deflect the strike of just one of those lightning blasts?*

I'm not sure. Tom hung his head.

What if I help? She asked.

Tom looked up at her with his sapphire eyes, puzzled. *How?*

Well, look, Riana said. She reached toward the pink storm clouds and watched as the intensity in the local area she aimed her hand at lessened. *I believe my power is in my intention. I mean for that storm to allow us to pass, but like you, Tom, I'm young in my power. But, maybe, together, we can pass through.*

I am willing to try, Tom said.

The sharp sting of worry punctured Riana's momentary hope. So many lives were depending on this one moment. Rustofo and Donny were somewhere in that pink storm and would die in the limitless universe if she did nothing.

She steeled herself and approached the storm. She lifted a hand, but that really wasn't what gave her power. It was more to focus what she wanted. She wanted to get to her friends. She wanted to keep them safe. She wanted Elynda safe. She wanted to get to Elynda with her friends.

She wanted to go with her friends to get to Elynda. That deep desire resonated through her entire being, even a piece of herself she never knew existed. A deeper, older self she could just barely sense. A girl who had yet to become a woman, but had been a woman, grown and strong and confident in some other time and place.

She drew on that essence of self and pressed her light-filled fingers through the misty wisps of pink clouds drawing them in to their destruction. Beside her, Tom bowed his head, but it was not a gesture of submission. While his head was bent, his eyes were trained on the lightning that built in a bubbling blue orb at the base of the storm. His mouth stretched back to reveal canines that shone in the electric blue light of lightning and the whiter light of Riana's intention.

His long strands of scale-like hair floated around his head, interspersed with dancing flames of red and orange fire. He growled, the muscles of his jaws bunching with the effort. He stepped forward with Riana, his strong spirit illuminated and etched in the same shape of his feline and muscular body.

They reached forward together meaning to walk through the cloud and arrive to the rescue of their friends. A thunderous crack resounded around them, the flash of lightning consumed their vision and as they stepped into the storm, lightning slashed through the cloud formation, colliding into the two companions.

Riana hurtled away from the barrier. Tom was blasted in a separate direction. Pain splintered through Riana's entire being and the light of her intention extinguished. The pain brought on an overwhelming anger that sat in the pit of her stomach and burned.

She was a failure.

She tasted the words in her mind and swallowed them down her throat. With every moment that passed her friends' lives grew ever more tentative – and it was her fault. She'd dragged them along, pressed them into dangerous situations, and when the very worst encounter had been upon them, she'd injured herself, making herself a burden for them to carry.

She had failed to protect her grandmother.

Failed to protect her best friend.

Failed to protect Ribbit.

Failed to protect Kristopher.

And now the last hope she had of redeeming herself and protecting her friends lie on the other side of a space storm and she was helpless to get through it.

Riana clenched her fists, ground her teeth and sobbed at her sad state of ineffectuality. She raised her hands in front of her face and shouted into the eternity. It wasn't fair. It wasn't right. All she wanted to do was the right thing, yet she floundered to make it happen. That was not the way life was supposed to work. One who had a good heart and worked hard was supposed to accomplish what they'd set their mind to. Yet here she was on this side of the storm, and her friends sat on the other side. She slumped to her knees and let her hands fall on her thighs.

There is another way, a voice said.

Riana wrenched her gaze from her hands. In the distance, just around the bend in the massive storm, was the fierystwhiel. She stood; a function that felt odd where there was no ground.

The fierystwhiel stayed in one place, unmoving.

Riana recoiled, uncertain if the creature meant to attack or not.

I do not mean you any negativity. I am sorry for my previous behavior.

What did you mean about my blood? Riana asked. She wished Sela had told her her father's identity. It seemed she knew but had changed her mind about revealing it. She was sure her own identity would be much more understandable had she known who her parents were. And there were all these hints and hurts about who her father was – which she had nothing to do with. Why was it her fault her father was... whomever he was.

I sense in you the blood of my enemy, but I also sense in you the energy of our Mother.

Riana froze. The blood of her enemy hunted and killed magyses. Tingles ran down her spine. *The blood of your enemy is in my veins?* She whispered, not wanting to hear the truth, not wanting to know that the blood the fierystwhiel spoke of was the blood of her father and that blood belonged to the one on Tyrinth who had committed a five-century long genocide on those who possessed elemental and etheric magical ability. It was the only answer that made sense.

But stronger than that is the energy of Magloryn I sense in you. I missed it first. Then you used the Light. I've never seen another being use such a pure and solitary power as the Light. Yet, you have capacity for Shadow as well. First and foremost, though, you are a Creature Speaker.

Riana felt a warm sense of belonging in the title. She relished the pronunciation it. It felt right and it settled into her heart and mind and filled her with brimming joy. All this time since her grandmother's death, she'd felt the overwhelming need to fulfill the role of vineyard and winery owner. That wasn't what she'd been born to do. All this time she'd been fighting for a title that wasn't integral to who she was as a person.

She was a Creature Speaker.

You're more than that, you are a Dragon Speaker. And never before in the history of humankind has there been a Dragon Speaker for Magloryn. It seems now she needs one. And you are it.

I am she, Riana said, a certain weight in the statement that seemed to come from somewhere deeply inside herself. She drew herself up on a mental and emotional level, taking confidence in that she was tied to and a piece of Magloryn. That in some ways she was Magloryn, though she didn't know how that made logical sense.

We are running out of time, Tom said. He'd returned to her. He stood next to her in all his full-grown glory. His long, scale-like mane floated around him without the effect of gravity, his blue eyes crystalline in the blackness of nothing.

What other way do you have for us to enter and save our friends? Riana asked.

You must trust me, the fierystwhiel said.

Riana stared. *What do you mean?*

I have offended the Light, for which I am truly sorry. Now, the Light needs me so that you may enter the storm and save your friends. The friends who will assist you in freeing the Tyrinth from the rule of the one who murders magic. So, you must set aside your distrust because of how I acted previously.

I must forgive you, Riana said, with a certain clear-headed judgment that felt both compassionate and harsh all at once.

The fierystwhiel bowed its ginormous head, its electric colors vibrating and shifting. *Yes. Please forgive me.*

Riana considered. This creature was old. It wasn't like the fire nymphs and antoli she'd made friends with in Landsend. This creature perhaps surpassed the age of the High King – her father. And the fierystwhiel was asking her for forgiveness. As if she had any right to give it. Yet, she somehow felt she did have a right. There was something unique about what she had to do in this lifetime, and it required the cooperation of the creatures she was directly supporting on some energetic level she didn't quite understand.

I forgive you, Riana said. Shame coated one side of her, while soft loving kindness reached out of her to the fierystwhiel and wrapped it up in love.

Let us move swiftly then, said Tom.

How do you plan on helping us? Riana asked.

The fierystwhiel lifted its head, turned one eye toward Riana and said, *Tell me where you wish to go.*

CHAPTER FORTY

Riana felt through the massive storm, through the flashes of lightning and crashes of thunder, and on to her friends whose lives and existence hung in the balance.

Where did she want to go? The question was so big and had so many answers she had a hard time figuring where to start.

She wanted to be wherever she could be to help Elynda. But she also wanted to help Rustofo and Donny. Her intentions ratcheted around, unable to focus on what to do in which order.

You must clear your mind and be careful and full of intention for me to get you where you want to go. To get where you want to go you must understand what you want.

Panic snaked up from her stomach and encircled her throat, squeezing out her ability to breathe.

Tom leaned against her. At first this felt like an unnecessary pressure on her leg and hip. Soon, Tom began a deep and insistent purr that drown out the rising panic. She closed her eyes, breathed deeply, and listened to the rhythm. The rattle of contentment came in the ebb and flow of inhale and exhale. She followed the breath and buzz and relaxed into the consistency.

In her mind's eye a potential timeline stretched out in front of her. First: collect Rustofo and Donny. Second: retrieve Elynda, Ribbit and Kristopher. Third: find a place of absolute safety for them all to continue saving other Magys-kind.

Once she had the feel of the potential, she repeated it in her mind: save Rustofo and Donny, save Elynda, find a safe place.

Riana's front side of her body tingled. She opened her eyes to the new sensation and found herself face to face with the fierystwhiel. She stretched her hand out and placed it on the creature's nose while she maintained contact with Tom.

As she touched the fierystwhiel, she was consumed by the same sensation when using the portal. The three of them were pulled into the pink clouds and yanked sideways. Riana couldn't be sure she'd even moved; it felt as though the universe had moved around her rather than they who were moving through the universe.

Lightning crackled below them, blue sparks skipping through layers of fog. The lightning piggy-backed over itself, climbing ever closer to Riana and her two creature companions. Thunder shook her insides. Riana let out a warning scream, but as the lightning skipped to just under her feet the fierystwhiel shifted and they were in the eye of the storm. The universe around them erupted in pale blue light.

Riana released her hand from the fierystwhiel and looked around her, searching for her companions. Donny and Rustofo were both limp, their bodies strewn across an invisible plane. Riana rushed to them, followed closely by the fierystwhiel and Tom. She grabbed Rustofo's hand in her left and Donny's in her right. Tom pressed his body against Riana's leg and wrapped his tails around her calf.

The fierystwhiel touched Riana's back with its nose.

Riana was tempted to close her eyes at the sensation of squeezing darkness and the vertigo of traveling through the ether.

She resisted. *Eyes wide open*, she told herself.

CHAPTER FORTY-ONE

Elynda approached the High King, working to keep her face from wrinkling at the stench of his decaying body. She'd never smelled such a foul odor on a living body. It was almost as if the body was dead and still animated.

She'd been thinking about the last time she'd been here. How the shadow had touched her mind. How Magloryn had conversed with the entity through Elynda. Perhaps that was the wisdom to follow. What had Magloryn done to make the Shadow retreat from them?

Her hands tingled as she stepped toward him, their intuitive knowing and automatic intention unaware that the healing they wanted so desperately to provide would revive and reinvigorate a man that could end her for the very thing that would save him.

Magloryn had not attacked, as one would believe should be the best course of action. She'd said things about Shadow that Elynda would never have considered. She'd always thought of darkness as evil, negative. In the darkness, people stumbled and fell. In the darkness, men and women were known to do hateful things. In the darkness, secrets were concealed.

In the darkness is where truth is revealed. Magloryn's voice spoke into her mind.

We do not conquer, you and me. We are not overthrowers. Our power does not elevate us over others. This power is nothing but love. And love is always the answer.

Elynda shook at this unanticipated answer. What would her fate be once she'd healed the High King? If she gave into the deep need gnawing at her insides to heal, wouldn't the king be in greater power to continue his own conquering conquest?

Listen well, child of light. It is no mistake you are here now, in this place, with this person. The Shadow within the man is distorted. We were never strangers before this man took Shadow into his being. But now, Shadow sneers, hates, and belches anger. Shadow is now addicted to it and chooses not to heal itself. Heal the man and the wounded Shadow will continue to rot him from the inside out. Trust your power. Trust Love.

She didn't know if she trusted the voice, but she had seen herself what Magloryn meant about the power of the Shadow lurking within the High King. She looked at his majesty and assessed what she wanted the outcome to be. She was so good at healing the corporeal body. With any patient, she could root out the cause of their symptoms and then focused on eliminating that cause. This meant the patient was often not comfortable during the process of healing, but they did heal. There were tinctures for the pain. Let the pain be handled by mundane means while the healing she worked was so much more inexplicable than the effect of certain flower essences on the nervous system.

The High King turned to her, his face slack, his mouth gaping, lungs working hard to draw in breath. His eyes were glossy and blood shot and his skin was waxy.

Elynda knew what she had to do. She grimaced.

Captain Luther prodded her with a sheathed knife. "Go on, now. You don't want yer friends gettin' more beaten than they already are."

Elynda tripped forward, falling to her knees at the side of the bed. She reached out to catch herself, but her hands found the arm of the High King like magnets drawn together. Her head yanked back; mouth wrenched wide open in a silent scream. Tingles started at her crown and coursed through her head, throat, chest and arms. The energy blasted through her.

The compulsion was overwhelming. Elynda was meant to trust in it. As if the power had a mind of its own, it sped through her body and into the High King, delivering powerful doses of healing energy.

All without the tamping effects of pain killer elixirs.

The king's body went rigid, stretching out like a stiff board. The muscles under Elynda's hands tensed and pulled, hardening to strands of solid steel-like muscle. Elynda could feel the fibers expanding, as if laying down new tissues. She'd never felt anything more extreme and as much as she wanted to slow the process, she felt enslaved to the healing. She was its servant.

Elynda was filled with light and love. She hated herself for it but loved the moment so much, the sensation of joy and purity. She cast aside any intentions and allowed the energy to consume her.

After a moment being caught up in the healing energy, a slow whistle escaped the High King's mouth. The wheeze grew to a groan and then to a scream. Elynda could not move or shift or do anything except grip the High King's arm and let the energy flow through her.

The High King's scream reached a climactic high. Elynda wished she could cover her ears. All at once the power blasted through her with one final dose. It stole her breath and squeezed her insides. She closed her eyes against the wringing sensation.

The High King's scream stopped.

The energy petered out.

Elynda opened her eyes weakly. The High King was covered in sweat, eyes closed, arms flung out and limp. Elynda put an ear next to his face and felt the faintest whisper of air moving through his mouth.

"What's happened to him? Did you kill him, girl?" Luther asked and he did not seem upset at the prospect.

"No," Elynda said. "He's just passed out from the pain."

"Good," he said. He moved away from the king and Elynda to the cupboard and swiftly fiddled the locks until it opened. He withdrew the dragon's eye and turned to her. "Ya know how long he might be out?" he asked.

"Uh...," Elynda said dumbly. "Minutes? Maybe hours? I don't know. I usually dose people for the pain first."

"Then we best hurry," he said. He grabbed Elynda's upper arm and hauled her to her feet.

Elynda crashed back to the floor, her body jittering and jumping and weak. She'd had milder versions of these symptoms previously with powerful healings. This one took the cake.

"Come on, girl," Luther growled. "Unless you want to find out what our monarch is capable of in perfect health." He nodded toward the inert form of the High King.

Elynda was unsurprised to find the body was beginning to repair itself. Already his skin grew more elastic, his muscles grew, his hair filled in.

Elynda pushed her shaking form up from the ground and lurched toward Luther.

He led the way out of the room.

Elynda hardly saw what happened next. A blast of warm light hit the female guard who was thrown against a stone wall. She slumped to the ground, eyes closed.

"Did you just kill her?" Elynda asked while following Luther in a rubber-legged version of running.

"No, but you may wish I had."

Elynda looked over her shoulder as they rounded a corner in the corridor and caught a glimpse of the beautiful soldier's limp legs strewn across the stone floor. "What are you doing? Where are you taking me? Why are you helping?"

"Save the air for breathing," Luther fired over his shoulder. He turned down a connecting corridor and pelted down its length.

Elynda pushed her body, but she was never a strong runner. That was Riana's strength. She tripped, banging her knees against the hard floor. She yelped in pain, throwing out her hands to catch herself. The gritty stone floor scraped against her skin and broke it open in small scratches. Before she could gather herself, Luther yanked her up from the floor.

"Come on, girl. The High King won't care about your skinned knees," Luther said. He scooped a strong arm around her waist and hauled her forward. Ahead of them a steel door glowered in the shadows.

"Is that where they're keeping Ribbit and Kristopher?" Elynda asked.

Luther grunted and let go of Elynda. He stumbled the rest of the way to the door, the dragon's eye tucked beneath his arm. Luther peered into a small window lined with bars.

"Ribbit? Kristopher?" Elynda yelled. "Are you in there?"

A rattle of chains was the only answer.

Luther wheeled around and put a finger over his mouth in shush gesture. "You'll scare her," he said.

"I don't understand. Where are Ribbit and Kristopher if they're not in there?"

Luther ignored her and turned back to the door, gently wrapping his fingers over the window's ledge and pressing his face against the bars. "Fae?" he whispered, his voice turned soft and anxious.

Elynda leaned against the wall and worked to catch her breath. Exhaustion stole over her body and made her mind whir in confusion. "I don't understand. Who is Fae? Why are you helping me if that's what you're doing? And where are Kristopher and Ribbit?"

Luther didn't answer. His body was pressed to the door, face stuck between the bars he gripped. "Fae," he called again. The scraping metallic of chains being dragged across the stone floor echoed through the small bar-covered window.

Shivers washed over Elynda's arms, prickling her skin in gooseflesh.

The chains stopped. A feminine voice rasped through the door.

"Dad?"

CHAPTER FORTY-TWO

Hurtling through a galaxy of stars, Riana held a tight grip to Donny and Rustofo, petrified of her grip slipping and losing them somewhere in this space terrain. She held the thought of Elynda as tightly in her mind as she held Donny and Rustofo with her hands. The fierystwhiel had been clear: she must mean to end up where she wanted. Without her utter focus, they would be lost, and she wouldn't risk their safety again.

Tom was pressed against her leg and his warmth and presence was an extension of strength she needed. Her brain still buzzed and swam from the knock to the head.

We must get to Elynda, she thought.

The fierystwhiel's nose pushed them forward. Riana reveled in the odd sensation that it was not them that moved but the reality around them. As if it slipped over them without any locomotion on their part, like pictures passing by.

Focus, child, the fierystwhiel warned.

Riana gripped her companions tighter as Tom purred loudly. She mentally shook herself. They needed to get to Elynda. Elynda, her best friend. They had to get to her. And then they had to find someplace safe to stay.

One step at a time, said the fierystwhiel.

We must get to Elynda. Elynda, where are you?

There! Tom said.

Approaching them was a tunnel of white light. It expanded and in its center a picture of Elynda grew clear. Riana's heart leapt at the sight of her best friend. Tears filled her eyes. Elynda was alive. Her stomach squeezed in on itself. She had survived. A sob burbled up from her depths. "Elynda!" she screamed.

Elynda's head yanked up but her eyes didn't meet Riana's. She seemed confused. She mouthed something. Riana recognized her name as Elynda repeated it but couldn't hear it. Elynda turned her head, peering down at something next to her.

I sense others with power, the fierystwhiel said.

Yes, Riana confirmed. *Elynda is a Magys.* Her friend might be the most powerful sort of Magys there was: a healer.

There are others, the fierystwhiel noted.

Riana nodded. Of course, Ribbit and Kristopher had also turned out to be Magyses.

You are nearly there. Please be careful. I sense some great darkness on the other side of this portal.

But, aren't you going to help us get to safety?

Yes, I will be here for you when you enter the portal.

Thank you. For everything. We owe you our lives, Riana said.

On the contrary, we will owe you more than that, should you succeed. Restoration of the balance between dark and light is in your hands.

Riana faced the growing light and braced for impact. Hard stone floors met her feet, which had grown accustomed to standing on nothing. Her knees buckled and she fell to the ground. Her hands let loose of her tireless grip on Rustofo and Donny who slid over the ground and stopped. Riana looked around as the world solidified. The constant movement in the ether made the sudden stillness nauseating.

She squeezed her hands to her head and rolled onto her side, curling her knees into her chest.

"Riana!"

It was Elynda's voice. Elynda's sweet voice. She'd missed it so much. She tried to open her eyes and look at her best friend and closed them once more. The world wobbled under her. Elynda's hands touched her shoulder and head. Riana was filled with instant relief, warmth and energy. She allowed the soothing sensation to flow through her, feeling as though it were stitching her back up again in all the parts that had torn and ripped.

She breathed in deeply, immediately recognizing the aroma of soil and dirt and stone and water and pushed herself up into a sitting position from the gritty ground. She was in a dark and dank room, her body situated outside the circle of another portal.

A small shaft of light shone in from a crack in the upper wall. Water trickled down the sides of the old stones. Moss clung to fissures and aging mortar. The roots of a tree had long ago explored the cavern seeking new sustenance and found it in a pile of dirt occupying one corner. Ivy covered the wall nearest the pillar of light. The square room seemed clearly underground, but she'd thought that before.

Tom was next to her, purring and his mane was back to its previous length. He nudged her arm with his head. Riana's body turned the direction his nudge pushed her body and saw Elynda with alert eyes. Riana grabbed her, afraid she would vanish on the spot, and squeezed her into a tight embrace. "You're alive," she said into her hair. She pulled her back and looked at her face. "You don't look well."

"Just a little rattled, is all. I'll be fine."

"I've missed you," Riana understated and pulled her back into an embrace. Elynda tapped her friend's arm until Riana let go.

"Let me look at the others," she said.

"Can you help them?" Riana watched as Elynda approached the first inert body closest to them.

Elynda moved swiftly to him, placing gentle hands on his shoulder and head.

Donny's breath quickened, then he coughed and groaned. His eyes slowly came open. Elynda wasted no time with a greeting but went directly to Rustofo, touching his giant chest with both her hands. Rustofo was breathing again in mere moments.

Watching her friend heal Rustofo and Donny was awe inspiring. She was so dumbstruck she barely noticed the movement in the shadows, just on the other side of Rustofo. She pushed herself to standing, feeling weak but not broken.

"Who's there?" she asked.

"Riana, wait. He's helping."

Riana was not surprised to see Luther creep out of the shadows. What did surprise her was the girl he accompanied. He held her shoulders tenderly, his eyes wide and pleading. Riana finally understood what he'd meant and why he'd helped her.

"This is your daughter," Riana said.

Luther nodded, although she didn't need his confirmation. The girl was a beautiful version of her father with warm, dark skin and wide eyes like his. But the color of them was different. "This is Fae," Luther said. "Fae this is Riana. She's gonna take ya to yer mama."

Fae looked at her father with striking gold eyes. "Mama?" she asked, her face confused.

"Shh," he told her.

Fae turned away from her father to look back at Riana. Riana guessed she was only a little younger than herself and Elynda. Fae shook slightly, dark smudges under her golden eyes hinting at malnourishment and perhaps disease.

"Fae is not well," Elynda spoke softly into Riana's ear. "She needs to be taken to her mother."

"Why her mother? Why not you?" Riana asked.

"Fae is suffering from the lack of an element," Elynda said, speaking quickly. "Think of it like not getting enough of a vitamin or mineral, or even food. The High King locked her up in a dungeon and kept her as leverage to keep Luther doing his dirty work."

"You're her chance to be free," Luther said. "I've contacted Mylah. She is waiting for you at the other portal."

Riana looked around the room. She counted them. Rustofo pushed himself to sitting, pulling his knees up and resting his arms on them, then lowering his head to rest on his arms. He looked awful. Donny was still flat on the ground, although he was holding his head in his hands as if he were afraid of it exploding and only by holding it just right, and remaining perfectly still, would he manage to keep it together. Elynda appeared absolutely fatigued, leaning against a wall, her head propped on a brick. And now this young girl and Luther. Plus, herself. Her ragtag team of misfits was growing, and they were all looking to her to keep them safe.

And then it dawned on her. There were two missing. "Where are Kristopher and Ribbit?" she asked.

Elynda glared at Luther. "Yes, why don't you tell them where our friends are."

This shook Rustofo out of his stupor. He looked barely coherent; his eyes wobbled in fatigue. "Where is Kristopher?" he asked. "Son? Where is my son?" And then he spoke Idalfynian. Riana assumed he was asking the same question in his native tongue.

Luther watched the giant struggle to his feet, an animalistic grunt escaping through gritted teeth. Luther took a step back, then pushed Fae behind him. "We will get him, I promise," Luther said.

"Very well," Rustofo said. "You must lead the way.

"I can't," Luther said.

"What do you mean?" Rustofo asked. He stepped toward Luther, hands clenching into fists. He towered over the henchman of the High King and Riana thought he would pummel him, depending on what his next words were.

Luther removed something he'd strapped over his shoulder. He held out the leather pouch which bulged. "This will show you where they're at and how to get there. Riana should be able to use it. I cannot."

Rustofo growled and the room around them rumbled. Riana backed away from the giant, wide-eyed. Luther did the same.

"I promise, I had no idea the High King had moved them. I only found out after they'd taken them. I think he suspects I'm working against him to save my daughter."

Riana approached Rustofo. She laid a hand on Idalfyn's king. His head whipped around to her. His gray eyes were like storm clouds and as he squinted in a pinched expression of anger, jaws tight, the small flicker of light from a nearby torch reflected, reminding Riana of the flashes of lightning they'd experienced in the ether.

"I think he's telling the truth," she said, and looked at Luther, hoping she was right.

Luther had a hand behind his back, holding his daughter behind him.

"You would vouch for the High King's henchman?" Rustofo bellowed.

Riana's ears rang. She breathed in deeply, steadying both her fear and her anger.

"No," she said, flatly. "But I would vouch for our ability to find your son and our friend. Especially with this." Riana held out her hands to Luther, her heart trilling.

Luther slowly extended his hand toward Riana, glancing between her and Rustofo, fear expanding his eyes.

Riana took the bag and quickly removed its contents. She cast the bag aside and held Magloryn's eye out for Rustofo to see. The eye was locked onto Riana. Riana could feel its gaze on her, but her eyes were locked onto Rustofo, pleading him to listen.

"How did you come by this?" Rustofo asked Luther.

Elynda spoke up. "He took it from the High King. He took it and me and brought me here to the portal room, along with his daughter. He stole it from the High King to keep it safe from him."

"A misstep I should have anticipated."

Everyone turned at the sound of the voice. Riana instinctively clutched the eye to her stomach, wrapping her arms around it in a protective embrace. She inched toward the portal circle, catching Elynda's eye and nodding in its direction. Elynda moved silently toward Donny, who still lay on the ground.

Rustofo stomped toward the High King, who looked vibrant and healthy.

Riana snapped a look at Elynda, hurt she would have healed him. "Why?" she asked.

"I couldn't help it, Riana. I don't know how to make the power not happen."

"That will be far enough, Captain," the High King said. He waved a hand in a circular gesture and a lasso of shadow whipped toward Rustofo.

Before the giant could take another step, the strand of darkness wrapped around him. He screamed. Shadow rose from his body as the and Rustofo went down to his knees.

Luther rushed toward Riana, pushing Fae at her. Riana reached out for the girl, her spindly body bony in her grip. "Go," he urged her. "You must use the portal and go quickly."

"But, where am I going?" Riana asked.

"My mother," Fae insisted, swaying on unsteady feet, leaning into Riana's grasp. "She'll be able to help us," she rasped.

"Yes, you must use this portal to get to Mylah. You'll be safe there." Luther instructed.

"What about you?" Riana asked, not believing the twinge of compassion in her heart for the very man who had murdered her grandmother.

"I'll hold him off for as long as I can. Save my girl, Riana. Please. I'm begging you." Luther's tears flowed freely.

"Luther, you've been a very naughty boy," the High King said.

Luther pushed Riana and Fae toward the circle. Riana grabbed Fae's hand and rushed to the southern point. "Elynda, take up the eastern point. Tom, you stay to the west. Donny seems to have the north taken care of."

Donny mumbled something unintelligible.

"Rustofo," Riana shouted. "Quickly! Get to the north with Donny!" Rustofo screamed, the dark tentacle climbing up his body.

Fae turned her golden eyes up to her. "I can help him," she said. Riana stared down at her. "Okay," was all she could manage.

Fae turned to the High King and flung her arms toward him. Flame erupted from her hands, dancing through the air and heating the room to a sweltering temperature. Riana watched the flames reach toward Rustofo's assailant. The High King broke his attention on the giant, gesturing toward the flames. The shadow released its grip from Idalfyn's king, snaking back to Achyla and forming a shield of darkness.

Fae inhaled deeply, her breath catching as her head shook slightly. When she exhaled it sounded to Riana like relief, as if the use of her power had relieved some pressure.

"I can't hold it for long," Fae said.

Rustofo pushed himself up and jogged toward the north corner of the circle.

Riana began the chant for the portal, fear kicking her heart into overtime, Fae at her back, blasting flame at the High King. Fae grunted, falling to a knee, arms dropping as the fire in her snuffed out.

Luther gasped, reaching for his side. His dark blade whipped out of its sheath and was instantly ablaze. The knife flew, a dart of flame streaking through the darkened room.

The High King waved a hand, and the knife flew off course, sticking in the crumbling wall behind him. With the monarch distracted, Luther widened his stance, gesturing toward the soil gathered in the corner of the room where the tree's roots had found purchase. With another wave of his arm, the soil erupted in hot blue flame. Luther grunted as he motioned with outstretched arms toward the burning mound of Tyrinth. Fire and soil roared, churning toward the High King.

Blue light bathed the room in an eerie glow, the heat billowing out at Riana and her companions, until she shielded herself from the heat. Beside her, Fae sucked in a breath as she straightened and faced the flame fully, like a snake eager to soak in the sun's warmth.

Achyla looked toward the moving wave of Tyrinth just in time for it sweep him up, rocks and dirt wrapping him up in a suffocating and burning grip. His face was awash in the light of the flame, shadows drawing to him in an instant. The king was slammed against the far wall. Ancient bricks, wayward vines, and dirt skittered to the floor, rocks bounding away.

Riana turned her shielding arm from the now extinguished flames to the ceiling as knots of soil fell on them and in the circle. She continued calling on the elements in turn. Rustofo knelt and scooped Donny into his massive arms. Fae stayed put next to Riana, but she watched her father with worry on her face.

"Dad!" she screamed, tears flowing. "Hurry. We're leaving!"

The pile of dirt under which the king was buried vibrated. Luther turned to Fae.

"I love you, sweetheart. I don't wantya ta ever forget it or doubt it. No matter what you hear, darlin' you best know everything I've ever done has been for you."

The king broke free of the encasing soil, his handsome pale face now smeared with dirt, a sneer twisting his mouth into something ugly, blue eyes sharply trained on Luther.

He extended an arm and shadow shot out of the soil and wrapped Luther in darkness, hoisting him into the air. Luther inhaled sharply as the shadows coiled around him. Pops and cracks rent the air, and Luther tipped back his head and screamed.

Riana squeezed Fae closer as the girl screamed, a hand reaching for her father, tears springing into her fear-filled eyes.

"You've disobeyed me for the last time," the king said.

Each of the stones set in the directional quadrants were ablaze with purpose. "Creation," Riana called to the element in the center, in the depths, the darkness that was not evil, but from which all was born. The shadows gathered around them seemed to shiver, to pause if only for a moment.

The shadows wrapping Luther in a killing grip eased. He panted, head lolling forward.

"Please help him," Fae said to Riana, her eyes pleading. Riana opened her mouth to answer, how she didn't know, when she sensed a presence within the shadows. She reached out to it and felt a wash of familiarity, like kindred spirits having met for the first time.

The king grunted, falling to a knee amidst the rubble, a silver necklace shaking loose from under his shirt. He gripped a small black talisman hanging from the chain and the shadows around them quaked before rolling back to the king.

"Go!" Luther said to Fae. "Please, if you love me, leave me and go."

"Dad," Fae sobbed. "No."

"Yes, doll. Let me do this. For you." He opened his mouth to say more but the shadows twisted tighter around him. He screamed again.

"And where do you think you're going?" Achyla said to Riana.

Riana's heart galloped as the High King turned his attention on her even as the shadow at his command deconstructed the Captain of the Tyrmini Guard. Time was out. They had to go. Riana grasped Fae's hand as the shadow gripping Luther squeezed.

A cacophony of snapping and popping ground through the darkness and then were drowned out by Luther's screams. His body twisted, his lower body turning one direction while his top half swiveled the other, as if the shadow were wringing him like a rag. Riana covered the girl's eyes with her free hand as Luther's body twisted unnaturally. His screams crescendoed and with one last mighty crack of breaking bone, cut out altogether.

"Dad," the girl cried and clawed at Riana's hand.

Luther gurgled and Riana watched in horror as blood gushed from his mouth, splattering to the floor. Riana didn't dare ease her grip on Fae's face, trying desperately to spare her from seeing her father squeezed to death by shadow. Fae thrashed against her, and Riana was grateful for the girl's weakened state. She kept hold of Fae as she inhaled to call out to the last remaining element. The shadow eased, expanded, dropping the remains of Luther's inert and mangled body to the ground.

The shadow coalesced around the king, who gathered it to himself before flinging it toward Riana. It shot toward her, its ebony etheral essence undulating through the room with barely trackable speed. She nearly yelped, nearly lost all control of her voice as she saw the essence of creation trained on her. That same force that had just gruesomely slaughtered Luther.

"Love," Riana screamed the last element. The crystal suspended in the air at the center of the circle spun and glittered, casting rainbows against the darkness shooting toward her. The ether expanded around them. Shadow wrapped around Riana's neck. She gagged against the force crushing her throat. It burned and froze. Pain seared her skin, muscle tendon and tissue. Everything was on fire. She wanted to claw at the shadow gripping her, but one hand held the dragon's eye and the other gripped Fae's face.

She struggled to breathe, even while they sped through the universe.

No, no, no. That simply won't do. The voice of the High King was thick in her ears. *I have seen many Tyrmini in my time, but I've never seen such as you. How did you use the portals? How is it so? How did you escape my traps? You saw through the mirage at the second portal and you escaped the Inilu. How?*

You don't know what I am, Riana said. *Nor who I am.*

I think I may have a hunch. By the way, I'll be needing my eye back.

The shadow from her neck snaked its way down her body, like a sick tentacle reaching for Magloryn's eye. Riana could feel the life leaking from her, escaping with every missed breath. Yet, she could not let go of the eye and she would not let go of Fae.

You must let go. The new voice was one she hadn't heard since the very first portal they'd jumped through in Lanadsend. The sound of it soothed her, but the words pricked at her logic and heart.

But, we need it to find Ribbit and Kristopher. And I want to return it to you. I want you to be whole.

I don't need it. And you don't either. Riana, you are like me. You are part of me and so you do not need any talisman to see clearly, to see far and to see truly. But the High King does not know that. You must let it go.

Riana had pangs of doubt. She had the power to see as Magloryn saw? How could that be so?

You cannot consider any longer. You must trust yourself and let go.

Did she have any idea what she was talking about? Trust herself? How? How could she trust herself when she didn't even understand her true nature?

Your nature is my nature. Now, trust me or all will perish. You. Me. Your friends. All but the High King. Choose your path.

Riana gripped the eye as tightly as the shadow gripped her throat, strangling her. She looked at her best friend, the girl Fae, caught up in her hands that were now blue. Rustofo held Donny. Tom swished his three tails, hissing at the shadow that had wrapped his companion in a death grip.

The tendril of shadow touched the hand holding the dragon's eye. He could not have it. He could not be allowed to see as Magloryn sees any longer. They would not be safe if Riana allowed that to happen.

What had she intended when the fierystwhiel had instructed her? She had intended to save her friends and get to safety. She still intended that. Stars danced in her periphery. Darkness closed in on her vision. Dizziness swept over her. She closed her eyes, wished for safety, and let go.

CHAPTER FORTY-THREE

The eye dropped away from her.

No! the High King shouted.

Riana inhaled deeply as the shadow released her and chased after the eye. The eye sped through eternity, the shadow following. A ring of red exploded through the universe and through it the fierystwhiel flew. The red ring of energy hit the eye, the glass shattered, the eye incinerated, sending rainbow sparks out into the vast eternity. Sparks caught the shadow and burned it away until it was no more.

Riana faced Donny and Rustofo who represented the north. She removed her hand from the girl's eyes and held on to her shoulders. They had to get to safety. Riana led them through the ether with single-minded intention.

The light on the other end of the portal illuminated their path. Riana felt the familiar tug as they hurtled through the break in time and space and the ground appeared beneath them. Riana gently touched down, careful to hold the girl up against the awkward rush to stability. Rustofo and Elynda fell to their knees. Rustofo carefully laid Donny on the floor. Elynda crawled over to him. Tom landed springily on all fours, looked around the circle, and with a shake of fur and scales, transformed into the ginger cat disguise he'd used while in Landsend.

"Donny?" Elynda asked, her voice came out harsh and weak. She placed both hands on his shoulders. Donny stirred, looked up at Elynda, then slowly rolled his eyes toward Riana.

"Are we there yet?" he asked in a hoarse voice.

Riana gripped her painful neck and cleared her damaged throat. She inhaled to speak, but her voice would not work. She nodded and hoped it sufficed.

Fae wandered away from her, arms wrapped around herself as sobs ripped from her core. Riana's heart broke for the girl, even with the warring emotions inside her. The man who had killed her grandmother was dead again, but that was Fae's father. Riana didn't know what it was like to have a father who loved her so much he was willing to die to protect her. She did know her grandmother had done very much the same thing as Luther: given her very life to protect Riana. She hung her head as she watched their new companion's heart shatter.

Riana tore her gaze from the teen and looked around her. The glittering crystal in the center of the tile winked in rainbows. The maze carving underneath her boots glowed and pulsed in waves of blue. Lights bloomed in sconces positioned on the walls around them.

Riana recognized this place.

Elynda rushed to her, gripping her in a fierce hug. "We're home!"

"Mom?" Fae asked through sobs into the surrounding darkness, her voice broken and hopeful.

A beautiful woman strode from a darkened corner and into the blue light, her hair a mass of dark waves, her eyes the same striking gold as Fae's, her skin a gorgeous brown. She wrapped her arms around Fae's shoulders and closed her eyes as tears streamed down her face. At her side, a small bright gold fox-looking creature trotted along, looking up at the child and the mother.

The woman was robed in white, loose clothing. She loosed the grip on Fae.

Fae looked into her mother's face, tears streaming as she sobbed. "He killed him," she said, hiccupping through the words. "He killed dad."

Mylah gripped her daughter's face in her hands, shock widening her eyes. New tears welled and spilled down her golden-brown cheeks. She tipped her head back, face lifted to the ceiling of the domed room. Pain creased her features, a sob escaping her mouth, before she wrapped her daughter back into an embrace. She pressed her chin into Fae's hair as Fae gripped her mother. The two passed several minutes this way, clinging to each other as grief stole over them.

Riana could do nothing for them, except allow them these moments to share in their suffering. She wandered to Elynda, wrapping her hand in hers, leaning into her best friend. She was selfish with the gratitude that Elynda was still alive. Selfishly grateful she wasn't mourning like this new stranger and her daughter. Riana pulled Elynda down into a sitting position on the grooved floor, and in silence, they waited through the pair's storm.

After long minutes had passed, the tears had slowed, the sobs growing quiet, and the two released each other. The woman named Mylah, this dark beauty with now-puffy golden eyes, red-rimmed, approached Riana.

Fae lowered herself to the ground, wrapping her skinny arms around her knees and rocking herself, tears silently flowing. Riana stood and Mylah extended a hand. Riana took the offered hand and let the woman pull her into an embrace. Riana stiffened.

The woman pulled herself free and looked deeply into Riana's eyes, seemingly struck in awe as her mouth hung open slightly and her eyes went wide. "It is you," she said. She wrapped Riana's hands with her own and squeezed them. "I am Mylah. I've been waiting for you. But I never thought you would also reunite me with my daughter. You truly are the miracle you were born to be."

"You've been waiting for me?" she managed to squeak out the words, thinking the reverse was true. "We just used this portal days ago and you were definitely not here."

Mylah bowed her head as if in shame. "Please forgive me. I tried coming earlier but was caught up in affairs in Sylvanea." She paused, distracted and touched Riana's neck. "The shadow has scarred you."

Riana was shocked to discover she did not feel Mylah's exploring fingers.

"It's numb," she said, her voice no more than a harsh, tight whisper.

"Let me look at it," Elynda said. She crossed the maze stone, casting a distrustful gaze at Mylah.

"There is nothing you can do for this," Mylah said.

Elynda turned to her with fierce emerald eyes. "I'll be the judge of that," she said. She looked over the wounds while Riana shot a question over her head to Mylah.

"Why did you come here to Landsend?" she asked.

"Luther contacted me when he worked out a way to free Fae. The timing lined up with you coming of age."

"My birthday," Riana said, stunned, her voice catching roughly in her painful throat. "What day is it today?"

"Today is the first full moon of Tijilou," Mylah stated and smiled. "Happy birthday."

"Oh," Riana said. "I'm sixteen now. I can stay in my home again." She didn't speak the other truth: that she now had ownership and responsibility for Starliss Vineyard and Winery. She would not be able to fulfil that obligation and track down and rescue her two other friends. If she even had a vineyard and winery still standing and operating after Mr. Fraely had had his meddlesome fingers in her business.

She couldn't summon the normal venom she usually had when her thoughts wandered to Fraely. She was exhausted.

"We have to find my son," Rustofo said. "Riana, where is the eye?"

Riana didn't want to use her voice and wished it hadn't been working moments earlier so she could use it as an excuse to not explain. "I had to let it go," she said.

"You what? My son could be on the brink of death and you lost the only implement to find him?"

"She does not need the eye," Mylah said, folding her arms under her wealth of bosom and fixing Rustofo with a stern gaze. "And you should not speak to the daughter of Magloryn in such a way."

"The daughter of...," Donny said, finally standing, though rubbing the back of his neck with purpose.

270

"She is the only one who will finally dismantle that old Usurper, who you know as the High King. She has no need for talismans of the Dragon of Light. She is her own Light, blessed by Magloryn before her birth."

Riana swayed. That was why she had so many similarities to the dragon. Magloryn had bestowed her power upon Riana. The chant that had started months ago thrummed to life inside her. *Magloryn. I am Magloryn. Magloryn.*

"I am Magloryn," Riana said out loud, fighting against the strained and bruised muscles in her neck and throat. "I am."

She put a hand to her heart, suddenly full of an overwhelming love.

"Yes," Mylah said. "Yes, of course. Did your grandmother tell you nothing?"

Riana hung her head. "She wanted to protect me."

Mylah seemed to weigh her response, eyes casting over Riana's body. "I see. Well, then, we must catch you up while we rest, eat and drink... and mourn." She lowered her head at this, inhaled, and exhaled slowly. She lifted her head after a moment. There were fresh tears shining in her eyes. She placed a hand on her chest, rubbing what Rianna knew must be a deep ache brought on by sorrow. "We cannot take long, though. I'm certain Achyla will send word soon to the various regions' law enforcement. Still, we can take a day or two to prepare for our next move."

"What's that?" Riana asked, voice harsh and painful. She looked around at the others, who all stared at Mylah, seeming as unsure as Rianna.

"Isn't that obvious?" Mylah asked. Fae wandered toward them, one hand gripping her other arm. She looked at Riana and then at Mylah and nodded, shuffling from foot to foot.

Riana stared, nonplussed. "You mean rescuing Kristopher and Ribbit?

Mylah looked at her daughter, wrapping an arm around her, and hugged her tightly. Fae leaned her head against her mother's shoulder, her eyes swollen, cheeks tear-stained, expression distant. Riana couldn't help but imagine all the girl had been through, locked in a dark cell, deprived of light and food and love. Her freedom had been hard-won with her father's sacrifice and rebellion. He'd known that could be the cost, and he'd rebelled anyway, his love for his daughter transcending his own need for survival. It was then she realized that perhaps all of Luther's choices had been in the service of that one goal: to keep his daughter safe. Riana wondered what other sacrifices she'd see made to save those suffering from Achyla's rule. She wondered what she herself would sacrifice for the cause.

Mylah turned from Fae to Riana as she swayed, Fae locked in her grasp, as if she meant never to break that closeness again. "Oh, I suppose that's part of it, yes."

Rustofo approached and crossed his arms over his chest. Donny stared flatly at this desert beauty. Elynda stopped probing Riana's neck long enough to fix Mylah in her gaze.

Mylah looked at them each in turn. "I would have thought it was obvious."

"Humor us," Donny said.

Mylah fixed Riana with an intense golden gaze and said, "What comes next is we help you usurp your father's throne."

CHAPTER FORTY-FOUR

There was one piece of business Riana knew she had to sort out immediately on her birthday. Despite the deep fatigue sinking into her bones, despite the ache in her neck muscles and the chill she couldn't shake, she'd made her way into town and found Captain Steph of the Baron's Guard.

Before the afternoon could expire, Riana found herself in the winery office, gripping the official document of inheritance in her shaking hands.

The office was a mess; he'd wasted no time in settling into the desk that had once seated Sela Starliss and countless other Starlisses before her. His cloak hung on the coat rack in the corner. His hat laid on the desk. Even a handkerchief with his initials embroidered into it was wadded and set on top of the book of accounting he was apparently perusing. Riana's nose wrinkled.

She tried to stop her speeding heart, but it raced on. She anticipated a fight. She was also nervous about the things she'd stolen from her guardian before she'd left Landsend. Captain Steph stood beside her, grinning from ear to ear under his auburn moustache and rocking from heels to toes as he hummed. Word had not caught up to the Landsend region of Riana's rebellion against the High King, though she could not count on that for long.

They heard him approaching before they saw him. Riana was all too familiar with the heavy stomp of his gait. She inhaled deeply, closed her eyes, and steadied herself as best she could.

The door to the office burst open. "You forfeit your inheritance when you left Landsend. You have no right!"

"As it turns out, Mr. Fraely, she does," Captain Steph said. He turned to Riana. "Happy birthday, dear."

Riana nodded in thanks to Captain Steph.

Mr. Fraely stared, open-mouthed, like a surprised fish.

Riana held out the document before him.

Mr. Fraely ground his teeth one way and then the next.

"If you'll read the following paragraph," Riana started, "and settle any debt with me you may have incurred by withdrawing funds from the Starliss accounts, you can then be on your way."

"I had to take care of business while you were gone," he growled.

"Certainly, and so it states in the inheritance document that should you personally profit from the business, all monies shall be returned to the benefactor when she comes of age," Riana stated, pointing to the words in the document as she read them aloud. "You have one moon from today to return my property."

"Property!" he bellowed. "You're one to talk about returning property. What about all the things you stole out of my shop?"

She'd asked Steph about this.

"Ah," Steph interjected. "Riana tells me she took clothing, food, and a light source, all of which you are required by – Riana may I see the document, please?" he asked.

Riana handed it to him. He surveyed the long piece of parchment briefly.

"Here it is," Steph said. "The sole guardian shall provide basics of survival and thriving, including food, clothing, light, warmth, and shelter."

"And what do I get out of this?" Fraely raged. "What do I get for sharing my space, my food, my inventory with the likes of her?"

Captain Steph seemed not to notice Fraely's tantrum and simply glanced over the document for a long moment, gloved hand gripping his chin. "The guardian shall receive payment of one-hundred gold coins for the safekeeping of the benefactor. Should the benefactor's safety be at risk in the guardian's keeping, all debits of good faith are canceled." Captain looked up at Fraely, a broad smile stretching over his face.

Fraely gaped at him. "Nothing. I get no thanks for what I've done here." He gestured around the office, as if he'd done her a favor by stealing money from their account.

Riana stood rooted to the spot, hands interlaced, composed. Memories of the nights he'd beaten her, of days spent starving from lack of food, of being forced to work, yelled at, belittled, prodded and insulted flashed through her mind – and she had not even a shred of sympathy to send the man away with zero compensation.

He was still in her office, though. She decided to rectify that. She walked to the coat rack and pulled Mr. Fraely's cloak from the peg. She held it out to him.

He sneered at her.

"I believe you know your way out," Riana said, her voice still harsh. "Leave now, or I will press charges for assault, extortion, and theft."

He snatched the cloak from her grip and closed in on her.

"Or do you need an escort?" a voice boomed. Rustofo bent to enter the office.

Mr. Fraely took several steps back, leaning away from the giant. "I – I think I can manage," he said.

Rustofo exited the office and held out an arm to show the Fraely the way.

Roy Fraely considered her for a moment longer, unable to keep a look of disgust from his face. Riana stared back at him, no longer afraid of him or the abuse he'd previously doled out. Mr. Fraely turned, snatched the handkerchief from the accounting books, and stomped out of the office.

Riana followed him, wanting to see him leave. When the doors finally closed behind his retreating figure, Riana breathed a sigh of relief.

"Well done, my dear!" it was Ms. Hightower. She threw herself onto Riana gripping her shoulders in a wiry embrace. "You have no idea how good it is to see you."

Riana smiled and ducked her head. "Yes, I figured you might feel that way," she said. She turned to Steph. "Thank you, Captain. Just one more thing before you leave. If you would please witness what I say next." She turned back to Ms. Hightower.

"What's this?" Ms. Hightower said, looking suspicious at Riana.

"Ms. Hightower, you were my grandmother's right-hand woman. You've tendered my apprenticeship over the last several months. It only makes sense I appoint you as the keeper of Starliss Vineyard and Winery."

"But... where are you going? What will you do?" Ms. Hightower asked.

"For now, I have another job to do. And it requires some travel."

Note from the Author

Did you like this book?

Readers rely on reviews to decide if a book is worth their time and money. Therefore, I greatly appreciate any rating or review you're willing to give, whether it's just clicking the number of stars you believe it deserves or writing out what you most enjoyed about the book. I can be found on amazon.com and goodreads.com.

Get immersed in the world of Tyrinth. Sign up for my e-newsletter for exclusive access to creature art, character descriptions, maps, and more at raynalstiner.com.

Thank You!

www.ingramcontent.com/pod-product-compliance
Lightning Source LLC
Chambersburg PA
CBHW021219250626
47155CB00008B/2871